"I swore I wasn't going to do this."

"Do what?" Alexis whispered.

"This."

They came together with a shudder of need. Her hands slid over the silky panes of Wyatt's chest to wrap around his neck in a silent plea. Wyatt's lips covered hers.

It wasn't enough. Not nearly enough. She nipped at his lip in demand and the kiss went hot and wet with hunger. She felt him stir against her, hard and wanting, the way she wanted with a burning fierce intensity that consumed her.

Wyatt released her and stepped back, breathing hard. "Go to bed."

Alexis wondered if she'd lost her mind. They didn't know each other. Wyatt didn't even know her real name! She trembled. "Come with me."

Dear Harlequin Intrigue Reader,

The holidays are upon us! We have six dazzling stories of intrigue that will make terrific stocking stuffers—not to mention a well-deserved reward for getting all your shopping done early....

Take a breather from the party planning and unwrap Rita Herron's latest offering, *A Warrior's Mission*—the next exciting installment of COLORADO CONFIDENTIAL, featuring a hot-blooded Cheyenne secret agent! Also this month, watch for *The Third Twin*—the conclusion of Dani Sinclair's HEARTSKEEP trilogy that features an identical triplet heiress marked for murder who seeks refuge in the arms of a rugged lawman.

The joyride continues with *Under Surveillance* by highly acclaimed author Gayle Wilson. This second book in the PHOENIX BROTHERHOOD series has an undercover agent discovering that his simple surveillance job of a beautiful woman-in-jeopardy is filled with complications. Be there from the start when B.J. Daniels launches her brand-new miniseries, CASCADES CONCEALED, about a close-knit northwest community that's visited by evil. Don't miss the first unforgettable title, *Mountain Sheriff*.

As a special gift-wrapped treat, three terrific stories in one volume. Look for *Boys in Blue* by reader favorites Rebecca York, Ann Voss Peterson and Patricia Rosemoor about three long-lost New Orleans cop brothers who unite to reel in a killer. And rounding off a month of nonstop thrills and chills, a pregnant woman and her wrongly incarcerated husband must set aside their stormy past to bring the real culprit to justice in *For the Sake of Their Baby* by Alice Sharpe.

Best wishes to all of our loyal readers for a joyous holiday season!

Enjoy,

Denise O'Sullivan
Senior Editor
Harlequin Intrigue

THE THIRD TWIN

DANI SINCLAIR

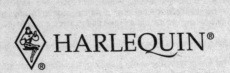

HARLEQUIN®

TORONTO • NEW YORK • LONDON
AMSTERDAM • PARIS • SYDNEY • HAMBURG
STOCKHOLM • ATHENS • TOKYO • MILAN • MADRID
PRAGUE • WARSAW • BUDAPEST • AUCKLAND

For Natashya Wilson—I can't thank you enough.

Ditto to Roger, Chip, Dan, Barb and Judy Fitzwater, who hung in there when I wasn't sure I could.

And special thanks to Max, Mischief and Possum, the best stress relievers a writer could have.

ISBN 0-373-22742-6

THE THIRD TWIN

Copyright © 2003 by Patricia A. Gagne

This edition published by arrangement with Harlequin Books S.A.

Visit us at www.eHarlequin.com

Printed in U.S.A.

ABOUT THE AUTHOR

An avid reader, Dani Sinclair didn't discover romance novels until her mother lent her one when she had come for a visit. Dani's been hooked on the genre ever since. But she didn't take up writing seriously until her two sons were grown. Since the premiere of *Mystery Baby* for Harlequin Intrigue in 1996, Dani has kept her computer busy. Her third novel, *Better Watch Out,* was a RITA® Award finalist in 1998. Dani lives outside Washington, D.C., a place she's found to be a great source of both intrigue and humor!

You can write to her in care of the Harlequin Reader Service.

Books by Dani Sinclair

HEARTSKEEP

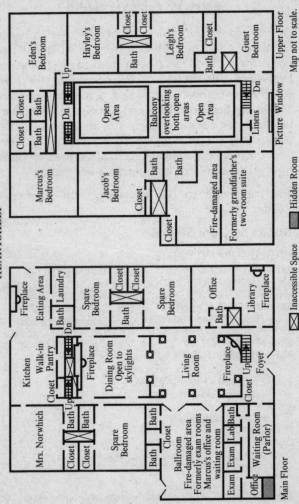

Main Floor

Mrs. Norwhich | Closet | Bath | Closet | Bath
Kitchen | Walk-in Closet | Pantry | Fireplace
Eating Area | Bath | Laundry

Spare Bedroom
Bath | Closet | Closet
Spare Bedroom

Dining Room Open to skylights

Living Room

Office
Bath

Library
Fireplace

Fireplace

Dn | Up

Spare Bedroom
Bath | Bath | Closet
Ballroom
Fire-damaged area
Formerly exam rooms
Marcus's office and waiting room

Exam | Exam | Lab | Bath
Office | Waiting Room (Parlor)

Fireplace | Closet | Up | Foyer

Upper Floor   Map not to scale.

Eden's Bedroom

Hayley's Bedroom
Closet | Closet
Bath

Leigh's Bedroom
Bath | Closet

Guest Bedroom

Closet | Closet | Bath | Bath
Dn | Up

Open Area

Balcony overlooking both open areas

Open Area

Dn | Linens

Picture Window

Marcus's Bedroom

Jacob's Bedroom
Closet
Closet

Bath | Bath

Fire-damaged area
Formerly grandfather's two-room suite

⊠ Inaccessible Space   ⬛ Hidden Room

CAST OF CHARACTERS

Dennison Hart—Was the Hart family patriarch murdered because he learned what had been done twenty-four years ago?

Amy Hart Thomas—Could a mother not know she gave birth to a child?

Brian and Lois Ryder—Did they know the truth all along?

Alexis Ryder—Who is she really?

Wyatt Crossley—A cop with a murder to solve.

Marcus Thomas—Was he blackmailed or the blackmailer for all those years?

Eden Voxx Thomas—If the truth comes out, she'll go to jail.

Jacob Voxx—How far will Eden's son go to protect his mother?

Mario Silva—What does the ex-con know about the past?

Livia Walsh—She was devoted to the Hart family. Too bad she can't talk anymore.

Kathy Walsh—Livia's daughter may know the answers if they can find her in time.

Bernie Duquette—Did Kathy's boyfriend take one gamble too many?

George and Emily Walken—Were they more than family friends and neighbors of Heartskeep?

Hayley and Leigh Hart Thomas—They need to find Alexis first.

Bram Myers/Gavin Jarret—They are committed to protecting the women they love.

Dear Reader,

Heartskeep has been eerily watching, waiting for this day to come. The estate is willing to divulge its secrets to the right person—providing she can stay alive long enough to find the answers.

Alexis Ryder lives a normal life until the day she comes home from work to learn that nothing about her life is what it seems. Her parents aren't really her parents, and her real family has reason to want her dead—and only part of that reason is a briefcase full of money and instructions to trust no one. Running from faceless killers, Alexis has no choice but to go to the small town of Stony Ridge looking for answers. But all she finds are more questions and an incredibly handsome stranger who mistakes her for someone else. If she can ignore the compelling attraction between them long enough, she just might learn what she needs to know.

Police officer Wyatt Crossley has a seven-year-old murder to solve and a family debt to repay. He never expects to find himself so attracted to one of the Thomas twins. Their dislike of the police in general, and the Crossley family in particular, makes his investigation into their mother's death hard enough without becoming personally involved with one of them. Wyatt knows that Alexis— smart, sexy, yet beguilingly vulnerable—is keeping secrets from him. Unless he can earn her trust, those secrets may get them both killed.

Join me once more in the shadows of Heartskeep, where only love can dispel the darkness of betrayal and open the future for the Hart family heirs. Enjoy!

Happy reading,

Dani Sinclair

Chapter One

The smell hit her as she pulled the key from the lock and her apartment door swung open. The pungent scent of whiskey had become all too familiar since her mother had died. Alexis Ryder felt her stomach churn in revulsion and anger.

What was her father doing here, in her apartment? He'd only been here once since she'd moved in with her college roommate, and then only because she'd felt compelled to invite him. He was her father, after all. But he'd arrived so drunk, he'd passed out five minutes later. He'd spent the night snoring on their couch.

Why was he here now? Why tonight of all times? She had a date in less than an hour.

Alexis strove to control her bitterness. "Dad?"

Dropping her purse and the mail on the table by the door, she bent to retrieve an envelope that had slipped to the floor. That was when she saw the blood. A vivid dark red, the splotch of color glittered against the faded gold carpeting.

Fear slammed into her. Instinctively she reached for the door handle, ready to flee even as her eyes traced a trail of drops to their tiny excuse for a kitchen.

Common sense kicked in. The smell of whiskey told its own tale. This was no burglar. What had her faher done?

"Dad?"

There wasn't a sound from inside. She was unsurprised when he didn't respond. No doubt he was passed out in there.

Releasing the door handle, she stepped into the room far enough to see the kitchen through the breakfast bar. The cupboard where they kept their meager supply of alcohol yawned open. A once-full bottle lay on the counter on its side, no longer able to dribble the rest of its golden-brown contents onto the floor.

Blood smeared the label. It streaked the cheap white cupboard and the countertop. Spilled whiskey mingled with the shattered remains of a glass, the shards glittering on the white linoleum floor.

Fear returned. What had he done? The meager trail of blood led away from the kitchen, down the hall toward the bedrooms. She took a step in that direction. The drops of blood on the floor grew larger. A smear streaked the white wall, as if someone had rested a second before moving into the bathroom.

Her chest felt incredibly tight. The sound of her heart beat loudly in her ears.

"Dad?"

Their cluttered yellow bathroom was barely recognizable. She hadn't known that blood had an odor. It did, and it was one that even spilled whiskey couldn't mask. A wadded, bloodstained dish towel lay in the sink.

The medicine chest stood ajar. Cosmetics and bottles of lotion had crashed to the floor. A tube of antiseptic cream lay on top of the toilet tank, a frightening testimony to an attempt to bandage a wound. What had he done?

"Dad!"

She was breathing too fast. A shaking had seized her taut limbs. Alexis stared at another blood smear near the doorknob of her bedroom. Her door wasn't shut all the way. The latch didn't always catch if she wasn't careful. She'd been careful this morning.

For a moment her knees threatened to succumb to the weight of her fear, but she had to know. It might not be that bad. Obviously her father had cut himself and come here for help. He must have drunk himself into another stupor.

She nudged the door open with her foot.

For one very bad second she thought she would lose control over her stomach. The room grayed as a rushing sound filled her head. She stumbled toward the still figure lying on her bed.

"Daddy?"

She hadn't called him that since she'd been a little girl—back when he'd still been her hero. Her vision blurred. She rubbed at her eyes to clear the tears sliding down her cheeks.

"Don't be dead. Please don't be dead."

The whispered words sounded far away. As if they'd come from some other source.

Brian Ryder was sprawled on his back across her pastel bedspread. He didn't move. His thin features were haggard with pain and his pale skin looked more like carved wax than living tissue. He'd pulled up his shirt. His abdomen was covered with one of her yellow bath towels. Blood stained the towel and the bony fingers that pressed the terry cloth against his abdomen.

There was another smell mixed with the foul stench of blood and whiskey. She'd never encountered the odor before, but she recognized it. The smell of death.

Alexis shut her eyes. Sobs tore from somewhere deep in her chest. She heard them, strangely detached from the sound.

She should have been a better daughter. She should have tried harder to understand. Alcoholism was a disease. It made people do things they wouldn't ordinarily do. It destroyed fortunes and families. It wasn't entirely his fault that he'd stopped being her hero. Her mother had died on a rain-slicked street and her father hadn't been able to handle the loss. He had loved her mother more than anything in the world. Now they were both gone and she was alone. And he'd died without knowing that his only daughter still loved him.

The sobs tore from her heart.

When she opened her eyes, he was staring at her.

"Daddy!"

She flew to the bed.

"Oh, God. It's going to be okay, Daddy. I'll get an ambulance. Lie still. It's going to b—"

His hand snaked out to grab her wrist, staining it with his blood. "Listen."

"Yes. I will. I promise. Just let me call—"

"Listen!"

For a second his voice was as strong as his grip. She leaned over him, inhaling the scent of whiskey on his breath. But the glaze in his eyes wasn't alcohol-induced.

"Get out of here! Now!"

"Daddy…"

"…be coming…here…next." He struggled for breath, pushing out the words with desperate effort. "Take… briefcase. Don't let any…one…get…it. Run! Promise… me!"

His fingers clawed her arm for emphasis.

"Yes. I'll run." Anything to make the nightmare stop. "I'll take your briefcase," she promised. "I'll run. I won't let anyone get it."

The fingers relaxed their fierce pressure, though he continued to hold her. His eyes closed in pain or exhaustion or both.

"Should…have told you…truth."

His chest heaved with the effort. There was a rattling sound that terrified her.

"Never mind! Don't try to talk anymore, Daddy. Let me call an ambulance."

He opened his eyes. The glassy look faded. For a minute he looked right at her. In his eyes was the father she remembered.

"I love you, Daddy."

His lips worked into a smile. A trickle of frothy blood leaked from the corner of his mouth. "Good...daughter." He whispered so softly she had to strain to make out his words. "Made...her...happy. Wish...you'd...been mine."

"What?"

The rattle intensified. "Run!...Hart...keep."

More spittle dribbled from between his lips, frothy with blood. His chest heaved with that terrible rattling sound and then he sighed. The hand clutching hers went limp.

"Daddy!"

She shook him. His eyes were fixed and empty. His features were oddly peaceful in death.

Alexis didn't know how long she stood there, holding his dead hand and crying, but her body was tight with pain when she straightened. Her head throbbed. She swayed slightly, feeling light-headed and weak. Every muscle in her body felt stiff and uncoordinated. And she was so cold. Her teeth chattered uncontrollably.

Swollen red eyes stared back at her from her reflection in the mirror over her dresser. Her face was blotchy from her tears. There was blood on her wrist. She used a corner of the towel to wipe it off.

The apartment buzzer sounded—an imperious summons from someone in the downstairs lobby. She'd forgotten all about her date. It didn't matter. He'd have to wait. Everything would have to wait. Her father was dead and she didn't even know what or who had killed him.

Like a somnambulist, she left the room, barely able to think past the horror. The buzzer sounded again, impatiently this time. She couldn't deal with a date right now. Her father was dead. He'd been so still in death. He'd always been so animated in life.

She entered the living room. The buzzer was an irritant.

She wished it would stop. She was so terribly cold. Moving automatically toward the door she paused, staring at the shiny spot of blood on the floor.

"I need you, Daddy."

The whispered words ended on a broken sob. Except she couldn't cry anymore. She felt spent. Besides, tears wouldn't bring him back. Yet her eyes continued to burn with fresh tears.

The buzzer stopped its annoying sound. She swayed, feeling sick. She couldn't seem to think. She should call for help. Only there was nothing anyone could do to help. Her father was dead.

Run!

He'd told her to run.

Fear slipped past her barrier of shock and grief as the memory of his broken words surfaced. She hadn't given real thought to how he'd died or why, too caught up in the horror of his death. Now she tried to wrap her sluggish mind around that thought.

Her father had ordered her to go. He'd used his last remaining strength to tell her to run. She pictured the blood, the towel pressed to his abdomen. This hadn't been some careless, drunken accident. Something far more horrible had happened.

Run!

Her gaze fastened on a large suitcase-shaped briefcase. The dull black leather was nothing like the worn brown case he usually carried—the one her mother had given him years ago when life had been fun and happy.

Lifting the unfamiliar case, she was surprised by its weight. The case was sticky with his blood. Adrenaline shoved aside her shock. Her father had died, struggling to tell her to take the briefcase and go.

She looked around for something to wipe the blood from her hand. Linda's favorite throw pillow was the closest object. She didn't care. She had never had liked that shade of orange anyhow.

In the hall outside her apartment, the ancient elevator ground to a halt. The sound was alien. Menacing. No one who lived in the building ever used that elevator. Most visitors took one look and opted for the stairs.

Heavy footsteps started down the hall. Terror seized her. She realized she'd left the front door ajar.

Someone would come here next. Run!

She'd waited too long. Now there was no place to run. Clutching the briefcase against her chest, she snatched up her purse. Mail fell to the floor. She ignored it and darted inside the miniscule hall closet, pulling the door closed.

Her heart threatened to beat its way free of her chest as she heard the footsteps stop in front of her apartment. She sensed more than heard the front door swing open.

Alexis held her breath. With every thud of her heart, she waited for someone to fling open the closet and to kill her, too. Seconds passed. What was he doing? What was he waiting for?

Heavy footsteps moved into the living room. Panic held her immobile as she strained to listen.

The sound of glass crunching beneath an incautious foot put the intruder in the kitchen. Alexis opened the closet. He'd closed the front door. Her fingers felt numb as she turned the handle and slipped into the hall.

The elevator yawned open across from her. A death trap, more so now than ever. But someone was coming up the stairs. In seconds the person would be in view. Or worse, the intruder inside her apartment would open the door at her back.

Alexis ran for the elevator. Flattening her body against the dirty metal panel, she prayed she was hidden from direct view while she strove to control the sound of her raspy breath. The person on the stairs was coming down the hall. Terror left her muscles straining with tension as she battled an urge to run.

Her apartment door opened. "What are you doing here?"

A man's voice. She didn't recognize it. She missed the low-murmured response. "Forget it, she's gone. We'd better go, too."

Mrs. Nicholson's dog began yipping in pleasure as animal and owner headed down the main steps from the floor above. The sound covered what the voices were saying.

"...find her. Get inside."

Her apartment door closed. Alexis pressed the button that would take the decrepit elevator up to the next floor. The old metal doors crawled closed. Sounding as if any second might be its last, the elevator rose with painful slowness.

She stayed pressed against the side until it finally ground to a halt and opened once more. The hall beyond was empty and silent. Alexis pressed every floor, sending it on up, then ran for the back stairs.

But running was bad. Running would attract attention. She mustn't draw attention. They'd be watching for that. She didn't know what these people looked like, but it was certain that they would know her. Her car was in the garage down the street. She'd have to walk around the block to get there.

Walk. Don't run.

They'd expect her to use the back door out of the building since they'd come in the front, so Alexis forced herself to walk down the hall toward the main entrance. She squirmed out of her white summer blazer and folded it over the briefcase as she stepped onto the noisy, dirty street outside.

She welcomed the people moving past, intent on getting home and out of the city heat. The ninety-seven-degree temperature didn't faze the ice in possession of her body. With each step, she fought the panic screaming inside her head. Panic that urged her to run, urged her to look back to see if she was being followed.

A horn blared so loudly that it made her jump. Balanced on the razor's edge of hysteria, she averted her head and kept walking. Other horns joined in screaming protest. They weren't honking at her so it didn't matter. Let them honk. This was rush hour in New York. Everyone used their horns. Her brain filtered out the noise and kept her moving.

She was deaf with fear by the time she reached the busy garage. It took every bit of strength she had not to break into a run to the safety of her seldom-used car. At each step, she expected to be stopped by a hand on her shoulder—or worse.

She nearly sobbed with relief when she reached her car. Putting down the briefcase, she searched desperately through her purse for the keys. She was shaking hard by the time she found them. The automatic button released the lock. She tossed the briefcase onto the passenger seat and slid inside, locking the doors and slumping down to allow herself the luxury of sitting a few minutes until the worst of her shaking had passed.

When she could manage it, she put the key into the ignition and backed slowly from the narrow parking space. She rarely drove and this was the height of rush hour. Inhaling deeply, she plunged into traffic. Normally a timid driver, she pushed the small car recklessly through the crowded streets until she had no choice but to slow down in the bumper-to-bumper traffic waiting to cross one of the bridges leading out of town.

It didn't matter which bridge or where she headed. She only needed to leave the city behind. Panic still hovered on the edges of her mind as she followed the flow of traffic until she found herself on an interstate, still in New York state.

She had no idea where to go, what to do. She pictured the faces of friends and acquaintances. How could she drag anyone else into this? She didn't even know what "this" was all about.

Her father was dead. She didn't know why or even

how. There was no family to turn to. Her mother had been an orphan. Her father had been the only child of elderly parents. If there were cousins, she didn't know about them. She was totally on her own.

Alexis shuddered. She reached for her jacket and struggled into it as she drove. She was so cold. So scared. She should go to the police. Only, her father hadn't told her to go to the police, he'd told her to run. Why?

Alexis shot a glance at the briefcase on the seat beside her. She was loath to touch the heavy object again. Like Pandora's box, opening that briefcase might turn loose the evil that had killed her father.

She tore her gaze away and kept driving until the gas gauge warning light came on. She'd forgotten to fill the tank again. She'd have to stop somewhere. Surely she was safe now. No one could have followed her. Even she didn't know exactly where she was.

Exhausted, she watched for signs for the next gas station, finally pulling off the road at a rest area. Parking as far from other cars as possible, she sat for a minute trying to decide what to do. She couldn't just leave her father there. She should call someone.

Who? What could she tell them?

Her fingers trembled as she reached for her seat belt. There was no choice. She had to open the briefcase. Surely the contents would tell her what this nightmare was all about.

Even though she'd parked near the end of the lot, Alexis scanned the area to be sure no one was nearby. If an inanimate object could be evil, surely this briefcase was evil. She had to force her fingers to reach for the locks so she could peer inside.

A scream of protest filled her mind, but never made it past her lips. Beneath a thick manila envelope, the briefcase was filled with stacks of what appeared to be hundred-dollar bills. She closed her eyes tightly, wishing she could make them disappear by thought alone.

What had he done? Dear God, what had he done? Her father didn't have this kind of money. Only drug dealers or kidnappers had this sort of cash.

Her moan of anguish escaped, shockingly loud in the tense silence of her car.

No wonder he was dead. No wonder someone wanted this case. But where had it come from? Her father wasn't a drug dealer. He wasn't a criminal. He worked in the insurance industry.

Money laundering?

Oh, God. She knew nothing about that sort of stuff. Could a criminal launder money through an insurance company? And even if they could, why would her father have this briefcase full of money? He wasn't a crook, he was her father!

She snapped the case closed and shut her eyes. What was she going to do? Opening her eyes, she stared at the parking lot. What would happen if she simply carried the case over to the large trash can sitting several feet away and left it there? The idea was dangerously tempting.

Except, whoever wanted this case wouldn't stop looking for her just because she'd thrown it away. No matter where she ran, they'd follow. The money made that a certainty.

There had been an envelope. Maybe the contents of the envelope would tell her what to do, how to get this money back where it belonged. She forced her fingers to reopen the case. Lifting the envelope, she turned it over and stared in horror at the bold printing across the front.

Her eyes burned with the need to cry again, but she'd used up all her tears. Too bad she hadn't used up the fear, as well. It threatened to consume her at the sight of her name.

She should go to the police right now. It would be best if she didn't even look inside the envelope. But she knew she would. He had been her father, whatever else he may have been. He had brought this briefcase to her apartment for a reason. She owed him a hearing, even in death.

With a heavy heart, Alexis lifted the unsealed envelope flap. On top was a sheet of lined paper, ripped from some sort of notepad.

Darling Alexis,
If you're reading this note it means I'm in trouble and never got a chance to explain. Hang on to this briefcase. A woman named Kathy can tell you the rest. I don't remember her last name, but I'm sure she'll be in touch.

So typical of her father. He could never remember names or details. Kathy might really be Suzy or Betty or something that wasn't even remotely close to that.

Don't let anyone know you have this in your possession. I'm sorry to put this onus on you, but I may not have a choice. I'm not sure about the legality of this money. I trusted the wrong person years ago and a lot of people were hurt as a result. It's too late to make amends to some of them, including you, but I'm going to try. I'm sorry, Alexis. I know I've been a lousy father. I wasn't the best husband, either. Lois deserved so much more than I could give her.

Alexis wiped at her burning eyes. Whatever else had been wrong with his world, her father truly had loved them both.

Saying I'm sorry really doesn't cut it, but it's all I can say. I can't make the past go away or change the decision that we made. I'm a weak man, Alexis. A stronger, better person would have told you the truth a long time ago.

The note was rambling. He must have been drinking when he'd written it. The penmanship was sloppy, but it was definitely her father's handwriting.

I'm sorry for that, too, but as it turns out, even I didn't know the truth until recently. I still don't, at least not all of it. God, I wish I'd told you this in person! Your mother and I couldn't have children, Alexis.

What? Her heart began to pound as his words burned away her entire life.

Lois wanted a baby desperately, so we applied to adopt. We were told it might take years. You know how much I loved her. I would have given Lois the moon if it had been possible. I knew it would kill her to wait indefinitely, with no certainty that we'd ever get a baby to call our own. Instead, I knew someone who knew of a doctor that might be willing to bend the rules for us. I'm sorry, Alexis, I knew it would be an illegal adoption, but I didn't care at the time.

She was adopted? It couldn't be true. It mustn't be true. Her whole life had been a lie? She wanted to crumple the damning paper in her hand and throw it away, but he'd looked at her through eyes that were dying and had said he'd wished she'd been his.

The paper shook so badly she could barely hold it still enough to continue reading.

The doctor claimed he knew an unwed girl willing to see her baby go to a good home for enough money to go to college and start over. If we could cover his fee and pay the girl, he was willing to take a chance and help us all. I'd like to believe if we'd known the truth, we wouldn't have gone through with your adoption, but Lois wanted a baby so badly, I don't know.

What truth? What had he done?

We didn't ask any questions. We never met your birth mother. You were only a few hours old when the doctor's nurse placed you in Lois's arms. You were such a beautiful, perfect little baby girl. I wish you could have seen Lois's look of joy. It was worth everything. You may not have been our biological child, but we always thought of you that way, you have to believe me. We loved you, Alexis. I loved you. I know I haven't been there for you since Lois died. I let my grief consume me instead of thinking about you like I should have. It's too late to make that up to you now. All I can say is I'm sorry, Alexis.

She wiped at the burning tears that slipped down her cheeks. The car was so hot she was suffocating. She turned on the ignition to let the air conditioner run, wiping at her tears until her vision became less blurred.

It wasn't entirely his fault. She should have tried harder to get him to seek help. If she'd been a better daughter…but she wasn't really his daughter. The enormity of that was still hard to accept.

Alexis stared at the money. Once again, fear gripped her. Had her father done something awful in an attempt to make things up to her? She gripped the note, fearing the answer it must contain.

I just learned that the doctor who forged your birth certificate was murdered recently. I did some snooping and learned the awful truth. Your real mother

*never gave you up for adoption, Alexis. I don't think
she even knew you existed.*

How was that possible? This made no sense. She didn't
want to read any more. Her father's words were tearing
her world to shreds. How could he not have told her this?

The doctor had been murdered. Now her father had
been murdered. If she wasn't careful, was she the next in
line to be killed?

*When I realized what that man had done, I was
sick. I think if he hadn't already been dead I'd have
been tempted to murder him myself. How could any
man, especially a doctor, have no soul? He pulled
you from her body and gave you away with no remorse. It still sickens me to think about it. I'll carry
this horror to my grave. I wonder if God will forgive
me for my part in this. I guess I'll know soon enough.
I've been lying to you, Alexis, about more than just
your birth. I know you thought my drinking was simply grief over Lois's death. And it did start out that
way, but the truth is, I've been ill for some time now.
I'm dying, Alexis. The cancer is inoperable. I didn't
want you to know. The alcohol helps dull the pain.*

Shock blurred the words on the page. She pictured how
thin he had grown…and knew the words were true. Why
hadn't he told her? Why had he lied and lied and lied to
her?

Grief mingled with anger and guilt. He hadn't been the
best father since her mother…since Lois had died, but
what sort of daughter had she been? So angry over his
drinking and his refusal to get help, she'd stopped paying
much attention to him. For a second her eyes closed in
grief and self-recriminations. But she had to finish, to
know it all. There'd be time for castigation later.

I've been trying to make things right as much as I can, but the truth of your real parentage, well, I can't give you back those years. Not you or your real family. But I've gathered together all the proof you should need to convince them of the truth. The only thing is, the more I learn, the more the situation makes me nervous.

Her real family. She had a real family. Why hadn't he told her this? How could he have let her go on living every day without telling her?

The nurse who brought you to us was there at the cemetery that day.

What cemetery?

I'm pretty sure she saw me. She isn't going to want you to come forward, Alexis. It's the last thing she'll want. What she and that doctor did wasn't just horrible, it was illegal. She could go to prison. She should go to prison. She's as guilty as he is. So you're going to have to be real careful, Alexis. I figure you'll need help before you go to see your family. The truth is, I'm not sure what sort of a reception you'll get from any of them. You're one of the rightful heirs, you see.

No, she didn't see. She didn't understand any of this. It was like a bad movie script. How could this be happening?

This envelope contains all the proof you need to claim your birthright. Take it to Ira Rosencroft. He's an attorney in upstate New York.

This couldn't be real. Her father had made some horrible mistake. Horrible enough to get him killed.

> *The town is small. It's horse country. Stony Ridge, the town is called. I checked around and from what I could learn, Rosencroft has a reputation for being honest. He's the trustee for Heartskeep, he'll help you. He has no choice. Just be careful, Alexis. Don't trust anyone. I wish there had been time for me to do this the right way, but I think my time is running out. I think someone was watching the house today. Maybe I'm getting paranoid, but I'm scared. Not for me. For you. Show Mr. Rosencroft the contents of this packet, but don't show him this letter and don't tell him about the money. Don't tell anyone about the money until you talk to this Kathy. I think you can trust her, Alexis. If she hadn't found me, I would never have known this much. You're the best daughter any man could ever want. I know it's selfish, but I'm glad you were ours. I only wish you had been ours in every way.*

The tears she'd thought were used up fell despite her best effort to keep them at bay. She could barely finish the last two lines.

> *Please don't think too badly of me. You will always be the daughter of my heart.*
>
> > *Your loving father,*
> > *Brian Fitzpatrick Ryder.*

For what seemed like a very long time she simply sat there and cried. She tried to make sense of all this, but nothing made sense. Not this rambling note, not the money in the briefcase, and certainly not her father's death.

He wasn't her father.

The world she had known had just dissolved.

A car pulled into the lot, alongside hers. She stuffed the letter back inside the briefcase and snapped it shut. The parking lot had filled with cars and people. A young couple sat arguing in the car parked beside her. They didn't even glance her way, but she couldn't afford to sit here in plain sight with a briefcase full of money.

Her engine suddenly sputtered and died. The car had finally run out of gas.

With the care reserved for handling fragile items, she lifted the heavy briefcase and got out of her car. She'd never heard of Stony Ridge, and she had only a New York City map in the glove compartment. She'd have to go inside the restaurant to see if she could buy a map. Then she'd have to get the gas can out of her trunk and go to the gas pump to get enough gas to drive her car over to fill it up. And as she trudged through the busy parking lot, one thought kept running through her mind.

How could a woman not know her child existed?

Chapter Two

Wyatt Crossley didn't like having time on his hands. He understood why his uncle, as chief of police, had no option other than to place him on leave while the shooting of Nolan Ducort was investigated, but Wyatt didn't have to like it. Stony Ridge had a major murder investigation under way. His investigation.

Unfortunately the Ducort family was politically well-connected and they were demanding answers. He and the two state police officers who'd fired their weapons two nights ago were being forced to wait until ballistics determined which gun had fired the shot that had struck Ducort and the investigators were satisfied that the shooting had been justified.

The outcome wasn't in question, really, but the three of them had been relieved of their duties until the panel cleared them of any wrongdoing. Wyatt was determined not to let that keep him from conducting some unofficial investigative work.

The bones discovered on the grounds of Heartskeep almost certainly belonged to Amy Hart Thomas. Everyone believed she'd disappeared in New York City seven years ago—everyone except her identical twin daughters. Now it looked as though the twins had been right all along and sloppy police work—specifically, his uncle's sloppy police work—had let the murderer go undetected for more than seven years.

Leigh and Hayley Thomas had always insisted that their father, Marcus, had killed their mother. Now that Marcus Thomas was dead, there was only one person left who might have the answers to what had really happened seven years ago.

Wyatt frowned as he thought about Eden Voxx Thomas. The R.N. had worked with Dr. Thomas since before his daughters had been born. The obvious scenario for Amy Thomas's demise would be a love triangle that had ended in murder. But where the Hart family was involved, Wyatt had learned to keep an open mind. Events were seldom as simple as they appeared on the surface.

He hoped finding Eden would solve a big portion of the mystery. The way she'd taken off and disappeared the moment Amy's body had been discovered implied some prior knowledge of guilt.

His uncle had turned the investigation over to the state police. Stony Ridge didn't have the manpower or the equipment to deal with a case of such magnitude. Wyatt was the only officer on the small force with a background in criminal investigations. That was why his uncle had assigned him as liaison to the state police. Their forensic team was slowly exhuming the body's remains while another team concluded a search of the massive estate for possible evidence. Since Wyatt couldn't continue his role, he figured he'd do some unauthorized investigating on his own.

Eden had tried to remove everything she could carry from the house after her husband's death. When Amy's remains had been discovered in the overgrown maze behind the house, Eden had fled, leaving behind a stack of books. Inside those books had been several blackmail notes.

They now knew Marcus had misappropriated more than six hundred thousand dollars from the Heartskeep estate, yet he had died broke. On the surface it appeared he'd stolen the money to pay blackmail demands. But Wyatt was still leery of the obvious. If the auditors that attorney Gavin Jarret had hired were able to match the blackmail demands to the amounts on the forged bills Marcus had submitted on behalf of the estate, maybe Wyatt would be able to tell if Marcus was the one being blackmailed—or the one doing the blackmailing.

Not for the first time Wyatt wished those notes hadn't been so ambiguous. Not only didn't they tell him who was being blackmailed, they didn't give him a clue as to why that someone was being blackmailed.

Wyatt itched to be back at Heartskeep right now, supervising the search of the enormous mansion instead of driving into town looking for Gavin. But he'd already been reprimanded for going back out to Heartskeep the day after shooting Ducort.

Since the estate was off-limits, he'd driven out to the Walken estate this morning. Being their closest neighbors, and Gavin's former foster parents, Emily and George Walken had opened their home to the twins and Gavin. Unfortunately, Wyatt had made the trek out there for nothing. Only the Walkens' housekeeper had been present. Nan had informed him that everyone had left, planning to stay elsewhere until the media frenzy died down.

The day had been a fruitless waste of time so far. With any luck Gavin had gone to his office to supervise the audit. Otherwise, Wyatt was going to find himself twiddling his thumbs most of the afternoon.

Parking was at a premium in town. The only spot open was in front of the remains of the dry-cleaning shop and what had once been Gavin's rented apartment above. The burned-out shell of a building was a silent reminder of how far a person would go to keep a secret. Wyatt wondered how far Eden would go.

He climbed out of his car into the hot, muggy air and wiped at the beads of sweat that immediately formed on his forehead. June was setting records, both for high temperatures and an unusual number of fierce summer storms. Stony Ridge had been fairly lucky so far. Located far enough north of New York City to sit high over the Hudson River, temperatures were generally milder here and the storms tended to give them more of a glancing blow.

Striding down the street, he exchanged greetings with several people without slowing down. The Hart family and Heartskeep had been a source of conversation for the locals since the day the first Hart had set foot in Stony Ridge. The town already hummed with gossip and speculation about the body and recent events at the estate. Wyatt wasn't about to add to the fodder.

As he neared the narrow brick building that housed the law offices of Rosencroft and Associates, luck finally beamed a smile his way. Leigh—or Hayley?—Thomas stood on the sidewalk out front clutching an oversize briefcase to her chest.

Having met the twins several times now, he was surprised by an unexpected twist of physical awareness when he first caught sight of her. They were attractive young women, but neither of them had ever sent his pulses leaping in anticipation before. Of course, he'd never really seen one of them alone before. Hayley was rarely without Bram Myers at her side. She'd staked a clear claim on the rugged blacksmith and he seemed perfectly content to be claimed—even if her wealth was still an issue between them.

Wyatt decided this must be Leigh. She and Gavin had seemed pretty tight, and he certainly couldn't blame his friend. Wyatt was struck by the way her chin-length hair shimmered more gold than brown beneath the unrelenting noon sun. The twins were slender, attractive women with identical heart-shaped faces and delicate bone structures. But exhaustion tugged at her expressive features, bowing the graceful arch of her neck.

He shouldn't be noticing his buddy's lady this way, but

it was hard not to. She had surprisingly long, graceful legs for such a petite woman. And there was definitely something appealing about the way she stood there in her wilted, bright green-and-white blouse and trim navy skirt. The outfit was hardly provocative, but it did show her figure to good advantage.

She turned away from the building and caught him staring. His chagrin was forgotten when haunted blue eyes regarded him with no trace of recognition. Wyatt took a chance on the name.

"Leigh? Is something wrong?"

A stupid question given the current circumstances. No purse, he noticed, but she clutched the large, scuffed briefcase against her chest. Stained and battered, the case wasn't the sort of accessory he'd associate with a Hart. He set that thought aside as his attention was drawn back to those wide, crystal-blue eyes. Fatigue mixed with sorrow dulled them—a painful reminder that his "case" was her mother's death.

Wyatt closed the distance between them. "Is Gavin inside?" He nodded toward the door at her back.

Her forlorn expression changed to one of confusion. Her gaze flicked toward the building and back to his face, sliding away quickly.

"The office is closed."

Her soft voice came out flat and empty. He barely controlled the impulse that started his hand in the direction of her slim, bare arm.

"Has something else happened?"

A flash of fear came and went so fast he wasn't positive it was what he'd seen.

"Excuse me," she said more firmly. "I have to go."

Her reaction was all wrong. So was her appearance. Where was Gavin? Or her sister, for that matter? Leigh shouldn't be out here alone. She looked like someone running on empty.

Wyatt blocked her path and nodded at the case. "Are those your grandfather's files?"

Her knuckles whitened as she hugged the awkward case more tightly to her chest.

"I have to go," she repeated.

He touched her shoulder, stopping her. She raised startled eyes to his. The tip of her tongue touched her lips. The nervous gesture was not the least bit erotic yet it made him sharply aware of her as a woman.

She took a quick step back. Wyatt let his hand fall to his side. Her wary expression made him frown.

She raised her face. "What is it you want?" she demanded.

Several totally inappropriate answers sprang to mind. What the devil was wrong with him? This was Leigh. He was almost positive it was Leigh. While he barely knew the twins, Hayley's ability to put a man in his place was legendary.

"I'm not your enemy."

"Glad to hear it. Now, if you'll excuse me..."

"Can we talk?"

"Another time. I have to go."

"Where?"

The question stopped her. For an instant she stared at him in consternation. He would have sworn there was a hint of desperation, even fear, in those expressive eyes. Something was wrong here.

"Let me pass."

Her voice was still firm.

"I could make the request official."

Definitely a lick of fear.

"What do you mean?"

His conscience gave a guilty twist. Her vulnerable expression was getting to him. The last thing he wanted was to make her afraid.

"I know we haven't met under the best of circumstances, but I'm not my uncle, Leigh. I'm on your side."

She inhaled visibly. Watching her marshal her mental defenses took only a split second, but it revealed quite a bit about her. Leigh would face whatever life tossed at her. He should have known that from the way she'd handled herself when Ducort had threatened to kill her. Still, his admiration went up another notch as she raised her chin another notch and held his gaze.

"What side would that be, exactly?"

Mentally he applauded the challenge. "Let me buy you a cup of coffee and we can discuss it."

"It's ninety-eight degrees out here."

"Good point." He offered her a wry smile. "How about an iced tea instead?"

"Thanks, but I have to go…home."

The catch in her voice gave him another glimpse of her vulnerability. Wyatt shook his head. "I'm assuming you don't mean home to Boston, but if you mean to the Walken estate, I just came from there. Nan said everyone left to avoid the media. They're still camped out in front of both estates. And if you meant Heartskeep, the state police haven't finished their investigation yet."

Panic flared in her expression. While she had plenty of reason to distrust the police, panic made no sense. Yet she looked ready to bolt.

"One drink," he said gently. "Better yet, what about an ice-cream cone?"

"Ice cream?"

She formed the words as if they were foreign to her. Her eyes skimmed the street—searching for a way to escape? What the devil was going on? He'd take bets it had something to do with her death grip on that case.

This didn't seem like a good time to remind her of the talk they were supposed to have about the events surrounding her mother's disappearance.

"Ice cream," he said calmly. "You know, that frozen stuff that melts on your tongue when you lick it."

Her eyes widened. He hadn't meant a sexual connotation, but even to him the words came out sounding that way.

"I can't."

"We don't have to talk, Leigh," he coaxed gently. "I told you I'd make an appointment for that. I'd just like some company right now. I'm not used to having nothing to do all day."

She stared at him blankly.

Tempted to explain his temporary suspension, he decided it was better not to remind her of the events of the other night. She'd come far too close to being killed as it was.

"We could drive out to Golden's, grab a cone and come right back."

She was shaking her head back and forth even before he finished.

"You could call Gavin and invite him to come with us," he added.

"No!"

Instant and vehement. So there was some sort of problem between them. A lovers' spat? He'd never realized his friend was an idiot. Wyatt shouldn't have liked the fleeting notion that maybe their relationship wasn't what he'd thought.

"I don't want to talk to Gavin right now," she amended quickly. "I'm not... I don't feel like talking to anyone right now."

That was pointed enough, but he wasn't about to let her go when she was so obviously upset.

"Then we won't talk," he agreed. "But let's get out of this sun before we fry."

She studied his face. Wyatt was relieved when, after a moment's hesitation, she fell into step beside him. Despite this unexpected jolt of attraction to her, he had no intention of encroaching on his friend's relationship with Leigh. This was strictly business. He was a cop with a case to solve, and the contents of that briefcase were of

major interest to him. He'd keep things light and imper-
sonal. Once he gained her trust, he'd ask her about the
case.

Of course, gaining her trust would be the hard part.

ALEXIS WONDERED if she'd taken leave of her senses. Going anywhere with this incredibly handsome stranger was
pure folly, yet she'd taken one look into those warm
brown eyes and felt an instant connection to this man.
The impact had rattled her more than she cared to admit.
He wasn't breathtakingly handsome, but he was the sort
of man a woman would always notice.

What on earth had possessed her to let him believe she
was someone else?

Because it had seemed the quickest way to get rid of
him. Obviously that had been a big mistake on her part.
What would he do if she told him she had no idea who
Leigh or Gavin were? Or him, either, for that matter?

The thought was dangerously tempting. She was so
tired she couldn't seem to think past her fear and exhaustion. Her father's note had told her to come here for answers, only there were no answers for her here. Ira Rosencroft was dead.

Alexis had wanted to ask the woman inside how he'd
died, but a man had come out of an office to ask a question. Maybe this Gavin person. The receptionist or whoever she'd been had asked the man to wait while she
offered Alexis an appointment to see a Mr. Jarret next
week.

Alexis declined. Her father's note had said not to trust
anyone except the lawyer and someone named Kathy. But
when she had asked the woman if a Kathy worked there,
the woman had shaken her head. With the man standing
there waiting, Alexis had thanked her and left. Now she
didn't know what to do.

An uneven bit of pavement sent her stumbling. The
man beside her had a firm, strong grip as he took her bare

arm to keep her from falling. His touch reinforced her vibrant awareness of him. Under other circumstances, she might have welcomed the unexpected reaction. As it was, she wished he'd go away and let her think.

"Easy, there."

His voice was soothing to nerves that felt stretched far too tight.

"Why don't you let me carry that case for you?"

Panic lifted her eyes to his. "No!"

Instantly his expression changed. What was the matter with her? She'd overreacted, made him curious. Calling his attention to the briefcase like that had been stupid. He'd already expressed an interest in the contents. If he saw all that money...

"Sorry. I didn't mean to snap at you like that. I haven't had much sleep and my nerves are a little shot right now," she told him truthfully.

His expression relaxed. Her stomach gave a funny little lurch at the compassion in his eyes.

"I know," he told her. "It's okay. Come on. I'm parked right over here."

There was nothing for it but to resume walking. The kindness in his warm brown eyes was dangerous. Dangerous, because she wanted to trust him. She was so tired. So scared. Grief had vied with fear all night long. She'd taken a room at a motel right off the highway last night and had lain sleeplessly, going over and over her father's death, wondering what she could have done differently.

The half cup of coffee she'd managed to swallow this morning was still burning a hole in her stomach lining. It was so hard to think.

Her roommate was in California for the week, which meant that no one had yet discovered her father's body.

Except his killers.

She shouldn't have run. She should have stayed and called the police. She nearly had called more than once last night. But each time she'd reached for the telephone, fear had stilled her hand. The police would have questions. Alexis didn't have answers.

She'd thought if she talked to this Mr. Rosencroft first, everything would make sense. But if he was dead, too, she didn't know where to go next. Had he been murdered, as well?

Her father had said his killers would come after her next. He'd been right. But who were they? What was she supposed to do with all this money?

Her companion stopped at a car parked in front of a fire-gutted building. Alexis had noticed the burned-out remains earlier on her way into town. He opened the passenger door of the trim black sedan and began stacking several files sitting on the seat.

This was insane. What was she doing, getting in a car with a total stranger? Only a fool would do something so stupid. She wasn't a stupid person. Yet she had no desire to turn and run in the opposite direction.

He cleared the passenger seat of papers and folders, dumping everything on the back seat, which was already littered with other items.

"Sorry. I'm afraid I've been using the car as something of a spare closet."

His embarrassment was sort of reassuring. Tall and lean, with a thick head of dark, curling hair, he had an easygoing manner that offered her frazzled nerves a false sense of security. There was confidence and a sense of strength about him. More important, he knew things. Things she desperately needed to know.

Who was Leigh? Undoubtedly related to her if they looked enough alike to be mistaken for one another. Stony Ridge did have answers after all. So did this man. All she had to do was to ask the right questions.

Alexis hesitated, debating her options. She glanced at the building behind her. A smoky scent lingered in the heavy, humid air. The fire must have burned hot and furious, because the insides had been destroyed with savage completeness.

"You and Gavin were lucky the other night," he said in a hard tone of voice. "If you'd been upstairs when that gas line blew…"

Upstairs? She raised her eyes and realized there had been living quarters above the shop. The thought that anyone might have been inside was horrifying.

"You want to toss your briefcase back here?" he asked, dismissing both the fire and the building.

Should she go with him or stay here?

He waited calmly, as if he sensed her indecision. There was nothing remotely threatening in his manner. She liked that he was giving her time to decide. But when it came right down to it, she had nowhere else to go.

Alexis handed him the heavy case. He set it on the back seat without a word about its weight and stepped back, holding the door open for her.

The car was low. Her skirt scooted up her thigh as she sat. She felt his stare as she struggled to pull it into place. If his expression had been the least bit lecherous, she'd have been out of the car instantly, but his gaze held only a masculine appreciation she might have enjoyed if things had been different.

Watching him stride around to the driver's side, Alexis had all sorts of time for second and third thoughts. Going anywhere with this vibrant stranger was a really stupid thing to do. He thought she was someone named Leigh. How long could she maintain the pretense before he saw through the sham? She wasn't up to this. Heck, she didn't even know who *she* was anymore.

He offered her a smile as he slid behind the wheel. Her clenched muscles began to relax. The man had a breathtaking smile.

"I'm afraid it'll take a second or two for the air conditioner to put out anything like cool air. Jezzy here isn't up to dealing with this sort of heat."

"You named your car?"

His grin widened unselfconsciously. "Blame it on my mother. She and my sisters always named our cars. I guess I picked up the habit."

There was something rather endearing about that, which was ridiculous. So what if the man had a mother and sisters? Even serial killers had family.

"Jezzy?" she asked nervously.

"Short for Jezebelle. You'll notice the faded leather seats and all the fancy dashboard equipment. At one time this girl was loaded with all the extras, flashy and pretentious for such a cheaply made little car. When I found her on the used car lot, she reminded me of an abandoned harlot, past her prime but determined to make the best of what she still had."

"Oh."

He chuckled, a warm rumbly sound that was as oddly soothing as the man himself.

"Don't worry about it. My family thinks I'm a little nuts, too, but it isn't contagious."

"Too bad."

He tilted his head. Alexis squirmed. "I just meant that it's a nice sort of nuts to be." That grin of his was dangerously disarming.

"Thanks."

Alexis looked away quickly. The man gave a whole other meaning to the words "perfect stranger." She was suddenly all too aware of how rumpled she looked. She'd done the best she could this morning considering she'd had no fresh clothing and only the contents of her purse to work with. She'd only wanted to look presentable when she spoke with the lawyer. Now she wished she'd taken the time to stop and buy a clean outfit. There was nothing she could do about it at the moment, but she'd noticed a dress shop in town. She'd go there as soon as they returned. Hopefully the prices wouldn't be too outrageous. Her bank account was a little slim these days.

With a start, she realized he'd spoken to her again. "I'm sorry, what did you say?"

"I just said you look tired."

"I am tired." A gross understatement. Alexis closed her eyes in despair.

"It's going to be okay, Leigh."

Her eyes flew open. Who was Leigh? Cousin? Sister? Aunt?

"Look, I don't mean to be rude—"

"You aren't being rude. You're tired. You've been through a lot in the past few days."

Startled, she inhaled sharply. How did he know?

Puzzled concern creased his forehead. He didn't know, she realized. He'd meant this Leigh person had been through a lot in the past few days. He'd said the woman could have been inside the burned-out shell of that building back in town. It was simply an unnerving coincidence that this Leigh person had been through an ordeal, as well.

"Hey, how does a milk shake sound? Chocolate? Vanilla? One of the more exotics?"

A milk shake? Somehow she couldn't get her mind to focus on something so mundane. She was pretty sure she wasn't going to be able to swallow a single sip anyhow.

"Surprise me."

"Okay, but I like the exotics, myself. Some of those candy-flavored ones are dangerously addictive, you know."

It was impossible not to return that smile, even if hers felt weak and distant. She suspected candy-flavored milk shakes weren't the only things potentially addictive around here. Why couldn't someone like this have been her roommate's cousin instead of Seth?

Golden's Ice Cream turned out to be a drive-up place in the middle of nowhere. Yet, judging from the number of cars clustered around the parking lot, being in the middle of nowhere wasn't a drawback. A scattering of picnic tables sat in a grove of trees off to one side and all of them held people.

"Do you want to come with me or stay here while I get us something?" he asked.

"I'd rather stay."

He opened all the windows before stepping out of the car. "You sure you won't get too hot waiting for me?"

"I'll try to contain myself."

He winced in consternation as he realized how his question had come out.

"I meant, try not to melt before I get back, okay?"

That dredged a genuine smile from her. "You'd better quit while you're ahead."

"I think you're right. I'll be right back."

She liked him. Not only was he extremely good-looking, he was a genuinely nice guy, as well. She watched him stride toward the long line of customers waiting under the awning for service. More than one person called out a greeting as he passed.

"Hey, Wyatt!"

"Wyatt! Are we still playing ball tomorrow?"

"That's the plan, but if we get more rain, we may need snorkels."

His name was Wyatt and he played ball. She tossed the name around in her head. Unusual, but it suited him. Alexis could picture him as gunslinger in the Old West. Tall and loose-limbed, Wyatt had an athletic body that moved with a comfortable grace. Yet there was a sense of barely restrained energy about him. Wyatt never seemed to just walk. He strode with a sense of purpose, a sense of power. Like his namesake, the role of sheriff would suit him. Wyatt was the sort of man people looked up to, a natural leader.

What was the matter with her? She had no business sitting here thinking about some stranger, no matter how appealing he might be. She was in real trouble. She needed to stop thinking about Wyatt and to start planning a course of action.

Alexis leaned her head back against the headrest and closed her eyes. How could she plan a course of action when she lacked the most basic information? She was out of her depth and so exhausted she could barely think at all.

"Leigh? Wake up, Leigh."

The low, warm voice seeped through the barrier of half-sleep to stir her conscious mind awake. Alexis forced her heavy lids apart. For a second she had no idea where she was or why this incredible stranger was bending over her.

"I know you're tired, but it's too hot to sit in the car. I appropriated one of the tables in the shade. It may not feel all that much cooler, but the ice cream should help."

Loggy, she stared at his handsome features. Her fingers started a quest toward the strong line of his jaw.

"Hey, you awake?"

She lowered her hand, confused. "I'm not sure," she admitted.

He reached across her to unfasten her seat belt. Awareness tightened her nipples as his bare arm brushed her chest. He pretended not to notice, stepping back and extending his hand to her. Her body responded as if it was a different sort of invitation altogether.

His large, warm hand enveloped hers, making her feel small and delicate and surprisingly feminine. For a dizzy, disorienting second, their gazes locked. She came out of the car and swayed slightly.

"Easy, there," he said.

Anticipation rippled through her. He released her hand and stepped back quickly.

"Why don't you go over and have a seat? I'll grab our stuff and be right with you."

He'd felt it, too. His eyes had reflected the same spark of awareness that had sprung to life inside her, tightening her belly and making her aware of him on a sensual level she'd never experienced before.

What was she thinking?

Shaken, Alexis turned away and started across the parking lot. This was crazy. She was so exhausted that her mind was playing dangerous games with her. If she didn't get control she was going to make an utter fool of herself.

Relieved to see that the empty table he'd indicated was near the edge of the treeline, she headed there quickly. Several people nodded greetings as she passed. A few offered sympathetic smiles. Thankfully no one approached, wanting to talk. She sat quickly with her back to the other tables and hoped no one would.

Wyatt had said he didn't know Leigh very well. That was the only reason she'd gotten away with her masquerade so far. She'd never be able to maintain the pretense with anyone who really knew this Leigh person.

When he joined her a few minutes later she had her reckless emotions under control. Until Wyatt set down a tray full of food on the table.

"What is all that?"

"Lunch."

"You said ice cream."

"Yes, ma'am. Best milk shakes in the state." He placed an enormous paper cup full of thick liquid in front of her.

"I can't drink all this."

"They make great hamburgers, too. I figured we could share the fries."

Alexis stared at the thick hamburger in dismay. "But I'm…" On the verge of telling him she was a vegetarian, she stopped. Leigh might not be a vegetarian. That was something Wyatt might know about the woman.

"When did you eat last?" he demanded.

Her mind went blank. "I don't—"

"That's what I thought. You look like a stiff wind would blow you away. One bite. Please, Leigh?"

She looked at the hamburger, then at the determined

set of his strong, firm jaw. "Could I start with a French fry?"

He offered her another of those devastating grins. "Help yourself."

She was sure she wouldn't be able to swallow the thick, chewy potato, but at the first taste, her stomach let her know it had other ideas. She hadn't known she was hungry, but she was. The milk shake was so thick she needed a spoon, and true to his word, there were chunks of candy blended into the mix. The cold ice cream tasted even better than the French fry.

"Oops. Forgot the napkins. Let me return the tray and grab some. I'll be right back."

As Wyatt headed toward the building, Alexis quickly tore the meat from between the bun and tossed it into the underbrush nearby. With all the lettuce and tomatoes, maybe he wouldn't notice. She picked up the bun and bit into it. Her stomach eagerly accepted that offering, as well.

Wyatt returned, looking slightly more subdued.

"The Krolberths asked me to offer their condolences. I told them you weren't up to talking with anyone right now."

Alexis swallowed quickly. "Thank you."

Wyatt nodded and took a bite from his sandwich. For several seconds they ate in silence. She studied him covertly. Her instincts said she could trust him, and she needed to tell someone the truth.

"Do you want to talk about it?"

Her head jerked up. Her heart hammered against her rib cage. Had he just read her mind?

"Talk about what?"

"You could tell me what's bothering you," he said, "or we could start with your mother's murder."

Chapter Three

For a second Alexis thought Wyatt had said he wanted to discuss her father's murder. Her father had been murdered, the lawyer was dead, and now the mother of the woman who looked like her had also been murdered? Why? What was happening here?

The briefcase!

She couldn't believe she'd forgotten all about the briefcase full of money. She'd left it sitting in plain sight on the back seat of Wyatt's unlocked car! Not only that, she'd put her purse inside it this morning.

Alexis was on her feet and moving. Panic sent her running across the tarmac, dodging cars and people. The money must belong to someone. This Kathy person might want it back. What would Alexis do if it was gone?

Maybe she should hope it was. Maybe if the murderer got the money, she'd be safe.

"Leigh, wait!"

No one was near his car. She was almost there when Wyatt caught her by the arm and spun her around. Alexis jerked free. Her heart thudded painfully against her rib cage.

"Keep your hands off me!"

Wyatt sent a quick glance around. "Calm down."

So, he didn't want to create a scene. Well, too bad. A scene was exactly what he was going to get. If she could

make him mad enough, maybe he wouldn't push her for
answers she didn't have.

"I don't want to calm down." Alexis steeled her heart
against the genuine regret she could see on his strong,
handsome face. "'We don't have to talk, Leigh,'" she
mimicked. "'I'd just like some company.'"

"You're right," he agreed quietly. "I'm sorry."

His sincerity made it all the harder to pretend indiffer-
ence. She liked Wyatt. On some level she even trusted
him—but she couldn't tell him the truth. She didn't know
the truth. Besides, the truth could get him killed.

"Come back and finish your lunch."

"I am finished." Her personal feelings had no place in
this. She had to get away from Wyatt.

Pivoting, she turned back to his car. Despite the open
windows, the briefcase sat on the back seat, exactly where
she'd left it. Alexis breathed a sigh of relief.

"Hey, Wyatt. I thought that was your truck," a voice
called to them. "Hayley?"

"Leigh," Wyatt corrected tersely.

Alexis pulled the briefcase from the car and turned
around. Another good-looking, dark-haired man sauntered
toward them. He held an ice-cream cone in one hand and
a large paper dish of ice cream in the other.

"Sorry, Leigh. I never could tell you and your sister
apart."

Leigh must have a twin sister named Hayley. Alexis
couldn't have said why that knowledge was so frightening, but it was.

"Put the briefcase back in the car, Leigh," Wyatt said.
"I'll take you back to town."

"No, thank you. I'd rather walk."

He set his jaw. "I didn't think you were the petty
type."

Her mind supplied something he'd said to her earlier.
"And I didn't think you were like your uncle. I guess we
were both wrong."

Wyatt's lips tightened. Before he could respond, his cell phone rang. He reached for it automatically.

"I'm really going to have to work on my timing," the newcomer said wryly. "He isn't, you know."

"Like his uncle? I'll take your word for it."

Easy enough to do since she had no idea who Wyatt's uncle was. Wyatt growled into his cell phone. Alexis had a hunch her luck was playing out.

"Do you think you could give me a lift back to town?"

"Uh, I'm not going back into town right now. I have to swing by Heartskeep to pick up a piece of equipment."

Her father had tried to tell her something about Heartskeep, and Wyatt had implied Leigh lived there.

"Even better," she told him.

The man looked to Wyatt, but Wyatt's expression was intent as he listened to his phone.

"Uh, let me give Lucky this ice cream before it melts." Alexis followed the stranger to a well-used pickup. An enormous black dog of questionable parentage woofed a greeting and leaped down from the bed of the truck. She'd always liked dogs, but this one was a lot bigger than the apartment-size animals she was used to seeing. Fortunately his tail wagged in a friendly fashion.

"Here you go, Lucky."

Lucky looked from her to the ice cream. She was relieved when the ice cream won. He set to work inhaling the contents of the dish with a large pink tongue.

"I know it isn't any of my business, but do you want to tell me what's going on?" the man asked.

"Wyatt promised not to hound me when he brought me out here. Now all he wants to do is ask me questions."

"Official questions?"

I could make the request official, he'd said. What was wrong with her brain? She wasn't generally this slow on the uptake. Wyatt was a cop!

The other man was frowning at her, looking troubled. "I knew you should have told Wyatt about the hidden room. Did the police discover the entrance through the closet?''

Alexis tried not to gape at him. What was he talking about? Police and hidden rooms? She shook her head and picked what she hoped was a safe response. "I don't see how they could have, do you?"

He shrugged. "The cops have been combing the place since Lucky found your mother's grave. I would have thought it unlikely, but I suppose it's possible one of them stumbled on the entrance."

His dog had found a grave? Alexis floundered helplessly, but some sort of response seemed indicated.

"Is that likely?"

"I didn't think so. I patched the hole on the work side of the wall, and you know how well-concealed the closet entrance is. They would have had to run their hands all over the wood paneling inside the closet to find the depression that opened the door. But maybe they noticed the hole I patched on the other side. I didn't think anyone would notice since we're working in that room, but—"

He broke off abruptly, staring past her. Alexis didn't have to turn around to know Wyatt had come up behind her.

"R.J., could you give Leigh a lift back to Stony Ridge?"

She turned to face Wyatt, oddly disappointed by his change of heart.

"I have to go to Heartskeep," he explained.

"I thought you had nothing to do all day."

"Occasionally it pays to be related to the chief. I've been reinstated to active status." He looked at the man called R.J. "Pete's wife just went into labor. The chief had assigned him to take my place as liaison, but now I have to get out there and take over again."

"Guess we'll need another catcher for tomorrow's game then," R.J. said. "Actually, Wy, I was on my way out to Heartskeep myself. I need my portable generator. Think they'll let me remove it?''

"I don't see why that would be a problem. I'll get you inside. You'll be able to give Leigh a lift back to town?''

He looked pointedly at the briefcase in her hands.

"Uh, sure. No problem.''

"Thanks.''

Wyatt didn't look at her again. He turned and started back to his car. Her sense of loss was totally irrational. Alexis had wanted to get away from him. Even more so now that she knew he was a cop. She should be relieved.

A dark, furry head suddenly nudged her side, knocking her off balance. Lucky stared up at her with friendly, deep chocolate eyes. At least the dog liked her.

"I'd pet you, but I have my hands full.''

"Sorry, Leigh," R.J. said. "Let me take that and throw it in back.''

Alexis hesitated. She eyed the large dog as he sat on his haunches to lick traces of ice cream from his muzzle. "Will he eat it?''

R.J. paused as if considering that seriously. "I don't think so, but we'll let him ride in the back of the cab with us.''

Before she could protest, he lifted the briefcase from her hands and tossed it into the bed of the truck. It landed with a heavy thud.

"What do you have in that thing? Bricks?''

"Paper.'' Hundreds of pieces of expensive paper.

"Hop in. Wyatt's waiting.''

Lucky immediately jumped into the back. He wasn't interested in getting inside the hot cab of the truck and Alexis couldn't blame him. Not wanting to call any more attention to the briefcase, she assured R.J. it would be okay and crossed her fingers.

Climbing up into the high cab in her skirt wasn't easy. She was aware of Wyatt watching from his car as R.J. had to give her a boost up.

As he started the engine, R.J. immediately clicked off the radio, but not before she realized he had it set to a classical station.

"You can leave that on. I like classical music."

R.J. raised his eyebrows.

Because the real Leigh didn't like classical music?

"That's okay. I like an occasional change of pace from the country-western music most of my crew listens to all day," he said as if feeling a need to explain his choice of music.

Based on his dusty jeans, dark T-shirt, work boots and the fact that she'd noticed a hard hat on the back seat, Alexis deduced R.J. had something to do with construction. Those sinewy muscles didn't come from pumping iron in some gym.

"How's Gavin's hand? Think he'll be able to play ball tomorrow?" R.J. asked conversationally.

She wished he'd turned the radio back on instead of trying to make polite conversation.

"Do all of the men in town play ball with Wyatt?" she asked to avoid answering his impossible question. Then she realized Leigh probably knew the answer to that. Fortunately, R.J. didn't seem to think it an odd thing to ask.

"Most of them," he agreed. "If they don't play on our team, they play on Granger's team."

"Oh." She settled back, biting on her lower lip. She couldn't keep up this deception much longer. Sooner or later she was bound to say the wrong thing. She stared out the window as R.J. followed Wyatt's car onto the two-lane country road.

It wasn't long before stretches of field lined both sides of the road, tucked behind impossibly neat fences and massive old trees. Soon she began to catch glimpses of well-tended driveways that disappeared from sight, marked only by fancy-lettered signs and mailboxes. They were apparently entering the realm of country estates where breeding horses was a business as well as a hobby.

Alexis shifted nervously. Leigh and Hayley must have money if they lived near here. She was too tired to think through all the implications. Her thoughts weren't even making sense to her anymore. They just kept spinning in circles.

A yawn caught her by surprise.

"Why don't you lean back and close your eyes?" R.J. suggested. "You look tired."

"That's what Wyatt said." Instantly she regretted mentioning his name.

"You know, Wyatt's a good guy, Leigh. He and Gavin are close friends."

She attempted to focus on R.J. "Are you trying to make some sort of a point here?"

His shoulders rose and fell. "Guess not."

Maybe his cryptic words would make more sense if she could keep her eyes open and listen to what he was saying.

"I grew up with Gavin, if you'll recall," R.J. said casually. "When George and Emily first brought him to live with us, no one could get close to him. You and Hayley were pretty young back then and I know your mom and grandpa kept you protected, but I'm sure you heard some of the stories." He grinned impishly. "They were mostly true. The Walkens had their hands full with our wild group in the early days. Gavin was every bit as tough as they claim."

Alexis didn't know how to respond. Fortunately, R.J. didn't seem to expect a response.

"Wyatt's uncle had just been promoted to police chief. I think he always resented George and Emily for bringing juvenile delinquents to live in his community. I know Chief Crossley was always looking for an excuse to lock one of us up, especially Gavin. Gavin never backed down and he never gave an inch. Heck, if it hadn't been for you that last time, Crossley would have tried to pin old man Wickert's murder on him."

There was no way Alexis could mask her shock.

"Yeah, I know neither of you wanted anyone to know how you alibied Gavin that night, but you know how gossip flies in Stony Ridge. The story was all over town five minutes after they released Gavin. He never said a word to anyone about what happened, Leigh, but I know he was real upset when your dad shipped you and your sister off to Boston right afterward."

R.J. was painting a fascinating, if confusing, picture of the dynamics of Stony Ridge.

"Look, the point I was trying to make is that Gavin and Wyatt are both good guys. I don't want to see anyone getting hurt. Everyone knows how you and Hayley feel about cops, but don't play games with either of them, okay? If you and Gavin are having a personal problem, don't put Wyatt between the crosshairs."

"What are you talking about?"

"I'm not blind, Leigh. Even I could see the sparks flying between you and Wyatt a few minutes ago."

Alexis inhaled sharply.

"I'm not trying to get in your business. Just be sure you're straight with Gavin first. You don't want to pit two strong men like that against each other. The results would be ugly."

"I wouldn't do that." At least, not intentionally.

"Glad to hear it. You might want to scrunch down on the floor," he said. "We're coming up on the entrance and it looks like the press is still camped outside the front gate. If they catch a glimpse of you, we'll never get inside."

Alexis saw several vehicles parked along the side of the road up ahead. Still thinking about R.J.'s advice, Alexis slipped off her seat belt and tried to make herself invisible against the floor. The last thing she needed was to have a microphone thrust in her face.

As hard as it was to believe R.J. had picked up on her

attraction to Wyatt, she appreciated the warning. She didn't need to complicate someone else's love life, either.

She *was* attracted to Wyatt, but she certainly wasn't going to act on that attraction. She already had one man too many in her life. She was still trying to convince her roommate's cousin, Seth, that she wasn't interested in the young vet as more than a friend.

Of course, after the way she'd stood him up last night, that was probably no longer an issue. She would have preferred a kinder way to let him down, but she could hardly have answered the door with her father lying dead in her bedroom.

Still, she couldn't afford to become embroiled in a farce here in Stony Ridge with her look-alike's men. She was going to have to find a way out of this mess, fast.

As R.J. brought the truck to a halt outside the gates, she thought about the insanity of the entire situation. She shouldn't have come here. Only how else could she learn the truth behind her father's note and all that money?

Lucky barked. R.J. waved to someone and the truck began moving again. It bounced around as if they were driving off-road.

"Sorry," R.J. said. "The crew is scheduled to start work on your driveway the day after tomorrow. I hope Wyatt will let me know whether I should cancel the gravel delivery. I hate to have to reschedule with those people, but I guess that's going to depend on the cops. We're out of sight of the gate. You can get up now."

"Think so?" she asked wryly as the truck's front wheel hit a rut deep enough to swallow a lesser vehicle.

"Sorry," he repeated.

As she climbed back onto the seat, Alexis found herself riding beneath a canopy of old trees whose limbs stretched to obscure the sky. This was a driveway? It meandered more like a road. Alexis had to stifle a gasp of shock as Heartskeep appeared around a bend. This was Leigh's idea of a *house?*

Only the very wealthy would call a massive structure like this a home. The building rose against the sky, silent, defiant, eerie. In the section of New Jersey where she'd grown up, a place this size would qualify as a hotel.

R.J. pulled into the circular driveway, already filled with state police cruisers and other vehicles. One wing of the building appeared to be undergoing major renovations. Judging by the heap of rubble piled inside an enormous Dumpster container, fire had struck Heartskeep as well as that building in town. A shiver of apprehension traveled down her spine.

"This should only take me a minute or so," R.J. told her.

Wyatt had already stepped out of his car. Lucky gave a happy woof and leaped down to join him. Alexis opened her door. Wyatt came toward her with an inscrutable expression. His hands went to her waist and he lifted her clear of the truck without effort.

Her heart hammered recklessly at the intimate touch. He set her down and her hands slid along his shoulders in an unanticipated caress. Her skirt had ridden up her thighs once more. Feeling the heat scalding her cheeks, she smoothed it back into place, grateful to have a reason to look away from those knowing eyes.

R.J. came up behind them and Wyatt turned.

"Get what you need," Wyatt told his friend. "If anyone says anything, tell them to see me."

R.J. frowned. It was obvious he wanted to say something. He looked from Wyatt to her and then shrugged. With casual thanks, he mounted the porch steps and disappeared inside the house, Lucky at his heels.

Wyatt turned back to face her. Alexis found herself wishing she didn't find him so fascinating. He wasn't doing a thing to exert this sensual pull, yet it was there between them all the same.

"I owe you an apology," he said without preamble. "I want to help you, Leigh. If you'll let me."

For one crazy, reckless instant, she was once more tempted to hand him the briefcase and to tell him everything. The relief would be exhilarating.

He pulled a pen and notebook from his pocket. Scrawling something on one of the pages, he tore it off and handed it to her.

"That's my cell phone number. It's always on. Call me when you're ready to talk."

Her chest was so tight with suppressed emotions, Alexis thought she might explode. Watching him stride up the sagging porch steps and into the house, she wondered if she'd just made a terrible mistake by not telling him the truth. Then she noticed the uniformed officer leaning against the railing near a corner of the house. He'd been watching the exchange with interest and now eyed her curiously. Alexis made a snap decision.

"Excuse me, could you help me get something out of the back of the truck?"

Seconds later, the heavy briefcase in hand, she strode through the front door as if she owned the place. And came to a dead halt. Her entire apartment would fit inside the massive marble foyer. She'd never seen anything like this.

A grand piano sat beneath a wide, open staircase. Beyond that was the largest living room she had ever seen—big enough to be a hotel lobby, and about as inviting, despite the expensive-looking furniture. Almost completely open on three sides, the room seemed to stretch forever in all directions. Marble pillars supported a balcony that wrapped around the entire room. There was no ceiling. The room stretched upward like some dark wooden tunnel that peaked at two enormous skylights on the roof far overhead.

To her left was the roped-off area where construction had been started. To her right, one of a pair of double doors stood open to reveal what appeared to be a library. A fireplace stood against the far wall. The rest of the room was filled with books resting on floor-to-ceiling book-cases.

A flutter of excitement sent her moving in that direction. The answers to all her questions must be here, somewhere inside this vast house.

The library was spacious, as well, but in here at least there was a welcoming feel. She realized that the library connected with another room. Curious, she crossed to the partially open door and peered inside. An office this time, with a bank of computer equipment lining one wall. A comfortable-looking leather couch, several chairs and an absolutely gorgeous walnut desk didn't clutter the space at all. There were more bookcases here, as if it were a continuation of the library.

The proportions of the rooms were astounding. The house could have been designed for giants.

Leigh crossed to the desk and set the briefcase on the floor behind it. Her heart pounded with excitement. There were two more doors. One led back out to the hall, the other revealed a spacious bathroom with an exit into the hall. She closed all three doors, not wanting to be caught snooping.

Several framed photographs sat on the bookshelves. Alexis crossed to examine them and her lungs forgot how to breathe. Even though she'd begun to suspect as much, coming face-to-face with her own features filled her with so many conflicting emotions that all she could do was stand there and shake.

There was no way to tell how long ago the first picture had been taken, but at a guess, the two women were about sixteen. Despite the age difference between them, they didn't merely look like her—they looked *exactly* like her. Only their hairstyle was different.

In the picture their honey-brown hair hung halfway down their backs. Alexis had never worn her hair that long. Her mother always claimed long hair was too much trouble. She'd convinced Alexis to cut hers whenever it started to grow long.

Hair length aside, these women smiled for the camera with her smile. They stared into the lens with her eyes. Not cousins or aunts. Leigh and Hayley Thomas looked identical to her in every way.

"Oh, here you are," R.J. said.

Startled, she hastily set the photo down.

"I'll be ready to go in a minute," he said. "Wyatt says the state police expect to be finished with the house this afternoon. Do you want me to have my crew back out here tomorrow?"

"I guess so," she responded nervously. "As long as it's all right with the police."

"Okay, I just need to load the generator into the back of the truck and we'll be all set."

"I'm going to stay here."

"Um, Leigh, I don't think they'll let you."

She faced him squarely. "I'm not going to ask permission."

"Oh."

"R.J.? Thank you. I promise, no pitting."

For a second he looked blank, then he made the connection. "Glad to hear it. Are you sure about staying?"

"I'm sure," she said forcefully.

"Uh, all right, then. I'll let you argue it out with Wyatt. See you later."

"Yes," she agreed.

When he was gone, her eyes swept the shelves once more, staring at the scattered pictures. Most were of the twins at different ages, but there were also several pictures of a woman who could only be their mother.

Her mother.

Alexis stared at the woman's face. There was no mistaking the resemblance. Alexis had always known that she looked nothing like either one of the people who had raised her, but she'd never wondered about that. How could she have been so blind? Her entire life had been a lie.

The pain of the betrayal was so powerful she wanted to crumple into a ball. How? Why? The hurt was far too intense for tears. She felt numb to her soul.

Alexis lifted the photograph of the woman who was most likely her real mother. Despite the similarities of their features, it could have been anyone's face staring back at her. The woman was a total stranger.

Lightly she traced the heart-shaped face with a fingernail. She looked like her mother. Alexis's gaze flicked to the picture of her sisters. *They* looked like her mother.

How was this possible?

Why had it happened?

The questions repeated themselves over and over again. Alexis closed her eyes. Her throat felt squeezed so tight her breathing was labored, a loud harsh sound in the silence of the room. She opened her eyes. Hurt and anger would have to come later. Answers were what she needed, and time was running out. Anyone could come in and find her here.

Wyatt could find her here. And part of her wished he would.

She set the photograph down and stared at the two young women who bore her face. Leigh and Hayley. Her sisters.

How long ago had this picture been taken? The photograph itself gave no clue. She'd never heard of siblings looking so completely identical—unless they were born from a single egg. There was only one answer that made any sense. Her sisters weren't twins, the three of them were triplets. They had to be.

There. She'd acknowledged what she'd begun to suspect before she'd even arrived at Heartskeep. Why else would Wyatt and R.J. have accepted her as Leigh so readily? But, Alexis didn't look sixteen, so these must be older photographs. She began to hunt for proof.

Judging by the desk drawers, she wasn't the first to go hunting for something in this office. The police would have searched it, of course, but there had to be something that could give her a few answers.

How had their mother been murdered? More important, when had she been murdered? Did it have something to do with the money in the briefcase? Everything kept coming back to that cursed case.

Alexis moved back into the library and scanned the bookshelves. She stopped when she came to an old family bible dating back several generations. In the back were pages for listing family members. It wasn't the past that interested her, but the final three entries held her riveted.

Alexis Mary Ryder had been printed with a careful hand in blue ink. A bold line with an arrow had been drawn from her name at the end of the column, to an insertion point above Hayley Hart Thomas. The letters *DBH* were written in the margin beside the line.

Alexis didn't have to go far to link the name that went with the initials. DHB: Dennison Barkley Hart, her maternal grandfather.

Instead of answers, she only had more questions. One in particular overrode the rest. How had her grandfather known of her existence? Was this why she'd been warned not to trust anyone?

Her gaze swept the room. She took in the expensive furniture, the rows of books, the lovely stone fireplace. Was the money in that briefcase intended as a bribe for her father's silence? If so, who was Kathy?

Alexis scanned the list of names once more. No one even close to that name was listed in the bible.

A headache began to pound with vicious fury behind her eyes. Alexis bit down on her lip. The note's warning was obvious now. Her sisters had every reason to want her dead. Heartskeep should have been her home, too. She was an heiress. How was she supposed to deal with this?

Her fingers delved into the pocket of her skirt and

touched the folded piece of paper Wyatt had given her. She didn't need to call. She could go upstairs right now, find him and dump the whole mess in his strong, capable hands. He'd wanted her to talk. Well, she certainly had a story to tell him.

Except Wyatt was a cop. His warm, caring expression would change the minute she told him what had happened to her father—or rather, the man she had always believed to be her father. Someone had killed him for the briefcase—and maybe for what he knew. They would do the same to her when they found her.

Her father must have known how dangerous the situation was, yet he hadn't sent her to the police, he'd sent her to a lawyer, but the lawyer was also dead. There had to be a reason.

If it had been hard to think before, it now seemed impossible. Alexis wasn't used to being indecisive. Working as she did with runaways and pregnant teens meant making decisions every day. Standing here like a vegetable would accomplish nothing. She needed to hide the money until she could figure out what to do—and who to trust.

Retrieving the heavy case, she peered into the hall. There were voices at the back of the house. She listened for Wyatt's deep tones without success. It was just as well. She had no idea what to say to him anyhow.

With no one in sight, she hurried up the front stairs. The second floor was eerily silent. The hairs on the nape of her neck bristled. She felt a stirring of malevolence, as if her presence disturbed something that didn't want her here.

The notion was ridiculous, simply the fantasy of a tired mind. Subconsciously her brain was trying to make her acknowledge that no one was going to want her here once they realized who she was.

An enormous window spanned the wide hall that divided the house into two wings. Without that light filtering in from outside, the upstairs would have been as dark as a tomb. Not exactly a pleasant image, but one that certainly fit.

Alexis crossed to the nearest door and peered inside. A spacious bedroom with an empty, unused feel. Probably a room for guests. About to leave, she stopped. R.J. had said something about a hidden room off a closet. He hadn't said which closet. Construction was actually being done across the hall, but it wouldn't hurt to have a quick look inside.

The closet was paneled in cedar. Empty hangers, spare pillows and several neatly folded blankets sat on a rather high shelf. Alexis studied the paneling, paying particular attention to the seams. If there was an opening, it was well concealed. R.J. had said the police would have had to run their hands over the wood to find the depression that opened the door. She didn't figure she had that kind of time. She could hear voices and they sounded nearby.

The sheets and pillows gave her an idea. If the room wasn't used often, it should make an adequate temporary hiding place for the money. Tugging a chair across the floor, she stood on it to reach the shelf and rearrange the blankets and pillows. Opening the briefcase, she removed her purse. One of the hundred-dollar bills clung to the white leather.

Alexis hesitated. She had about forty dollars in cash in her purse. Her checkbook was back at her apartment. She might not be able to use her credit card everywhere. While it felt like stealing, she put the bill and two others inside her purse and closed the briefcase.

About to step down from the chair, Alexis had second thoughts. Reopening the case, she retrieved her father's letter, and put it in the envelope. Hiding the briefcase behind the pillows and blankets, she replaced the chair, snatched up the envelope and her purse, and stepped from the room.

Halfway down the dark hallway she heard men's voices heading in what sounded like her direction. Alexis darted inside the next room. She didn't want to have to explain what she was doing up here. She wasn't entirely sure herself, except that she wanted a chance to explore and to learn as much as possible before facing her unknown family.

This room was entirely feminine, from the oil paintings on the wall to the bedspread. The occupant enjoyed reading and had rather eclectic taste in literature. Alexis set her purse and the envelope down on the end of the bed. Once again, she was drawn to the framed photographs sitting on top of a dresser. These were candid shots. She studied one of her sisters at a younger age, carving pumpkins with an older man. Dennison Hart or her real father?

The family resemblance to her mother was so strong that Alexis felt certain this was her grandfather. So why were there no pictures of their father? Had he died when they were very young?

From nowhere came a sudden thought that left her heart thudding. What if she wasn't the only baby the doctor had given away? Thanks to fertility drugs these days, it wasn't all that uncommon for people to have multiple births. What if Alexis wasn't a triplet, but a quadruplet or more? What if there were other sisters, even brothers, who knew nothing of Heartskeep?

The thought made her dizzy. She moved around the room touching items lightly until she found herself staring blankly into a neat but crowded closet. While Alexis preferred brighter colors to pastels, she applauded the classic styles and was impressed by the designer labels inside the array of clothing. The contents of this closet probably cost more than her annual salary.

It came as no surprise to discover that she and her sister wore the same size, right down to the shoes. This was one issue Alexis didn't have to debate. She needed a change of clothing and here were plenty of items she could borrow. She selected a pale yellow, sleeveless T-shirt to go with a pair of tailored white slacks. Her sister's taste in lingerie ran to simple yet feminine bits of lace and nylon.

Alexis gathered up what she needed and stepped into the bathroom. She'd never been in one that was bigger except a public rest room. The tub was almost a pool, and multiple people could fit in the separate shower stall. The bathroom connected with another room. A glance at the double sink had already told her that two very different individuals shared this bathroom.

Alexis peered inside the second bedroom. Posters and other decor indicated a teenager's room. Nothing she'd seen so far had indicated any younger siblings. Puzzled, she stepped inside. There were different pictures in here, but mostly of the same people she'd seen next door and downstairs. This closet yielded brighter colors and several outfits that had been trendy when she was in high school. Alexis was too tired to work through the significance at the moment. Besides, she had to hurry before she was caught.

The shower stall was tempting, but the last thing she wanted was for Wyatt to find her naked in the shower. Her adrenaline rush was fading. Clean clothing and washing her face weren't enough to blunt the lethargy pulling at her. Keeping her eyes open was becoming a real effort.

When she let them close for a minute, she had to force them open again. She needed to lie down for a few minutes. She couldn't afford to fall asleep, but she was nearly asleep on her feet as it was. If she could rest for a few minutes, she might be able to summon the energy to continue.

She stuffed the large envelope inside one of the pillow-cases and lay on her sister's bed. She was going to have to ask Wyatt for help. What did she really think she was going to accomplish by wandering around a place like this on her own?

Alexis struggled to open her eyes, but the lids refused to budge. She mustn't fall asleep. Goldilocks had been discovered by bears, but she was apt to be discovered by something far worse if she let sleep claim her.

Chapter Four

"What do you mean, you didn't take Leigh back to town?" Wyatt demanded of his cell phone.

"She said she was going to stay at Heartskeep," R.J. replied, sounding troubled. "I couldn't force her to come with me. I figured she wanted to talk to you."

Wyatt swore under his breath. Unless someone had come to pick her up, Leigh was still at Heartskeep—alone.

"All right, R.J. Sorry to snap at you like that. Thanks for letting me know. I'll check on her. And yes, as far as the police are concerned, your crew can resume work tomorrow. I'll talk with you later."

He disconnected and punched in the number for Gavin's cell phone. Gavin hadn't answered his calls all day, nor had he returned any of the messages Wyatt had left for him. The conclusion was inescapable. Gavin was avoiding him, and Wyatt suspected the reason had something to do with that briefcase Leigh had been toting. Given the way Hayley and especially Leigh seemed to attract trouble lately, the briefcase was of real concern. Gavin knew better than to withhold information.

Wyatt should have remembered he was a cop first and a friend second. He should have pushed Leigh for answers this afternoon. Ducort was no longer a threat, but the house was dangerous with construction under way and the broken balcony. On the other hand, Heartskeep was her home. Still, the idea of her there alone worried him. That far from town, she'd likely lose the electricity and maybe even the phone service if the weather predictions proved accurate.

Stony Ridge didn't need another storm, but rain was turtle-crawling its way in their direction at a leisurely pace that meant probable flooding in the low-lying areas around town. Wyatt had just come from briefing his uncle on the state police investigation. The house search had yielded no information and his uncle had only listened halfheartedly because another storm meant overtime the department couldn't afford.

Wyatt drummed his fingers against the steering wheel and stared at the dark band of clouds moving in. His uncle Nestor's budget worries weren't his concern. Leigh was. Dinner would have to wait. Wyatt was going back to Heartskeep to find out what Leigh had been carrying in that briefcase.

On his way through town, a small blue compact car caught his eye. The car looked forlorn and totally out of place parked near the office buildings. Gavin's office was sandwiched between several other small brick structures, all of which would be closed at this hour. While the little blue compact would have been right at home in the city, in Stony Ridge, the locals, for the most part, drove trucks or high-end vehicles. The little blue car hadn't rated medium-end when it had been brand-new, and that had been at least ten years ago.

Wyatt's instincts kicked to life. Pulling in behind the car, he picked up his radio and called in the license plate. Dispatch came back with the name Alexis Ryder, and an address in New York City. No wants, no warrants, no alerts for a car like this, yet to find it sitting here at this hour was unusual enough to make him frown. Stony Ridge wasn't exactly a tourist trap like Saratoga Springs. For one thing, the town was a good distance off the highway. People who came here generally had a reason.

Alexis Ryder wasn't a known reporter, so who was she? More to the point, *where* was she?

Wyatt opened his car door. A gust of cold, damp air smacked him in the face. Retrieving his hat and slicker from the trunk, he put them on before striding over to examine the car. A map of New York State lay badly folded on top of a stained white suit jacket on the passenger seat. Okay, Alexis Ryder had gotten lost. Maybe she was having car trouble. From the age of the car, that was likely. If it had broken down here, odds were she'd wandered down to one of the stores that were still open closer in. Maybe she'd even walked to the gas station. That made the most sense.

He swept his flashlight over the interior. A sassy bright blue scarf protruded from the pocket of the white jacket. It was the only other item visible. He liked that scarf. Boldly cheerful, it made a statement of happy confidence. About to turn away, he focused the flashlight on the pocket right below the scarf. The stain bothered him. It looked suspiciously like dried blood.

Lightning burned its image across the sky. He was pulling his handheld radio from the kangaroo pocket of his raincoat to ask for a uniformed officer when he spotted his friend and fellow officer, Jim Lowe pulling up in a patrol car.

"Hey, Wyatt. What's up?"

"Have a look."

Mother Nature took that as an invitation, as well. She turned on the rain and sent another bolt of lightning to illuminate the scene. Wyatt was glad he could turn Alexis Ryder and her problem over to Jim. A nagging sense of urgency told him he really needed to get to Heartskeep.

ALEXIS HAD ALWAYS LIKED the scent of roses. Now the smell filled her head. Unseen hands gently shook her awake. She battled the dragging lethargy for control of her eyelids. Her dreams lingered, not yet ready to release her. She'd been trying to find Wyatt, but had become lost in a maze of ominously dark, oversize rooms. She kept hearing his soothing voice ahead of her, yet she couldn't seem to catch up with him no matter how hard she tried. Alexis called to him to wait, but the sound of her cry echoed down a long tunnel.

A woman's voice urged her to open her eyes. Reluctantly she managed the feat. Utter darkness surrounded her, yet she could still feel the light touch of the hand she'd imagined trying to wake her. For a split second she thought she could even still smell the faint trace of roses. A shiver went through her. She sensed no one in the darkness around her.

For a moment her sleep-drugged mind had no idea where she was. Confused, she lay still while her brain struggled between dream and reality. Finally it located the memories it needed. Her father's features, stilled in death. The worn briefcase, brimming with hundred-dollar bills. Heartskeep, towering against the sky. And two women who bore her face.

She was in her sister's bedroom, on her sister's bed—alone in Heartskeep.

Alexis sat up quickly. She'd fallen asleep! What time was it?

An explosive flare of lightning illuminated the room. The low growl of thunder sent adrenaline tearing through her bloodstream. Alexis scrambled off the bed. Her foot collided with her purse, which must have fallen to the floor while she'd slept. The skinny white bag shot beneath the bed as she groped for the lamp on the nightstand. She nearly knocked the lamp over, righting the base just in time. Rain assaulted the windows, unnaturally loud.

Stillness.

Why was the house so still—so dark? Where was everyone? Where was Wyatt? She was an idiot, falling asleep like that as if she hadn't a care.

Forcing her trembling hands to cooperate, Alexis ran

her fingers over the lamp until she found the knob. There was a click as she turned the switch, but nothing else happened. No light came on. She forced down instant fear. She had never liked storms or the dark, but the bulb had probably burned out. Maybe the lamp was controlled by a wall switch.

Another fork of lightning obligingly lit the path to the bathroom door. The blast of thunder was so loud, she cringed. She'd heard that sound in her dreams. Thunder had mingled with the sound of Wyatt's voice.

Never mind dreams. Alexis made her way to the open bathroom door. She wanted light, the brighter the better. How long had it been storming?

Her fingers felt along the wall until she found the switch. Nothing happened when she flicked it up.

She had to stay calm. She was no longer a child, afraid of the dark. Except that, even as an adult, while she tried to pretend it didn't bother her, she always kept a night-light burning in the bathroom, ostensibly so she could see in case she had to get up in the middle of the night.

She stemmed the rising panic by telling herself that the storm had simply knocked out the electricity. There was nothing to fear. There was nothing ominous in the dark. Hadn't she heard somewhere that electricity could be spotty in the country? There was no reason to panic. The police were here in the house somewhere. They had to be. She couldn't be here alone.

Alexis gripped the door frame, immobilized by sudden fear. R.J. had said the police had expected to be finished with the house today. What if they'd finished and gone? What if she was alone in the vast house? Her car was in town. She'd be trapped here!

She forced herself to take a deep, steadying breath. Her stiff fingers released the door frame. If she was alone, it wasn't the end of the world. Being alone in the house could be a good thing. She could search for information without interruption—if only the lights would come back on.

In the next brilliant flash of lightning, she charted a course back to the bed. There was a penlight on her key chain. If the battery wasn't dead, she could search her sister's nightstand for a flashlight. Surely her sister would keep one handy for emergencies. All she had to do was to stay calm, cross that black void, and wait for the next flash of light to look under the bed.

A soft thud came from somewhere inside the house. She wasn't alone, after all. Everything was all right.

Except, it didn't feel all right. It felt terribly, terribly wrong.

A ghost of warning sent her gaze flashing toward the bedroom door. Lightning obligingly illuminated the knob. As she watched, it twisted slowly, as if an unseen hand willed it to be silent when it opened. Thunder crashed overhead. Alexis didn't pause to think. With the dire sound echoing in her ears, she dropped to the floor and slid under the bed. She scraped her head and her shoulder on the side rail as she forced her body to squeeze into the tight space.

She barely fit. Lying half on top of her purse, she was unable to pull it free or to even move. She wasn't even sure how she'd get back out. What a stupid thing to have done.

But the thought died even as it formed. The bed skirt settled back into place as the beam of a flashlight swept the room.

Alexis froze. Heavy footsteps crossed to the bathroom door. After a second, they moved to the closet. Hangers were jostled. The beam of light skipped around the room. She pictured the person shining the light in search of her.

More frightened than she'd ever been in her life, she felt paralyzed as the footsteps approached the bed. Her body would have left an indentation in the pillow and the comforter. He had to know someone had lain there.

Blood pounded in her ears. She was deaf to everything but her racing thoughts. Someone named Ducort had tried to kill Leigh. Had he come back to finish the job?

Or worse, was this one of the people she'd heard outside her apartment? Had they located her somehow?

The footsteps stopped inches from where she lay. Alexis had never known such helpless terror. She was trapped. Any second now the bed skirt would lift and the flashlight would reveal her hiding place.

Lightning and thunder cracked as one. The explosive noise was so loud, her body twitched in reaction. Above her, a man's voice growled an obscenity.

Heart hammering, she held her breath and waited to be discovered. Had she made a sound? Had he heard her?

The footsteps moved away. A second later she heard his shoes on the tile floor of the bathroom.

Alexis longed to squirm out from under the bed. Why had she chosen to hide? Why hadn't she used the self-defense training she taught so blithely?

Because part of the training was to avoid situations where you might be forced to use the training. Hiding was common sense. *Avoid confrontation if you can!* How many times had she told her classes that?

So, even when her muscles began to cramp, she forced herself to wait. She couldn't have said why she was so certain the man wasn't a police officer, she only knew every instinct insisted she mustn't be found.

That was also part of her training. *Listen to your instincts. If something feels wrong, it probably is wrong.*

As seconds became intolerable minutes, she wondered how long she had before he returned—and this time peered under the bed. She had to move.

Summoning the dregs of her courage, Alexis forced herself to squirm out from under the bed. She bumped her head and scraped her shoulder in the process, but those small noises didn't matter. Nothing mattered except get-

ting away. Though she quaked from head to toe, it was a
tremendous relief to be able to stand.

In a splinter of lightning she saw that he'd left all three
doors open. If he'd heard her, he would return at any
second. She wanted to run for the hall, but what if that
was what he was waiting for? He must know she was here
somewhere.

Don't make it easy for him. She'd be vulnerable in the
hall. He had her at a serious disadvantage. She didn't
know this house. The only place she knew to go was back
the way she had come. And then what?

Alexis crossed to the closet. No sooner had she stepped
inside than she heard him coming. His flashlight swept
the room ahead of him. She flattened herself against the
wall beside the open door. A weapon would be nice. Why
hadn't she thought to grab her purse?

Minutes crawled past. She strained to hear, to figure
out what he was doing. He made a soft, grunting sound.
What *was* he doing? The tension was almost unbearable.

The sound of a zipper sent all sorts of horrible images
dancing through her mind. Did he know she was in here?
Was he toying with her?

She forced her mind to grow calm. Mentally she re-
hearsed the skills she'd so blithely taught but never used.

Abruptly the flashlight beam skittered past the closet
and moved away. Alexis didn't twitch. She waited, willing calm. She couldn't hear him anymore. Her imagination went on a rampage while her legs turned to rubber.

Where was he? Was he creeping toward her hiding
place or had he gone back into the hall?

Worse, was he waiting near the door for her to reveal
her location?

The tension was excruciating. She had to do something.
Even the wrong thing was better than standing here waiting to be attacked. If she could make it to the far side of
the bed undetected, she could reach her purse. Her cell
phone was inside. Wyatt's number was still in the pocket

of her skirt. Had she left that in the bathroom? It didn't matter. She could dial 9-1-1 and summon help.

Or could she? She didn't know the name of the street out front or have any idea what the house number might be. Would the operator know where Heartskeep was?

Worry later. Alexis forced her stiff muscles to move. As silently as possible, she inched to the opening and peered out. The room lay in dark silence.

Sensing she was alone, she scurried across the room. Dropping down on the far side of the bed, she lifted the bed skirt and scooted underneath again. Her hand sought for the soft leather of her purse to no avail. She wormed her way further under the bed. Maybe her body had dragged the purse closer to the opposite side. Her groping fingers found nothing. Her purse was gone.

The zipper sound! He'd looked under the bed for her and found her purse instead.

Alexis shunted panic aside. How many times had she stood in front of a class of battered, wounded women and told them that panic was their worst enemy? *Practice what you preach. Think!*

Odds were, he wouldn't look under the bed again. She could stay here all night if need be. She'd probably be safest if she did exactly that. The other option was to try to make her way out of the house. Less safe, and where would she go? She was miles from town, from her car. The storm didn't sound as if it had any intention of stopping soon. She'd be drenched before she got three feet from the front porch. Besides, with all this lightning, the last thing she should do is wander around under all those trees.

Staying put had the most to recommend it, but waiting held no appeal. If she could get to a working telephone, she could dial 9-1-1 and summon the police. A gigantic if.

Or was it? She didn't remember seeing one, but surely her sister had a phone in her room. There wasn't one on the nightstand nearest the door, but maybe there was a phone on the far side of the bed.

When minutes passed and she heard no sound beyond the rain and grumbles of thunder, she worked her way back out on the far side of the bed. Her fingers found the telephone. A base unit, not a portable one, thankfully. That meant it didn't rely on electricity.

But there was no dial tone.

She debated her options with her back to the window. A voice in the back of her head urged her to go—urged her to hurry. Leaving the sanctuary of the room made no sense, but the pressure became unrelenting. She had to get out of here!

Alexis hurried across the room. Lightning and thunder crashed directly overhead as she reached the bathroom door. There was a cracking, splintering sound. An enormously heavy tree branch crashed through the window where she'd been standing only a moment earlier.

Alexis fled through the bathroom into the bedroom beyond. The noise summoned the intruder. He pounded down the hall. There was no time to make it to the closet or under a bed. As he raced past the open bedroom door, she glimpsed a shadowy shape behind a bobbing light.

Alexis darted into the hall as the light disappeared into her sister's bedroom. There was no option. She ran as silently as possible into the dark void of the endless hall.

WHEN WYATT FINALLY turned into the entrance of Heartskeep, he found the wrought iron gate standing open. He was pretty sure they had closed the gate when they'd left, making sure the press left, as well. Relieved that Leigh wasn't alone at the house, he made his way carefully up the long drive, eyeing the tall trees that bent and swayed overhead.

Visibility made it hard to avoid the huge ruts that sent his car bouncing and sliding as it struggled for traction in the muddy remains of the driveway. He took one pothole too fast as he came around the final bend and heard the undercarriage scrape. He hoped he hadn't damaged the wheel or the oil pan or anything else. He didn't need another big bill right now.

Cursing his stupidity, Wyatt was thankful when he pulled into the circular drive in front of the porch. There were no other cars parked in front, but that wasn't surprising. Gavin had probably pulled around back. Only, no lights shone inside the house.

Hitchcock-approved lightning illuminated the mansion. Wyatt wished he'd stopped by the Walken estate first. He was not going to be happy if no one was here and Leigh was safe and sound over there. But he'd tried their number when he'd left town and no one had answered. There'd been no point in calling Heartskeep because R.J. had disconnected the phone at the house so they wouldn't be bombarded with calls from the media.

Wyatt grabbed his heavy flashlight from the glove compartment and sprinted for the front door. Nothing happened when he pressed the doorbell. With all this lightning, more than one tree was apt to fall tonight. Power lines were probably down.

There didn't appear to be anyone inside the house. The front door was locked. No flicker of candles or flashlights when he peered through the nearest window. Not that he'd be able to see anything if they were at the back of the house or upstairs.

Rain swept across the front porch. He should get in his car and leave. His uncle was going to need every man he could get once the flooding started, but Wyatt was still bothered by the open gate. He resigned himself to the fact that he was going to have to check the house completely, even if meant getting soaked.

Returning to the car, he retrieved his personal backup weapon and clipped it to his belt. Putting his handheld radio back in his coat pocket, he set off. Rain hammered him as he trudged around the side of the house. Periodic blasts from the heavens lit the grounds with surreal moments of light.

There were no cars parked behind the house. The side door near the kitchen eating area was locked. As he'd begun to suspect, coming out here had been a waste of time. Still, it usually paid to be thorough. He started around to the back door when a flash of light stopped him. The light had come from upstairs, inside the house.

He waited, but the light didn't come again and the rain was too heavy to see clearly. Maybe he'd only seen a reflection of lightning against the window. Wyatt strode to the back door.

Adrenaline shot through his bloodstream. The alarm system wasn't up and running yet, and the broken window over the door was telling. He reached into his pocket for the radio to call for backup. His ear filled with static. When he finally made the connection, the line was garbled and filled with bursts of static. He gave his location and the situation, repeating it when the reply broke up unintelligibly. The radio sputtered and fell silent. Either the stupid thing had gone wonky again or his new battery had failed. Procedure called for him to wait for backup. He'd left his cell phone plugged into the car jack. He knew he should take the time to retrieve it and to call in, but an inexplicable sense of urgency propelled him forward.

Wyatt pulled out his gun and reached for the door handle. A fierce gust of wind wrenched the door from his grasp. The explosion of thunder probably drowned out the sound of the door smashing against the wall. If not, whoever was in the house knew he was here. Wyatt forced the door closed and directed his flashlight over the kitchen. No wet, muddy footprints this time. Whoever was upstairs had gotten inside ahead of the storm.

With a gut-twisting sense of déjà vu, he clicked off his flashlight and headed for the back stairs. The cavernous house was a spooky place even in daylight. In the midst of a thunderstorm, going up against an unknown intruder alone was nothing short of stupidity. Except he figured the intruder was likely to be Eden Thomas. Wyatt would really like to get his hands on the woman.

As he made his way up the back stairs, the total absence of light was all too familiar. Wyatt paused just short of the landing to listen hard. To his right was the concealed door that led to the balcony, to his left, the corridor that spanned the back of the house. There were no windows back here and the landing sat in the center of the hall. That meant the minute he stepped onto it, he was vulnerable to attack from three directions. The flashlight had come from the corner room on his right.

Eden's former bedroom.

Wyatt stepped silently onto the landing. In the hall, even the storm's fury was muted. There was a disturbing sort of silence filled with ominous expectancy. No light. No sound of movement. Nothing to indicate if the person was still in Eden's room or not. The darkness was so complete he had to take a firm hold on his imagination.

An impossibly loud crack of thunder made him jump. There was the muffled sound of glass shattering and running footsteps. Years of training brought the order to stop to his lips. He didn't give the command voice. Wyatt started down the hallway to his right. Cautiously he turned the corner, directly into the path of a soft bundle of feminine flesh.

"Police—"

Bullets flamed toward them from out of the dark. He shoved the woman down, reaching for his gun to return fire. A sudden, sharp jolt to his hip sent him off balance before he could pull the trigger. Heavy footfalls raced away. Wyatt gave chase. He heard the attacker plunge down the main staircase.

As he ran forward, a blinding spiderweb of lightning illuminated the large picture window at the far end of the hall. Thunder reverberated in its wake. Wyatt reached the head of the stairs, but the figure had disappeared into the maw of darkness below.

Someone ran up behind him. He whirled, aiming his gun at the threat.

"Here, Wyatt."

Leigh.

Unaware of the danger, she thrust his flashlight at him. Wyatt was shaken by how close he'd come to firing.

"Get back!" he ordered gruffly. He snatched the flashlight from her hand and turned his attention back to the stairs. Below them, the front door opened. "Stay here."

He held the flashlight away from his body and swept the strong beam over the massive hall. Nothing moved. The front door gaped open. Wyatt inched down the stairs cautiously, aware it could be a trap. He'd make an easy target on the stairs in his bright yellow slicker, but there was no help for it.

No shots rang out. He strained to hear the slightest sound over the storm's fury. Out front, a car engine coughed to life. He raced down the remaining steps and reached the door in time to see Jezzy tearing back down the driveway. Wyatt cursed.

"What is it?" Leigh asked quietly.

He spun, shocked to find her standing only a few feet away from him.

"I told you to wait up there!"

"So someone else could grab me? No thank you."

Renewed tension flooded him. "There's someone else in the house?"

"I don't know, but I wasn't going to wait to find out. Please don't tell me that was your car."

Wyatt scowled and shut the door against the wind and rain. "Fine. I won't."

She muttered something under her breath.

"With any luck, he'll get swallowed by one of the giant potholes in your driveway," he told her.

"Let's hope not. I don't want him coming back."

Wyatt reached for his radio. His hand felt the damage even before he brought it out. His flashlight revealed a neat round hole through his heavy slicker, hip high. He remembered feeling the impact, but he hadn't felt any pain. He still didn't. Shock and adrenaline could cause that, but in this case... He held up his radio for a better view.

"Wyatt, you've been shot!"

"He shot my radio!"

He tugged his slicker around so he could see the exit hole. By some fluke of fate, the bullet had passed through his coat pocket and the radio without hitting him. The radio was well and truly dead.

"At least it wasn't your hip," she said with asperity.

"Yeah. Where's the telephone?"

"I already tried that. There's no dial tone."

He'd forgotten they'd been disconnected.

"I thought you had a cell phone," she said.

"I left it in my car."

"Well that's going to do us a lot of good."

"What about you?"

"Mine's in my purse." She turned her palms up. "Since he took that, too, I guess mine's in your car as well."

Wyatt swore.

"You already said that. What do we do now?"

"Nothing else we can do but wait and hope dispatch heard my location earlier through the static."

The house swayed beneath another blast of thunder. Wyatt looked around and lowered his voice. "Is there a chance anyone else is in here?"

"How should I know? There could be an entire marching band in here. He's the only one I almost saw."

"What are you doing here?"

"I was under the impression I owned the place."

"You know what I mean. You were supposed to go back to town with R.J."

"I didn't want to. I was tired. I haven't been sleeping much and I needed a nap."

"You took a nap?"

She lifted her face with a hint of defiance. "I didn't know napping was against the law."

"You knew the house was off-limits until the investigation was concluded!"

"R.J. said you were finishing up. I might have asked your permission, but you weren't around when I went upstairs."

"How hard did you look?"

She put her hands on her hips. "I didn't."

He started to swear again and stopped. He'd have a piece of someone's hide for this. He didn't know who was supposed to have checked the house before they left, but he intended to find out.

"Didn't you hear us leaving?"

"Sorry. I'm not sure I would have heard you on a megaphone. I told you, I was tired. When I woke up, it was dark and storming and someone was going through the house."

Remembering how tired she'd looked earlier, he tempered his response. "Who was it, Leigh?"

"I didn't catch his name."

She was full of snappy banter, but her eyes slid quickly from his. She was nervous. She was hiding something.

"Was it Jacob?"

Chapter Five

Alexis stared at Wyatt blankly. Who was Jacob? From his expression, it was someone Leigh knew and Wyatt didn't like. She'd never keep all these names straight.

"That wasn't Eden shooting at us," he said, "but he was inside Eden's room when I first arrived."

"He was searching all the rooms, looking for me."

"How do you know that if you don't know who it was?"

"Because I hid under the bed and listened to him! He wasn't going through drawers and stuff, he was peering into closets and corners."

"You hid under the bed?"

Embarrassed, she nodded. "I'd accidentally kicked my purse under there and was trying to get it out when I realized someone was sneaking around inside."

His eyes narrowed. "So how did he get your purse?"

"I forgot to take it with me when I moved to the closet," she shrugged, trying not to shiver at the memory. "He came back and looked under the bed."

"Are you okay?" he asked more gently.

"Sure. He never laid a hand on me." Alexis was surprised to find him regarding her with genuine concern. Her heart gave an extra little thump. Even scared and shaken, she was too aware of this man for comfort.

His expression softened. He touched her cheek lightly.

The roughened texture of his fingers against her skin created a new and very different tension inside her. He'd lowered the flashlight so it pointed toward the floor, leaving most of his face in shadows.

"You're trembling."

The quiet words only made it worse. He brushed at her cheek and pulled back.

"You had dust on your face," he told her a bit gruffly.

Wyatt wasn't immune to whatever was happening between them, either. But obviously he was uncomfortable.

"The maid forgot to dust under the bed."

"I don't think housework was high on her list of priorities lately. We need to get out of this hall."

"All right."

A muffled thumping, scraping sound filtered down the stairs. Frightened, she stared up at the darkness above them.

"Wait here," he whispered, clicking off the flashlight.

"No!" she whispered fiercely, grabbing for his arm. Her fingers slid off the slick wet raincoat. "You can't go up there."

"I have to."

He was going to go no matter what she said. "Then, we'll both go, but I want to go on record as saying this is a stupid thing to do. And," she added when he would have interrupted, "don't you dare tell me to wait down here."

She sensed he wanted to argue, but the sound was repeated.

"Stay behind me," he whispered, setting his damaged radio on the step. "Don't make any noise and do exactly what I tell you."

He removed his hat and peeled out of his raincoat. Setting them on the steps, as well, he handed her the heavy flashlight, pulled his gun, and started up. Alexis followed slowly, hanging back so as not to crowd him. A man with a gun was a terrifying sight, but not as much as the thought of standing alone anywhere in this vast house.

The minute he reached the upstairs landing, Wyatt gestured for her to wait. Her heart thumped madly as she pressed herself against the wall and strained to listen.

She could hear the scraping sound more clearly now. The sound of the storm seemed louder, as well. As Wyatt disappeared around the corner, she moved up to the edge of the landing. She could barely make out his light-colored shirt, until an exceptionally bright flash of lighting filled the black hall with a momentary glare.

Wyatt stopped outside the door to the bedroom she'd been using. Alexis barely heard the thunder over the blood pounding in her ears. She couldn't see him anymore. He must have gone inside the room. More than anything, she wanted to run after him, but she forced herself to stand there and wait. He reappeared quickly, a tiny flashlight in his hand, and motioned for her to join him.

"A tree branch came through the window," he whispered quietly.

Alexis nodded. "I know. I was standing in front of the window only seconds before it fell."

He took her arm and tugged her inside the room, closing the door. His shocked expression was understandable when she saw the damage. Long, leafy branches spread out from a large limb, reaching a surprising distance inside the room. The wet, dripping leaves waved grotesquely, like grasping tentacles. Rain fled before the wind, billowing the tangled sheer drapes in a ghostly fashion. Shards of glass glittered where the flashlight beam struck them. They lay sprinkled across the carpeting almost to the door.

"You were standing there?" Wyatt asked in a rough voice.

Alexis managed a nod. She didn't want to think about what would have happened if she hadn't had that premonition to move. The lamp and telephone had been wiped from the nightstand. The sound of a thick limb scraping across its surface was part of the noise they'd been hearing. Veins of lightning streaked the sky, but this time the resulting thunder sounded angrily muted.

Chilled at seeing how close she'd come to being speared or crushed by the tree branch, she tried not to shudder as Wyatt crossed the room and attempted to move it. The dripping wood didn't budge an inch.

"Forget it. We'd need a chain saw." He walked back to where she stood. "You could have been killed," he said, sounding angry.

"Tell me something I don't know."

He muttered an oath.

"I thought of a stronger adjective," she said shakily.

Wyatt shook his head. "You're pretty amazing, you know that? I've worked with trained officers who weren't this calm under pressure."

"You think I'm calm? Look closer. I'm shaking worse than those branches."

When he opened his arms she went into them as if it was something she'd done a hundred times before. His shirt was damp from trying to move the tree branch, but she didn't care. She laid her head against his chest and listened to his heart beat while she trembled from head to toe.

Alexis had been held by other men before, but it had never felt this right. He ran his hand up and down her spine soothingly, making her long to stand here forever.

Thunder trumpeted overhead. He released her and she stepped back, telling herself not to be foolish. This was hardly the time to be thinking the sorts of thoughts she'd been starting to have.

"Do you think the storm is ever going to stop?"

"Doesn't sound like it, does it?"

For a long moment they simply looked at each other. Once again Alexis experienced a sense of connection to Wyatt that had nothing to do with physical attraction.

"Thank you," she said simply.

Wyatt tipped his head. "For what?"

"Coming to my rescue."

"Yeah, I did a great job, didn't I?" he mocked. "Or did you forget we're stranded here?"

"At least I'm not alone."

The vulnerability in her words tugged at him. Wyatt didn't want this strong pull of attraction he was feeling, but a moment ago he'd come uncomfortably close to lifting that stubborn little face of hers and sampling the softness of those inviting lips. He had to keep reminding himself that Gavin had prior claim, but that was getting harder and harder to do.

"We need to get out of here," he told her abruptly.

"No argument, but I'm not real fond of walking in a thunderstorm."

"Are there any cars out back in the garage?"

Her hair swayed as she shook her head. "I don't know. Even if there are, I wouldn't have keys."

"That won't be a problem." He stiffened as a belated thought hit him. "Our trigger-happy intruder didn't walk here."

Her eyes widened in comprehension. "He must have driven. That means he's going to come back, isn't he?"

Wyatt nodded. "He won't want to leave his car. He must have driven in the back way and parked out by the old barns where Bram used to park when he was working on the gate."

Seeing her anxious expression, he touched her shoulder. She gave a start and he dropped his hand. "He won't come back inside."

"Why not? He knows we're stranded here. We even left the front door unlocked for him."

Leigh was right. The intruder had two ways back inside if he was so inclined. For certain, he'd circle back to get his car. "What does he want, Leigh?"

"How would I know? I don't even know what he was doing in here in the first place."

Wyatt thought about challenging that statement, but they were wasting time. If he cut through the woods, he might be able to intercept—

"No!" she said, grabbing his arm.

Wyatt stared at her in surprise.

"Don't go out there after him. He's got a gun."

"So do I," he reminded her.

"Well, I don't," she said firmly. "What am I supposed to do while you're out there looking for him? What if he comes in a different way? What if he isn't alone? What if someone else is in the house?"

Once again, she was right. He couldn't leave her and it was too risky to let her come with him outside. "Too bad Heartskeep doesn't have a safe room."

The small penlight didn't offer much light, but he saw her expression change.

"Maybe it does," Leigh said hesitantly.

"What do you mean?"

"There's supposed to be a hidden room behind the bedroom closet near the work area."

His gut clenched. "Supposed to be?"

"I haven't actually seen the room, I was only told about it."

"By who?"

"What difference does that make?"

"Why didn't you tell me about this before?"

She lifted her chin. "I'm telling you now."

"You didn't think the police would be interested in this room while we were searching the house?"

Of course she did, he realized. But Leigh didn't trust the police. She didn't trust *him*. The knowledge stung, more than it should have.

"Never mind. We'll discuss withholding information later."

"Good idea."

He could have shaken her in frustration. Why couldn't the stubborn woman see they were on the same side?

"Is that why you came back to the house today? To be sure we didn't stumble onto this room?" he challenged.

"No."

Her immediate response held the ring of the truth. The next flash of lightning showed the defensive set of her features.

"What's in there, Leigh?" he asked more gently.

"I have no idea. I told you, I've never seen the room. I only learned about it recently."

"How recently?"

She put her hands on her hips and glared up at him. "Shall we stand here in the dark and discuss all the whys and wherefores, or do you want to go see if my information is correct?"

They were wasting time, but the words grated all the same. Wyatt banked his anger. If there was a hidden room, he could stash her there, knowing she'd be safe while he found a way to get them out of here.

"We'll use the back hallway. Stay right behind me," he ordered gruffly.

"No problem. You make a bigger target anyhow," she scoffed. "I'll be your shadow."

Her quick rebuttal made him want to smile. "I think that's an oxymoron at Heartskeep even in daylight."

Some of the tension drained from her shoulders, as well. "I think you're right. Do you want your flashlight back?"

"No. I need my hands free. You hang on to it, but keep it off. I don't want to draw possible attention by using it. I know the floor plan well enough to find Jacob's room. If I don't, you can direct me."

Alexis shivered. He was so wrong, but his hand was already reaching for the doorknob.

Telling him about the room was a dangerous risk. She wasn't even sure she'd understood R.J. correctly. What if she was wrong? What if they went to the wrong closet? Even if this Jacob person's room proved to be the right place, she couldn't be sure they'd be able to open the hidden door. But the alternative was a game of cat and mouse with someone who had a gun and wasn't afraid to use it. Alexis didn't like the mouse role.

Wyatt crossed to the wall opposite the bedroom door. She stayed as close as possible without tromping on his heels. The back hall was a sea of oppressive darkness. Alexis decided she'd developed a strong distaste for the second floor of Heartskeep.

Wyatt came to such an abrupt stop, she ran into his back. Twisting around, he covered her mouth lightly with the flat of his hand. Fear chased up and down her spine. He bent his head to whisper against her ear.

"Go straight across as quietly as you can when I tell you to."

Straight across what?

He peered around an invisible corner then motioned her to go by him. Alexis hurried past, stopping after several feet to put out her hand until she felt the security of the wall on her left. Wyatt joined her. She was startled when he took her ice-cold hand in his and pulled her across yet another hallway.

"The balcony door was open," he said against her ear. "It was closed when I came up here. Don't make a sound."

Fear was a ghostly chill that spread from her hand to run straight down her spine. He freed her and began to move again. Her muscles quivered with tension as she followed.

Wyatt hadn't seriously considered there might be two people inside the house. He should have. No wonder Leigh didn't trust the police. His sloppy police work might get them killed yet.

He had to wonder if the entrance had been left open on purpose in an effort to lure him out there. He almost hoped so. Let them wait for him. He had no intention of taking their bait.

He hoped Leigh was right about the hidden room. He wanted her tucked out of harm's way fast. Jacob's room wasn't too far down on the right, as he recalled. And now that he thought about it, he was pretty sure he'd noticed a flashlight sitting on the dresser in that room. It had seemed odd at the time because there hadn't been anything else of a personal nature inside the vacant room. Now it made perfect sense.

How many other secrets were hiding in the darkness of Heartskeep?

With a mental shake of his head, he thrust aside his thoughts to concentrate on listening. The thunderstorm seemed to be abating, even if the rain and wind weren't. The house was surprisingly silent. Whoever else was inside wasn't making any noise that would help him pin down their location.

The minute his fingers touched the door frame, he stopped moving. Leigh stood silently at his back without fidgeting as he listened hard. The door was closed, as he'd expected. Reaching back, he found her arm and squeezed it in warning. She pressed her other hand over his in acknowledgment.

She continued to surprise him. She was as good or better than some of the cops he'd worked with over the years. Leaning in close to her, he whispered for her to wait and took the flashlight back from her. There was no reason to believe anyone waited inside this room, but he wasn't taking a chance.

The doorknob twisted almost silently. Wyatt sent the powerful flashlight beam in ahead of him as the door opened. Nothing moved, but he went in carefully all the same. The large room and the adjoining bathroom and closet were empty. He even stooped to check under the bed.

Leigh had obeyed and remained in the hall. Now he

motioned her inside, pleased when she quietly closed the door behind her. The flashlight, he noted, was sitting on the dresser as he'd remembered. He handed that to her.

"Show me," he said quietly.

She shook her head, her hair a minor distraction as it swirled around her face. "I'm not sure I can. I only know you're supposed to access the opening by running your hands over the paneling until you find a depression."

Wyatt frowned. They turned their flashlights on the inside of the large closet. If there was a door built into the old cedar paneling, someone had done a terrific job concealing it in the seams.

Leigh moved to the right corner of the back wall and began to run the flat of her hand down the paneling. After a second, Wyatt bent under the clothes bar and took the other corner, careful not to jiggle the clothes hangers. Together, they started working their way toward the middle of the closet.

Left of center, he inhaled sharply as his questing fingers found a depression.

"Did you find it?" Leigh asked eagerly.

The wall answered for him. There was a barely discernable sound, but where two boards met, one entire section of wall abruptly sank back several inches as if on springs. It slid back and to the side to reveal a small room.

"Oh!" Her soft gasp of surprise confirmed what she'd said earlier about not having seen the room for herself. Wyatt sent the beam of light dancing over the dark insides. An empty card table, a squat, metal filing cabinet, a folding chair and floor lamp were the only contents.

"What is this place?"

Leigh shook her head.

He took a minute to study the marks in the dust on the floor. They were by no means the first to find the room.

"Who else knows about this room?"

"I'm not sure. R.J.—"

"R.J. knows?"

Paw prints in the dust confirmed it. Wyatt could almost understand Leigh's reluctance to tell him about the room, but why hadn't R.J. said something? R.J. was supposed to be his friend. His sense of betrayal cut deep, and what stung the worst was that she'd trusted R.J. and not him.

"R.J. discovered this room," she said, as if reading his thoughts.

She pointed to the opposite wall where a hole had clearly been patched from the other side.

"He was asked not to say anything, Wyatt."

"Is that supposed to appease me?" The words came out more bitter than he'd intended.

"Sorry," she snapped, "I'm out of raw meat."

Her pointed words stole the heat from his anger. Too bad if his feelings were hurt, he had a job to do and he'd better darn well start concentrating on that. He returned his attention to the room. R.J. had not only patched a hole across from them, he'd nailed a board at the bottom of the wall so a second door couldn't be opened from the other side.

"I need to know who else knows about this room," he said more evenly. "Hayley?"

Leigh hesitated, then nodded.

"That means Bram and probably Gavin know, as well."

Leigh said nothing. Wyatt kept a firm chokehold on his emotions. This was why Gavin wasn't returning his phone calls.

"What did you do with the computer?" he asked tiredly.

Leigh's stare was blank. He pointed to the faint outlines in the dust on the table.

"I don't know anything about a computer."

He believed her.

"Shouldn't we go inside and close the opening?" she asked nervously.

"Give me a minute."

Wyatt studied the mechanism until he was certain he could get them back out again. Only then did he motion for her to go inside. He followed her and pressed the switch, watching the door move back into place. It was a tight, firm seal.

"You have to admit, it's pretty clever," she said nervously.

"More like ingenious," Wyatt agreed. "This isn't new construction, either. I bet this room was built when the house was built."

"I wonder why."

"Most likely, it was intended to store valuables." He hesitated. "Leigh, is there any chance Jacob knows about this?"

Alexis gazed into his dark eyes and knew that despite his calm tone, Wyatt was upset with her. She didn't blame him. She couldn't understand why Leigh hadn't told him about this.

"I don't know."

Wyatt looked grim. "Does he own a gun?"

She shook her head helplessly. Whoever Jacob was could own an entire arsenal for all she knew. "I don't know."

"Look, Gavin told me that you and Hayley have a blind spot where Jacob is concerned. I understand. The three of you grew up together. But you need to keep an open mind, here."

If only he knew how open her mind really was.

"Do you honestly think it's a coincidence that Jacob dropped from sight the same time as his mother? If you'd look at the situation objectively, you'd see there are a lot of things that make him a person of interest."

"What does that mean?"

"Among other things, he owns a very expensive car."

She shrugged at the non sequitur. "That's a crime?"

"That depends on how he paid for that car. He told you and Gavin he worked for some company called Via-

Tek out of New York. We haven't been able to confirm that. We haven't even been able to confirm there is such a company. Since you told me the two of you had the best computer skills in the house, you have to admit he could easily have created those bogus bills Marcus submitted to Ira Rosencroft.''

Leigh had good computer skills? Alexis certainly hoped she wouldn't have to put *her* skills on display. ''Why would Jacob do that?'' she asked anxiously.

''To help his mother? For a cut of the money? Who knows? Think about it, Leigh. We know there's at least six hundred thousand dollars missing.''

Her heart sank to her toes. She thought about the money in the briefcase. She had no idea how much was in there, but there was quite a lot, and it was money she had no way of explaining.

''Given those blackmail notes you found—which I will remind you were also computer generated—who was in a better position to try a little blackmail? Jacob spent a lot of time here at Heartskeep, right?''

''I guess so,'' she said reluctantly, hoping that was true.

Wyatt nodded as if it was a given. ''So he had access to all sorts of information. And before you go getting all defensive, I'm not saying Jacob had anything to do with what happened to your mother seven years ago…''

Alexis inhaled. How could he know that her mother had died seven years ago?

''…but, for the sake of argument, let's say either Jacob or Eden was blackmailing Marcus. They knew he wasn't in line to inherit anything and once your mother was declared legally dead, his free ride was over.''

Leigh's mother—her birth mother—had also died seven years ago? The coincidence sent Alexis's muscles contracting. But hadn't they just found her body? Alexis had thought Amy Thomas had just died.

''Jacob, alone or with his mother, could have been trying to get as much from the estate as possible. That would explain why they were so quick to remove everything that belonged to Marcus from the house. They wouldn't want to risk someone finding any evidence like those notes to incriminate them."

Alexis felt ill. What sort of family was this? She didn't want to be related to these people. She longed for the comfort and safety of her old life. Except there was neither comfort nor safety there anymore, either.

He must have seen her consternation, because Wyatt reached out and touched her arm.

"I'm sorry, Leigh, but you have to understand, it may have been Jacob who was shooting at us tonight."

"Why?"

"I don't know. I can't help but wonder if it has something to do with what you have in that briefcase you were carrying this morning."

She turned away and closed her eyes. Wyatt was right. Jacob had to be after the money. That was why he was looking for her. But how could she tell Wyatt the truth now? She still didn't know who Kathy was. What she did know was that the man who had raised her had a much stronger motive for blackmailing Marcus than this Jacob and his mother.

Opening her eyes, she stared at the file cabinet. What if her father's note had been a lie like everything else? What if Brian Ryder *had* been blackmailing Marcus Thomas?

"Leigh?"

For a second she considered lying to Wyatt, but she couldn't bring herself to do that. Her chest was so tight, she wasn't sure she could speak at all.

"Is that what you had in the briefcase?" he persisted. "Files?"

Alexis squared her shoulders. She faced him sadly. "The briefcase isn't important right now," she told him. Amazingly, her voice came out strong despite the racing of her heart. "But I'm thinking these files might be."

His jaw tightened in anger. She deserved his anger, but the flash of hurt she glimpsed jabbed at her conscience. Alexis turned away and opened the top drawer of the small cabinet.

Wyatt felt his guts twist. What had he expected? Just because they were attracted to one another didn't mean she'd open up to him. Instant trust was too much to expect, but it smarted all the same.

"It looks like someone's taken several files out of here," she said.

He didn't respond, afraid to trust his voice.

Closing the top drawer, she tugged on the bottom one. It opened a fraction and stuck.

"There's something jammed in here." She got down on the dusty floor and tried to work her hand inside to free the obstruction. "There's a file or something caught."

He watched her struggle with the drawer, trying to dislodge whatever was wedged in there. She wasn't as calm as she was trying to pretend. Her hands were trembling. What the devil was she trying to conceal? And why? She wanted her mother's murder solved as much as he did. Didn't she?

Maybe a better question was, who was she trying to protect?

Wyatt gritted his teeth. Jacob was the only answer that came to mind.

"Are you just going to stand there and watch me break every one of my fingernails or are you going to help me get this drawer open?"

"Sooner or later, you're going to have to tell me, you know," he answered.

Leigh stiffened and stopped moving. Even in the dim light provided by their flashlights, he could see the haunted expression in her eyes.

Shunting hurt and anger aside, Wyatt dropped down on

the balls of his feet and nudged her aside. "Let me have a look."

She'd worked the drawer open far enough for him to get part of his hand inside. It was enough to feel what he guessed was a file folder wedged on top. After a minute of struggle, Wyatt realized it was going to require some sort of tool to work the obstruction free.

"I need something to hold it down," he told her. Wyatt stood, opened the door to the closet and listened for a moment. The only sound he heard was the drumming of rain against the bedroom windows. Removing a wire hanger, he stepped back inside and closed the door.

"The storm's dying down," he told her.

Untwisting the wire, he got back on the floor and worked the end inside the drawer. After several tries, Leigh got on the other side and used her hand to help hold the papers. Wyatt was finally able to push the folder down far enough to force the drawer open. Unfortunately the process tore the folder open. Several papers were ripped and crumpled. The rest scattered across the dusty floor the minute he pulled the folder out.

"At least you got the drawer open," she told him with a wry smile.

What was it about her that got to him so fast? He had only to look at her to want her. But it was more than just sex. He wanted to hold her, to protect her, to eliminate that haunted expression that lurked in her eyes when she thought he didn't notice.

It was scary the way she was getting to him.

Sitting on the dusty floor, Leigh reached for the nearest paper and began to smooth it out with long, graceful fingers. Her hair fell forward to shield her face and he found himself following the bow of that graceful neck with surprising hunger.

Wyatt pulled his gaze away and began to collect the spilled papers in reach, annoyed by his loss of control. It was nothing more than the intimacy of their situation.

Darkness, dim lights, danger, a beautiful woman—no wonder his libido was going nuts.

About to stuff the papers back inside the torn file folder, the logo on one caught his attention. Excitement churned inside him.

"No wonder someone hid these," he murmured as he realized what he was holding.

Leigh looked up. "What did you find?"

He held out the sheet of paper for her to read. "A handwritten note to your father on Marbury Clinic letterhead. It looks like it was written by Jackson Marbury himself!"

Leigh scooted over closer, adding her flashlight to his. He tried not to notice how feminine she smelled, forcing his attention from the silken spill of her hair as she poured over the note.

The handwriting would have been hard to decipher even in decent lighting. Wyatt wasn't surprised when she looked up at him shaking her head.

"I don't understand."

"If I'm reading this right, your father not only knew Jackson Marbury personally, Marcus was involved in his illegal scheme at the clinic."

She stared at him without comprehension. "Wyatt, I'm sorry. I'm feeling exceptionally dense right now. Spell it out for me, will you?"

"About ten years ago, Dr. Jackson Marbury and his fertility clinic made headlines for implanting women with fertilized eggs that weren't their own. Don't you remember?"

"Wyatt, ten years ago I was fourteen years old. I vaguely remember a scandal at some clinic, but…" She shrugged.

"Jackson Marbury was an obstetrician. He made a lot of money charging outrageous prices to help women conceive."

"So what?"

"So, he guaranteed success for any patient he agreed to take on. Women who'd been told they were infertile went to his clinic for a consultation. The ones he accepted as patients took the placebos he gave them, followed his instructions to the letter, and ended up pregnant."

"Sounds like a win-win situation to me."

"Uh-huh. Everyone was happy until a disgruntled husband found out his wife was having an affair. He challenged the paternity of her child."

"Let me guess. Marbury turned out to be the real father."

"Nope. Turned out the man was the baby's father after all—but his wife wasn't the baby's mother."

"What are you talking about?"

"Marbury had fertilized another woman's egg with the husband's seed and implanted it without telling the woman that it wasn't her egg. That's when the proverbial mess hit the fan. Turned out most of the women who came to see Marbury really were infertile. The doctor was buying harvested eggs from some never-identified sources and using them instead of the women's own eggs."

She uttered a shocked sound.

"Yeah. Unfortunately, Marbury learned of the police investigation in time to destroy most of his records. The authorities were able to shut him down and prosecute, but they never found out who was supplying him with the eggs. The speculation was that any number of women could be unwitting donors. DNA on the children born to his patients didn't match any of the mothers or anyone else in his records. The authorities lacked the evidence they needed to go after anyone else. The trial was a media circus."

Wyatt took another look at the note in his hand. "If I'm deciphering this scrawl correctly, your father was at least one of the doctors who sold him fertile eggs. Given what we know about Marcus, I can't say I'm surprised."

"That's awful!"

"The real shame is that so many of Marcus's records were destroyed in that fire downstairs. We may never know how many of his patients were victimized unless we can recover information from the damaged computers."

Leigh continued to stare at him in wide-eyed horror. "You're saying his patients could have children growing up that they know nothing about?"

"That's about the size of it." He turned back to the filing cabinet. "I assume these files belonged to your grandfather?"

"I don't know. Why wouldn't he have told someone about this?"

Wyatt slanted her a look. "Maybe he was trying to protect your mother."

"Oh, my God. Marcus could have stolen my mother's eggs, couldn't he?" she whispered. "I could be...I could have sisters, even brothers I know nothing about."

Chapter Six

"Doctors don't generally treat family members, Leigh."

"His name is on my birth certificate," she blurted.

According to the birth certificate she'd found in the bottom of the envelope her father had given her, Lois Ryder had given birth at home and Marcus Thomas had been the attending physician. But he was her birth father! Alexis felt horrified to her soul. The more she learned about this family, the more she longed to be able to claim the family she'd grown up with.

Wyatt scowled. "I guess that that explains your grandfather's reluctance to release this information. This is definitely going to give Gavin a few gray hairs."

"Gavin?"

"His job is to administer your grandfather's estate," Wyatt reminded her. "If there are more potential heirs out there, his job just became a whole lot more complicated."

Alexis felt sick to her stomach. Wait until Gavin discovered that one of those complications was sitting right here.

"Let's see what other little tidbits your grandfather saved for us," Wyatt went on, unaware of her internal turmoil.

She handed him the paper she'd just been looking at. "This is a copy of a birth certificate for Jacob Voxx. Why would this be in here?"

"I have no idea, but there must be a reason." He reached for another official-looking document. "This is a divorce decree for Eden Voxx and..."

He looked up at her with a stunned expression.

"I don't believe this. I really don't believe this. Who's listed as Jacob's father on his birth certificate?"

She brought the flashlight closer to the crumpled sheet of paper. "It looks like S-i-l-u-a."

"*V*," he said, nodding. "Not a *U*. Mario Silva."

Wyatt waved the copy of the divorce paper, suppressed excitement in his eyes.

"Maybe it isn't the same guy, but I figure the way things are going it has to be. Mario Silva and three other inmates escaped from the state penitentiary during a prison transfer two weeks ago."

Her stomach churned.

"This puts a whole new slant on things, Leigh. Eden's sudden scramble to clear everything away and her hasty disappearance could be tied to her ex-husband's escape."

"I thought she ran because you found the body out back."

His eyes glittered in excitement. "One doesn't rule out the other. I wonder where Silva was seven years ago. The state investigators are going to be very unhappy they didn't discover this room."

Alexis gripped his arm. "Do you have to tell them? I mean, couldn't you tell them we found these files somewhere else?"

Wyatt went still. She released his arm, but gazed at him with pleading eyes.

"What's the problem here, Leigh?" he asked quietly.

Alexis looked away. "What isn't the problem? My entire world is disintegrating around me. No one is what they seem to be, I've got people stalking me—"

"Yeah. I'm wondering about that, as well. Why is someone coming after you again?"

"Again?"

"Nolan Ducort?" he prodded. "He still swears you were there in the barn at the racetrack when he killed Martin Pepperton. If you didn't have such a good alibi, I'd wonder about that myself."

Like ice water dripping down her back, each word created a shiver. She had no idea who Nolan Ducort or Martin Pepperton were, but Alexis felt a sense of dread. She had gone to the Saratoga racetrack a couple of weeks ago with her roommate and Linda's cousin, Seth. The young vet had started working for a clinic whose biggest client had been Pepperton Farms. Seth had taken Linda and her to work with him that morning in an effort to impress Alexis.

Goose bumps skated across her arms. She'd gone to the ladies' room and gotten turned around. She'd wandered from barn to barn trying to find the one where Seth and Linda were waiting for her.

Nolan Ducort hadn't seen Leigh, he'd seen her!

But Alexis hadn't witnessed any murder. She'd barely glanced in each barn that she'd passed.

There had been one where a horse had been screaming and kicking in its stall. She remembered the barn had been dark and mostly empty. Someone had stood at the opposite end. He'd been backlit by the sun so she hadn't seen his features.

Dear God, her sister had nearly been killed because of a case of mistaken identity. Alexis closed her eyes. "This is like a farce without the humor."

"What is?" Wyatt demanded.

Alexis opened her eyes, feeling ill. "My life. Maybe you haven't noticed, but it seems to be spiraling out of control. If you'll excuse me, I think I'll just go over in the far corner and have a case of hysterics."

"You're shaking."

"I seem to be doing that a lot lately. Is there any way Ducort could be the one who shot at us?"

Wyatt's puzzled expression immediately told her that

she'd made a mistake. A frown pleated his forehead as he regarded her.

"Ducort's paralyzed, remember? He severed his spinal cord at the neck when he fell and hit the back of that chair."

Alexis shuddered and tried to cover her mistake. "Are they sure? He couldn't be faking?"

His expressive eyes darkened in suspicion.

"Well, he must have friends," she added quickly. Too quickly, because Wyatt did not look appeased as he studied her.

"You know better than that. Was he telling the truth? Were you there, Leigh?"

She couldn't look at him. She didn't want to lie, but she was afraid to tell him the truth. She ran her hands through her hair, wishing there was some way out of this hole she'd created.

"Would you believe me if I said I wasn't?"

"I told you before, I'm not your enemy, Leigh. Talk to me. Tell me what's going on."

"I don't know." She felt so cold she couldn't stop shivering. "I really don't, Wyatt. I didn't see anyone get murdered. I don't know who's in the house. I don't have any answers at all. You know more than I do. All I have are questions."

"All right," he said gently. "Take it easy."

"Sure. Easy for you to say. I suppose you get shot at all the time."

"I'll try not to take that personally," Wyatt said gently, with a surprising touch of humor. "Ironically, I've had more guns pointed at me here than I did when I worked in the city."

"You were a cop in New York?"

"Danbury, Connecticut," he corrected. He began gathering the scattered papers.

She seized on the information. Anything to have a new focus. "Is that where you're from?"

"A suburb near there."

"Why did you become a cop?"

"Now you sound like my mother." He offered her a smile. "As much as you probably don't want to hear this, my uncle Nestor first put the idea in my head. He talked about how rewarding the job could be. I've always been an active person. I couldn't imagine sitting inside a stuffy office all day, so I joined the Danbury force right after graduation."

"How did you end up in Stony Ridge?"

"My uncle invited me when a position on his force came open. I'd taken a lot of law and criminology courses in college, and I have a background most of his people don't have. The funny part is, I couldn't understand why he thought it would be useful in a quiet little town like Stony Ridge."

"Why did you come here if you thought your training would be wasted?"

"It seemed like a good idea at the time," he said ruefully. "I've got a pair of sisters who kept trying to fix me up with all their single friends. They have a lot of friends," he added with a wry twist of his lips. "I figured Stony Ridge was far enough away to give me a breather."

Alexis found she could still smile. "Poor baby. Hordes of women hot for your body, huh? It must have been tough."

"Go ahead and laugh. Escaping all those feminine wiles took skill and diplomacy."

"Uh-huh. I can imagine." She went to hand him several sheets of paper to add to the collection, but when their hands brushed, she dropped them.

"Sorry. I seem to be clumsy tonight."

Wyatt set the folder on the floor. His expression was tender as he gazed at her. "It's going to be all right, Leigh."

"Is it?" Her lips felt stiff.

He slid his arm around her shoulders. Without thought, she moved closer to his side.

"It is," he promised.

She let him press her head against his shoulder. The fit was perfect. Alexis closed her eyes. For a few precious minutes she allowed herself the luxury of simply being held by Wyatt. If things had been different...but they weren't, and she couldn't afford to relax.

She opened her eyes and pulled back. She couldn't read his expression.

"I should go," he told her.

"Where? Why would you go back out there?"

"We can't stay in here all night."

"Why not? It's better than being shot!"

"He's not going to hang around too long, Leigh. When he doesn't find us, he'll assume we left."

"No, he won't. You left your hat and coat on the front staircase. You wouldn't go out in the storm and leave them behind. When he sees the bullet hole in your radio, he'll know we can't call for help."

Wyatt swore softly. "You and Hayley are right not to trust the cops. A first-year rookie would do a better job than I've done tonight."

"Hey, we're still alive, aren't we?"

"No thanks to me," he said bitterly.

Alexis shook her head. "Self-pity doesn't suit you."

His gaze jerked to her face.

"I do it much better," she told him briskly.

He was slow to relax, but his teeth flashed in a sudden smile. "Think so?"

"I know so. I've had more practice."

"Yeah? How's that?"

"I was seventeen when my mother died. 'Why me' was a popular refrain."

He rested a hand on her shoulder. "That's an understandable reaction, Leigh."

She wanted to tell him her name was Alexis, not Leigh,

but the words caught in her throat. He leaned in closer. He was going to kiss her. She wanted that, as well. She raised her face in anticipation and the hidden door suddenly began to move.

Wyatt sprang to his feet, reaching for his gun.

Alexis scrambled to the far side of the door, out of the immediate line of fire.

"Wyatt? Leigh? You guys in there?"

"R.J.!"

Wyatt lowered his gun. A flashlight beam caught him full in the face.

"Yeah, I guess you are."

The light moved as Lucky bounded inside, his tail going a mile a minute.

"What are you doing here, R.J.?" Wyatt demanded.

"I got to worrying after I talked to you. I decided to head over and be sure everything was okay. When I found Jezzy under a tree down by the road, I knew they weren't."

"Under a tree?" Alexis gasped.

"Did you call for help?" Wyatt demanded. "You shouldn't have come in here."

"I tried to call, but we've got lines and trees down all over the place. Somebody spotted a funnel cloud outside town. You have no idea how bad it is out there."

"It hasn't exactly been a piece of cake in here, either," Wyatt told him grimly.

The men shared a look.

"I saw your coat and the radio," R.J. told him. "I assume you know a maple tree came down against the side of the house. Either of you hurt?"

"No."

Alexis let her hand come to rest on Lucky's broad head. The large dog wriggled in pleasure.

"You two want a lift?" R.J. offered.

"There may be a guy with a gun and a temper somewhere in the house," Wyatt told him.

"I don't think so. Lucky and I have been combing the place looking for you. He seems to think the house is empty."

Wyatt looked at the dog, then back at R.J. "You willing to stake your life on that?"

"I just did."

Wyatt nodded acceptance. "How bad is Jezzy?"

"Let's just say if she's repairable, you're going to make Beamer over at the garage one very happy, very wealthy mechanic."

Wyatt swore softly. He bent to retrieve the file and the few papers that still littered the floor. "Let's get out of here."

"What about the rest of the files?" she asked.

"I'll come back tomorrow."

Not we—I.

Lucky seemed unconcerned as he led them back down the main staircase, but Alexis noticed that Wyatt didn't tuck his gun away until they were crowding into R.J.'s truck. Being the smallest, she insisted on climbing in back with the dog.

"Just so you know, there's no one home at George and Emily's, but I do have a key to the house," R.J. told them.

"No," Wyatt said. "I hate to ask you to drive all the way back into town—"

"Can't," R.J. told him. "Not without going out to the highway and trying to come in from the east, and I'm not real sure that would work, either. The creek's already covered the roadway. My place isn't far. You two are welcome to bed down there if you don't want to go to the Walken estate."

Wyatt frowned. "Sure you don't mind?"

"Not if you don't mind roughing it. The only furniture I have is the stuff Emily gave me from her attic."

"You're talking to two people who've just spent hours sitting on a dusty floor," Alexis interjected. "If you have chairs, your place gets my vote."

"Yeah. I'd like to see this place you've been raving about for the past couple of months. Just make sure we aren't followed," Wyatt told him.

"Are you kidding? No, I can see you aren't. Okay, if I make it down this driveway, I'll keep a watch out."

They were nearly at the bottom of the driveway when Alexis saw the road was blocked.

"Uh, R.J., there's a tree," she pointed out nervously when he showed no signs of slowing down.

"It's okay, we can go around it. I told you you needed a truck to drive around here."

"I can't afford a truck," Wyatt protested. "I could barely afford Jezzy."

They passed Wyatt's crumpled car, protruding from under a limb that reminded Alexis of the one sticking into the bedroom of the house. The back end of the small black car was flattened beneath the branch.

"The driver was one lucky son—" R.J. stopped to glance at Wyatt.

He regarded the scene grimly. "Yeah," he agreed flatly.

For the next several minutes no one said anything. Rain began to hammer the truck, forcing R.J. to concentrate on his driving. Alexis was sitting on the edge of her seat by the time he finally turned down a rutted narrow lane.

"This driveway is in even worse shape than the one at Heartskeep," Wyatt complained.

"No, it's shorter. That's the problem with being a contractor. When the weather's good enough to do things around here, I'm too busy with work that pays. Buying this place took most of my savings, but it was too good a deal to pass up."

Alexis stared as the truck's headlights swept the sagging front porch steps, illuminating the peeling paint and cracked windows of the sprawling old farmhouse.

"I know it doesn't look like much, but it will once I get it all fixed up."

"I think it's great," she told him honestly. "The house looks warm and friendly."

"And about to fall down," Wyatt added.

"Ha! This old place will be standing long after you're gone. Stay to the left when you go up the steps to the porch, there's a loose board on the right that I've got to fix. Go ahead and get out of the rain while I check on the generator."

Alexis was shocked to discover R.J. hadn't even locked his front door. Lucky bounded after R.J. and she followed Wyatt inside the dark old house.

"Is this okay with you?" he asked her quietly.

"It's fine, Wyatt. No one will think to look for us here."

"Heck, they probably couldn't find the place even with directions."

She smiled up at him and everything changed. Her body responded to the raw desire she saw on his face. His touch was featherlight against her cheek. She raised her head and he lowered his. The door at their back swung open and Lucky bounded inside.

They sprang apart guiltily. If R.J. noticed, he didn't give them any indication. He turned on what proved to be the single lamp in the large, old-fashioned living room. A couch, matching chair and small television sitting on a stand of used bricks and scrap lumber comprised his furniture. The bits and pieces were almost lost in the large room.

"Sorry. I'm not exactly ready for company. There's basically only amenities for Lucky and me."

Alexis shook her head. Carefully she kept her eyes averted from Wyatt. "Don't apologize, R.J. This is a fantastic room."

"It will be once I get the fireplace cleaned up and slap some paint on these walls. Listen, make yourselves at home while I see what I've got in the kitchen."

"You don't have to feed us," she told him, even

though her stomach began to rumble at the thought of food.

"You've barely eaten all day," Wyatt complained.

Her stomach agreed, even as she shook her head. "I'm fine."

"Mostly, I grab meals when I'm out," R.J. told them. "But I know I've got a steak in the freezer and some frozen dinners."

"Not for me," she told him quickly. "I don't want anything that heavy this late in the day."

"Speak for yourself," Wyatt said. "We never finished lunch, if you'll recall."

The huge country kitchen boasted a card table and pair of mismatched chairs.

"The stove's gas, but I'm afraid the only thing I have hooked up to the generator in here is the refrigerator," R.J. said apologetically. From a cupboard, he withdrew a pair of large oil lamps and proceeded to light them.

"I've got plenty of sodas and beer," he offered. "Oh, and a bag of fresh peanuts."

"Why don't you guys take those into the living room and let me see what I can pull together?" Alexis offered.

"You cook?" R.J. asked in surprise.

"Of course I cook."

"Sorry. You always had a maid and cook at Heartskeep."

"But not when she lived in Boston, am I right?" Wyatt asked.

"Right." Since she had never lived in Boston, she didn't have to lie. "Would it be okay to raid your pantry?"

"Help yourself. You want a beer, Wyatt?"

Alexis scanned his meager offerings, relieved to find cans of soup, boxes of pasta, biscuit mix, and even cheese and a full half gallon of milk in his refrigerator. "No spices?"

"Salt and pepper," R.J. said sheepishly.

"It's a start. Have you got another chair for the table?"

"No, but I do have several TV trays. Lucky and I generally eat in the living room in front of the television set."

"Okay, if you'll set that up, I think I can come up with something edible." When she carried two bowls of steaming soup to them a few minutes later, they were watching the news. The rain had stalled over Stony Ridge. Forecasters predicted the storm wouldn't end until morning.

Alexis joined Wyatt on the couch a few minutes later, sure she wouldn't be able to eat sitting this close to him, but she was wrong. Hunger quickly claimed her attention. Over plates of macaroni and cheese, hot biscuits and canned fruit salad, they watched the news as police and rescue workers struggled with downed trees and power lines.

"I should be out there," Wyatt said.

"No, you shouldn't, R.J. argued. Your uncle's going to need you fresh for tomorrow morning. Leigh, this is terrific. You can cook for me anytime."

"Thank you, but all I did was open a couple of boxes and some cans."

Wyatt gazed at her. Alexis felt a flush mount her cheeks.

"It's great," he said simply.

"I've been thinking about the sleeping arrangements," R.J. said. "I've only got one bed upstairs so you can take that, Leigh. Wyatt can take the couch and I'll use my sleeping bag."

Instantly she and Wyatt protested, but R.J. wouldn't budge. "My house, my rules."

In the end Alexis found herself upstairs using one of R.J.'s old shirts in lieu of a nightgown. She finished rinsing her underthings and hung them over the shower rod, hoping they'd dry by morning.

She figured she wouldn't sleep after her long nap, despite the lethargy pulling at her. She'd spent the past couple of hours holding a mental debate while she pretended to watch television with the men. She'd finally concluded she needed to tell Wyatt the truth no matter what.

That he would be furious was a given. He might even arrest her. It didn't matter. She needed to tell him.

It was crazy the way just thinking of him seemed to make her heart beat faster.

She picked up the battery-operated lantern R.J. had given her and opened the bathroom door. Wyatt came off the wall where he'd been lounging in a fluid movement that drew her gaze to his bare chest.

"Oh! You startled me. I didn't mean to monopolize the bathroom."

"You didn't." He took the lantern from her trembling hand. "I was waiting to talk to you."

"I wanted to talk to you, too."

She tore her gaze from his chest only to find him staring down the deep vee created by R.J.'s shirt. Instantly her breasts grew heavy and full. The nipples tightened. Her stomach gave a funny little flutter.

His eyes fastened on her with a savage intensity that was exquisitely exciting. She could see him struggling to control his body's reaction.

"R.J.'s going to run me into town first thing in the morning. I think it would be best if you stayed here with Lucky," he said roughly.

"But—"

"R.J. will come back for you and take you to Heartskeep with him when he goes. I'll meet you both over there."

She flung out her hand to protest. The moment her fingers grazed his bare skin, the words died in her throat. She was suddenly, painfully, aware of her own body and the burgeoning heat of desire. She forgot to breathe, aware of the tension humming through him, as well. For a long moment neither one of them moved.

"I swore I wasn't going to do this."

"Do what?" she whispered.

Her mouth went dry as he set the lantern on the floor at their feet.

"This."

They came together with a shudder of need. Her hands slid over the silky planes of his chest to wrap around his neck in a silent plea for haste. Wyatt lowered his face and covered her lips with unbearable gentleness.

It wasn't enough. Not nearly enough. She nipped at his lip in demand and the kiss went hot and wet with suppressed hunger. She urged him on with soft mews of pleasure, running her hands over his smooth skin. When his large, rough hands slid over her hips to cup her bare buttocks, her hips tilted upward in invitation. He pulled her to him in shockingly intimate contact.

She felt him stir against her. Hard and wanting, the way she wanted, with a burning fierce intensity that amazed her, even as it consumed her.

"Hey," R.J. shouted from somewhere down below them. "Bring that back here, you stupid mutt."

Wyatt released her and stepped back, breathing hard. Her own lungs labored, as well, while tremors of desire rocked her.

"Go to bed."

Her lips trembled. "Come with me."

Her breasts strained against the rough material of the shirt as he stared at her with molten heat. Below them, Lucky barked. R.J. swore. A tremor went through Wyatt.

"I can't."

"No." Of course he couldn't. He was right. She knew he was right. But she wanted him.

"Get some sleep."

He had to know that was impossible. She doubted if either one of them would sleep much tonight.

Alexis stood there long after he disappeared from sight. Finally she bent to retrieve the lantern.

DUST MOTES DANCED in the sunlight that filled the room, streaming in past the bare windows. At least it wasn't raining anymore.

The sheets lay tangled around her, testament to her restless night. The memory of Wyatt's kiss rooted deeply in her mind. Alexis stared at the walls and their faded gingham paper and wondered if she'd lost her mind completely. She was pretty sure she'd lost her heart. It didn't make sense. They didn't even know each other. Wyatt didn't even know her real name!

She had to tell him, but the minute she did, everything would change. What if he didn't believe her? What if he thought she was part of the extortion plan?

Lucky climbed to his feet the minute she opened the bedroom door. Obviously he'd been waiting there for her to wake up.

"You're right, Lucky. I'm a slugabed this morning. Did they put you on sentry duty?"

The dog woofed happily. She'd always wanted a dog. Maybe not one quite this large. Still, she rubbed his head and patted his side, glad for his presence. What time was it? It felt late. The house was so silent she knew she must be alone. She'd meant to get up early this morning and to go into town with them, but she hadn't been able to sleep until late last night, trying to make sense of everything. She'd never heard them leave.

"Sorry, Lucky," she told the big dog when he tried to go in the bathroom with her. "I don't know about R.J., but I shower alone. I'll be out shortly, fella."

She'd slept in long enough for the panties to be mostly dry, if not the bra. She took a quick shower, smiling when she saw the unopened comb R.J. had left out for her. Tugging it through her wet hair, she decided it was a good thing that her style was low maintenance. A hair-dryer would have been nice, but the comb at least smoothed the tangles after she rubbed her hair as dry as possible with a towel.

The elastic on the bra and panties proved uncomfortably damp. Hesitating, she decided she could go without either one until she could get to Heartskeep to borrow another outfit from one of her sisters. She hoped R.J. wouldn't mind if she helped herself to another one of his shirts. Her sister's T-shirt was a little more revealing than she liked without her bra. Selecting a short-sleeved dress shirt with a badly frayed collar from R.J.'s closet, she put that on over her sister's blouse and gathered the ends, tying them loosely under her breasts. She let the tails hang down in front. She couldn't see a whole lot in the bathroom mirror, but she hadn't seen any other mirrors, so she decided the makeshift top would have to do. At least it was no longer obvious that she wasn't wearing a bra.

As she started downstairs she realized Lucky hadn't waited for her to come out of the bathroom. Hopefully she hadn't hurt his doggie feelings when she'd refused to let him inside with her.

"Lucky! Here boy. Lucky!"

She walked into the kitchen and jerked to a stop.

"I'm afraid I put Lucky outside," the genial-looking blond stranger said. He lifted a sheet of paper from the kitchen counter. "R.J. left you a note."

Alexis made no move to take it from him when he came forward with it extended.

"Who are you?"

"My name's Jacob. Jacob Voxx," he added with an engaging grin.

Fear washed over her.

"I see you've heard of me. All lies, I assure you. You're a hard person to find, Alexis."

Chapter Seven

It took her a minute to realize he'd called her by the right name.

"You know who I am?"

"Sure." He continued to smile. "Alexis Mary Ryder. Pretty name, by the way. I've been looking for you for several days now. We all have."

"All?"

"Your sisters. Bram. Gavin. Even Emily and George Walken, I suspect, but you probably don't know them yet." He shrugged. "Sit down. Have some coffee. It smells a bit strong, but it's likely been sitting here awhile. I could make some fresh, if you like."

"No, thank you."

Alexis forced herself to stay calm. He hadn't crowded her in any way, but Wyatt didn't trust Jacob. He'd even thought Jacob might have been last night's intruder. And despite Jacob's affable demeanor, she didn't trust him, either.

"How do you know my name?"

"I told you, I've been looking for you. Nice," he added, nodding to the bra and matching panties still in her hand.

She refused to let him disconcert her. "What are you doing here? How did you get in? I doubt you were invited."

"Technically, no, but the front door was unlocked."
He shrugged with a friendly smile. "We need to talk."

"About what?" She set the underwear on the counter
beside her. It was important to watch his eyes. The eyes
would give away his intentions.

"About the money Kathy gave Brian Ryder."

Fear slammed into her. She forced it aside. Her heart
hammered painfully while her head pulsed with questions.

"I don't know what you're talking about."

His features narrowed in warning. "Yes, you do. Don't
play games, Alexis. We don't have a lot of time right now.
I know you must be confused by everything that's happened. It must have been hard finding out you were
adopted. You haven't met your sisters yet, have you?"

Mutely she tried to think. Jacob appeared undaunted by
her silence.

"It's okay, you know. They really do look exactly like
you. It's amazing. What did Wyatt think when you told
him?"

Should she pretend to know more than she did?

"Ah, I see. He doesn't know who you are yet, does
he? Which one of them does he think you are, Hayley or
Leigh?"

Wyatt had said her sisters defended this man? Couldn't
they see past his youthful good looks and bumbling ways
to the hint of steel underneath that smile? Maybe they
underestimated him, but she wouldn't make the same mistake. Even without Wyatt's warning, she would have been
uncomfortable around a man like this. He was too glib,
too friendly, too sure of himself.

"You need to leave now," she told him firmly. "R.J.
and Wyatt will be back any minute. I don't think they're
going to like finding you in here any more than I do."

He shook his blond head, looking regretful. "Sorry,
Alexis. If you'd read his note you'd know R.J. won't be
back to pick you up until noon. I'm guessing that's a
conservative estimate. He took Wyatt into town this morn-

ing. The storm left the roadways a mess, so he was late getting out to Heartskeep to get his crew started. He has a lot going on over at the house today. I wouldn't be surprised if he runs quite late to pick you up. His note says you should help yourself to whatever you can find to eat. Do you want some breakfast?"

"What I want is for you to leave."

"I can't do that." His jaw hardened. There was determination in his ice-blue eyes. "If I found you, so can the others."

"How did you find me?" she asked stalling. He was still calm, still nonthreatening, except for the veiled threat beneath his words.

"Wyatt ran a make on your car's license plate last night. I heard the call go out over the police scanner. I figured you'd head for Heartskeep. Where else could you go?"

"I can think of several places."

If only she'd used any one of them instead of coming to Stony Ridge and walking blindly into this viperous trap.

"How did you find me here?" she demanded.

"I grew up in Stony Ridge. It's common knowledge R.J. bought the old Teller place," he told her with an easy smile. "Since I was looking for you, I was hanging around Heartskeep when I overheard R.J. on his cell phone talking to Wyatt. R.J. said he was going to pick you up around lunchtime, so I thought I'd save him the trip. Did you know R.J.'s people are going to tear down all those walls today?"

R.J. was tearing down walls? Which walls? Why? She longed to ask, but didn't want to reveal just how little she understood everything that was happening around her.

"What do you want from me?"

"I told you. I want what Kathy gave Brian Ryder before he died."

"What do you know about my...about what happened in New York?"

"You were going to say 'my father,' weren't you? He wasn't, of course, but you know that now. How much *did* Ryder tell you before he died, Alexis? Did you know you were Amy's firstborn child when you came here?"

"How did you know that?"

"I know a lot about the situation. For example, I know that your father and my mother sold you to the Ryders for fifty thousand dollars."

She couldn't prevent a soft gasp.

"Yeah. Only fifty thousand. I guess that's better than thirty pieces of silver, but I would have thought a baby, and particularly an heir to a fortune, was worth a whole lot more than that."

His sly innuendo didn't escape her. Her father's note had said he didn't know who she was. She wanted desperately to believe that much, at least.

"You want more?" Jacob asked. "I know that while my mother was bringing you to the Ryders, Marcus drove your mother to the hospital where he delivered your two sisters by C-section in front of an operating room full of witnesses."

Horror was tempered with a twitch of relief. At least she wasn't some stolen egg who'd been implanted at the Marbury Clinic.

"Nice parents we have, huh? They say you can't pick your family, but we really got screwed over with ours. At least neither of your parents ever went to prison—even if your father belonged in there with mine. Be glad you never met either of them. Marcus Thomas was one cold bastard. He married Amy Thomas for her money, of course. Must have come as a nasty shock when he learned old Dennison Hart disinherited Amy as a result of their marriage. You *do* realize that's what this is all about, don't you? Old man Hart left the bulk of his estate to his firstborn grandchild. That would be you."

She wouldn't give him the satisfaction of seeing her shudder. "Is that why your mother helped Marcus?"

"Good question. I've kind of wondered about that myself. Marcus and my mom always had this weird relationship, you know? Half the time I don't think the two of them even liked each other, but she worked for him even before I was born. When Dennison set Marcus up with an office at Heartskeep, she moved us here to Stony Ridge so she could keep working for him. And I know what you're thinking, but you're wrong. Mom wasn't in love with Marcus."

He chuckled and shook his head. It was all Alexis could do not to rub the chill from her arms.

"You haven't met my mother yet, but when you do, you'll understand. She can be passionate about things, but not people. I always thought of them as having a deeply committed business relationship. Even when she married him a couple of years ago, I figured it was because she liked the idea of playing lady of the manor, you know? Just business as usual with a few satisfying perks thrown in."

Alexis didn't understand how he could sound so complacent when describing such a bizarre situation.

"What about your father?"

All traces of boyish humor left his features. His expression hardened and his eyes grew cold. "My *father* has spent most of his life behind bars. Mom divorced him when I was a baby. I used to tell everyone he died before I was born. Mom said that wasn't far from the mark. Apparently he used to show up every so often, but only because he was looking for a handout—or a hideout. Mom kept him away from me. I don't really remember him, and it doesn't matter. He doesn't have anything to do with us."

She couldn't afford a stirring of sympathy for Jacob. "Did you know he escaped from prison a few weeks ago?"

Jacob stilled. "How did you know that?"

Alexis tried not to show her fear. "Wyatt told me."

"I didn't realize he knew anything about my father," he said thoughtfully.

"Maybe you should tell your mother," she said cautiously.

"Oh, she knows."

His dark expression was alarming. Alexis wished she hadn't brought the subject up. But then his features relaxed and Jacob looked at her again.

"You see? This is exactly why we need to work together. We can help each other, Alexis. I know things and you know things. What did you do with the briefcase Kathy gave Ryder?"

"There really is a Kathy?" she asked, trying again to buy some time.

"Of course. Did you think Ryder made her up?"

Alexis held her silence. She wasn't about to tell Jacob how bad her father was at remembering names.

"That's okay. Ryder probably figured the less you knew, the better off you'd be. He was wrong, of course. You're smack in the middle of this mess whether you like it or not."

She wanted to ask what mess she was in the middle of, but he continued blithely and she didn't want to interrupt him with questions when he was freely sharing knowledge she needed.

"Kathy Walsh and her mother used to work for your grandfather. They were devoted to Dennison and the Hart family. Naturally, they hated Marcus." He shrugged. "Can't blame them there. He was a real bastard. They weren't too happy with my mother, either. I think at first they saw her as a potential home-wrecker, but I have to say, they were always nice to me. Of course, the first thing my mother did after marrying Marcus was fire them. She'd been after Marcus to do it from the day they found your grandfather dead of a heart attack."

He paused and rocked back on his heels thoughtfully.

"You know, I always wondered about that heart attack.

Everyone knew the old man had a bad heart—including Marcus.''

"Are you saying Marcus murdered him?" It was too much. "Even soap operas aren't this melodramatic."

He grinned, suddenly looking young and carefree once again. "You're right. It's just a pet theory of mine. I never told anyone my suspicions. Marcus had nothing to gain by his death, but it did seem sort of…convenient or something, you know? I mean, a couple of months later, Amy goes to New York City and is never seen again. Quite a coincidence, don't you think? Hayley and Leigh always insisted Marcus killed her, but no one believed them. Of course, Chief Crossley's looking like a real fool now that her body finally turned up buried under Marcus's rose garden.''

Alexis stared at him in silence.

"Didn't you know that, either?" He shook his head. "Poor Alexis, you really are flying blind here, aren't you?" He tipped his head to one side and studied her. "You don't trust me, do you?"

"Why should I? I don't even know you."

"True," he agreed wryly. Once again he turned on the charm. "I wish I'd known about you sooner, Alexis. Maybe I could have protected you."

"Protected me from what?"

He looked toward the back door and frowned. Alexis realized she'd been hearing a scratching sound for several minutes now. But she'd been so focused on what Jacob was saying she hadn't paid any attention. Lucky wanted back inside.

"You know, I think we should go," Jacob said. "Come with me. I'll answer all your questions to the best of my ability."

"No." She wasn't going anywhere with him no matter how charming he could be. "You can answer questions here."

He glanced at the door again.

"Don't tell me you're afraid of Lucky," she said.

His lips pursed in a wry smile. "We need to leave."

"You go ahead. I'm going to wait here for R.J."

"Alexis, I told you, if I could find you, so could the others."

"You mean my sisters? Your mother? Your *father?*"

His open, friendly features hardened. She watched his eyes fill with steely determination. He was through being Mr. Nice Guy.

"I don't want to hurt you, Alexis. We can do a deal."

He closed the distance, reaching out to take her arm. Alexis didn't have to think twice. Years of training and conditioning took over. She met him halfway, taking his arm first. Using his own momentum against him, she sent him crashing to the floor, delivering three sharp kicks designed to immobilize him long enough to get away. Then she flew to the front of the house and out the door.

She heard him swearing painfully behind her. "Alexis! Wait!"

Lucky barked in agitation behind the house. Alexis didn't look back. She sprinted down the driveway.

"HEY, WYATT, where you been?" Jim Lowe called to him as he stepped out of his uncle's office.

"I can't talk right now, Jim."

Wyatt was in no mood for conversation after the tongue-lashing he'd just received from the chief. He was still dressed in yesterday's clothing. He hadn't even made it to his locker to don his spare uniform.

"I thought you'd want to know about the car you found yesterday."

Wyatt stopped moving.

"N.Y.P.D. wants it impounded. Seems they want to talk with Alexis Ryder real bad. Her roommate came back early from a trip and found blood all over their apartment. She found the Ryder woman's father shot dead in her bedroom."

"Better have someone check out that white jacket on the passenger seat," Wyatt told him. "I thought that stain I saw was dried blood. Do they think she killed him?"

"Either that or was taken away by his killer. They aren't saying much, but I gather they have something that indicates she was there in the apartment."

"The last thing we need around here right now is another murderer or another body."

"Tell me about it. Do you want to go in and brief the chief since you're the one who first spotted the car?"

He shook his head. "Not a chance. This one's all yours. I wasn't even on duty. Besides, I just came from in there," he admitted ruefully, nodding toward his uncle's office.

"Yeah. I heard you went silent on us last night. Dispatch was concerned."

"Hard to call in after your radio takes a bullet hole."

"Are you serious? What happened?"

"I went out to Heartskeep."

"No way."

Wyatt nodded. "I'll fill you in later. Listen, would you let everyone know I'm probably not going to make the game tonight?"

Jim shook his head. "Haven't you heard? The baseball field's under six inches of water. All games have been canceled for the rest of the week."

"I haven't been home to check my messages yet. Thanks for letting me know. Say, do we have a description of this Ryder woman?"

Jim flipped open his notebook. "White female, age twenty-four, five-two, one-hundred-fifteen pounds, chin-length brownish-blond hair."

An image of Leigh flashed through his brain. Not really surprising. He'd been having all sorts of images of her since last night. The one he liked best involved her naked in his bed, which was not exactly something he wanted to be thinking about right now.

"That fits at least four women I can think of here in Stony Ridge." Including Leigh and Hayley.

"Tell me about it. They're supposed to be faxing her picture over later this afternoon. She's some sort of social worker."

Wyatt groaned.

"Yeah. She works with runaways and pregnant teens. They say she has a tendency to bend the rules and get personally involved in her cases. They're looking into some possibilities there. She's also a volunteer instructor at a battered woman's shelter. Teaches some sort of self-defense classes."

"Terrific. That should make it much easier to spot her," he said sarcastically.

Jim grinned good-naturedly. "Keep your eyes peeled for a karate kicking do-gooder."

"Very funny. You wouldn't happen to know where I could find Emily and George Walken or Gavin Jarret, would you?"

"Sorry."

"Well, if you run into any of them, let them know I need to talk to them."

"Will do."

Wyatt headed down the hall to his desk. Several others stopped to say they were glad to see he was all right. Dispatch hadn't heard his location or his request for backup, but they knew he'd called in. When he couldn't be reached to verify his call, they'd put out an alert and notified his uncle.

Uncle Nestor was not happy to learn he was going to have to send more officers out to the estate to pore over the upstairs of Heartskeep looking for evidence of the shooting and break-in last night. R.J. wasn't going to be happy, either.

The only reason Wyatt wasn't back on administrative leave was that he hadn't returned fire last night. But being back on duty meant he had rules to follow and reports to type. He plopped the file folder down on his desk. His uncle had barely glanced at the information. He'd told Wyatt to deal with it himself.

Wyatt had spent the night reading through the file. Dennison Hart had compiled enough evidence to indict Marcus Thomas on a number of different charges. At the very least, Marcus would have lost his license to practice medicine if this information had gone public. So why hadn't Dennison used it to destroy a son-in-law he, from all reports, disliked?

The obvious answer was that he was trying to protect his daughter and his granddaughters from scandal. But that didn't jibe with what Wyatt had learned about the once-powerful head of the Hart dynasty. Dennison Hart had a reputation for playing fair and facing consequences no matter what. And there was no question that these files had belonged to him. There were several notations in the margin in his handwriting.

So, who else had this information? Had it been used to blackmail the doctor? Or had Marcus been blackmailed because someone knew he'd killed Amy Hart Thomas?

Wyatt's telephone rang the minute he made the mistake of sitting down. He answered absently and Tony Raine's voice filled his ear. Tony worked on the Saratoga Springs police force and played in their softball league on an opposing team.

"Hey, man," Tony greeted him, "don't you return phone calls?"

Wyatt winced. He'd intended to check his phone messages first thing, but it had taken them forever to get into town this morning and his uncle had nabbed him before he'd even made it to the locker room to change clothes.

"Sorry. I've been off for a few days, Tony. I just got to my desk. What's up?"

"You were so concerned about the Walsh case that I thought you'd want to know that Livia Walsh had a massive stroke and passed away without regaining consciousness."

"I'm sorry to hear that."

"The doctors said it was for the best," Tony intoned. "We got a lead on the daughter from the neighbor across the street. Katherine Walsh has been living in Canada with a man her mother didn't approve of."

"She was what, in her late forties?"

"Forty-five, but in this case, mother knew best. We lifted several sets of prints from inside the Walsh house. It wasn't ransacked by juveniles."

"The boyfriend?"

"Yep. A few years ago the Canadian police picked up Bernie Duquette during a raid on an illegal gambling operation. He was a customer, not part of the operation, but the arrest put his prints on file. At our request, the Canadians went over to have a chat with Bernie. His apartment was empty, but there were signs of a violent struggle, including blood."

Tony had his full attention now.

"They aren't sure whose blood, but neighbors haven't seen the couple in more than a week. They have, however, seen a couple of tough-looking strangers hanging around the place, and three of his neighbors reported burglaries in the last two weeks. Only cash and portable items were stolen, including a nine-millimeter semi-automatic and some extra ammunition."

"Meaning, Bernie's an armed thief?" Wyatt asked.

"Hard to say, but it looks that way. He doesn't have a criminal record other than that one arrest, but the feeling is he may be in to a loan shark to pay off some gambling debts. His résumé is remarkable only for the sheer number of menial jobs he's had and lost. Is this ringing any bells for you?"

"In a real undefined sort of way. Someone broke into Heartskeep last night and took a shot at me. Ruined a perfectly good raincoat and a handheld radio."

"Interesting way to spend an evening. The rest of us were simply battling torrential rains and downed trees and power lines."

"Yeah, well, you know how it goes. Some of us lead more exciting lives than others."

"To each their own. I'll take floodwaters over bullets any day. Do you think there's a connection between your thief and Duquette?"

"I don't know. What sort of M.O. was used on the apartments?"

"Strictly smash-and-grab—in through the patio window and out the same way. All ground-floor apartments."

"Our guy went in through a kitchen window by the door. If our people find any nine millimeter shell casings, or dig something interesting out of one of the walls, I'll be giving you a call back."

"Do that."

"Do the Canadians think Kathy Walsh is dead?"

"Let's just say they'd like to be shown otherwise. There were no bullet holes in the apartment."

"Glad to hear that."

"You'll keep me informed?" Tony asked.

"Naturally. And be sure to let me know if Kathy Walsh turns up."

"Will do. Your shortstop and his fiancée wanted to take Livia Walsh's body to Stony Ridge for burial, but we can't release it until her daughter is notified."

Fiancée? The word sliced past everything else. "Do you mean Gavin Jarret was there in Saratoga Springs?"

"Yeah. He's still your shortstop, isn't he?"

"What fiancée?" Wyatt demanded. But he knew, even before Tony began speaking again.

"Oops. I didn't know it was supposed to be a secret. Do me a favor and don't let on that I told you, okay? He and one of the Hart girls are engaged. Good-looking lady. I'm not sure how comfortable I'd feel about marrying someone with an identical twin. But that's just me. Her being an heiress is a nice perk, don't you think?''

Wyatt clenched his jaw so tight it hurt. ''Is Jarret still there?''

''Nope. They were going to drive to Canada to see if they could locate the daughter. I told them the police were already looking, but I got the impression the Hart women don't hold us dedicated law-enforcement types in high esteem.''

''They don't,'' he said flatly. He couldn't believe the wrench of betrayal clawing at his guts. ''How long ago did they leave, Tony?''

''Yesterday.''

That took a minute to sink in. ''What time yesterday?''

''Ten, maybe ten-thirty. Is there a problem?''

A huge problem. Leigh had been with him yesterday. It was possible, of course. She would have had to drive like crazy, but she could have left Saratoga Springs at ten and made it back to Stony Ridge in time for him to spot her standing in front of Gavin's office yesterday. And if she and Gavin had had a spat on the way home, it would explain her mood and that lost expression on her face when he'd first spoken with her.

He cursed out loud, remembering that kiss last night. If it hadn't been for Lucky and R.J., and a supreme show of willpower on his part, he might have done far more than kiss her.

''I gather something I said disagreed with you,'' Tony was saying in his ear.

Wyatt unclenched his jaw. ''Sorry. I'm a little preoccupied.''

She'd come on to him when she was engaged to Gavin? The knowledge was bitter. R.J. had tried to warn him. He should have paid more attention to what the younger man had been trying to tell him.

''Wy? Is something wrong?''

"It's been a rough couple of days, Tony. Thanks for the call and the info. I owe you one."

"Remember that when our team plays yours next week."

"In your dreams, pal."

Wyatt hung up to the sound of his friend's laughter in his ear. The last thing he felt like doing was laughing. Staring at his In basket, all he could see was the way she'd stood there, looking up at him last night. Soft, sexy, willing.

He cursed again. She'd been an incredible distraction, but maybe that's what she'd intended from the start. That sweet little come-on of hers had certainly kept him from asking as many questions as he should have.

His messages and his reports could wait. So could a shower and his uniform. That briefcase of hers was suddenly looking a whole lot more important. She'd sidetracked him every time he'd mentioned it. While he couldn't compel her to show him what was inside, he could certainly push a lot harder to find out what it was she didn't want him to know. Instinct told him it was important.

Wyatt locked Dennison Hart's file in his desk, pulled the keys to his cruiser from the pegboard and headed for the door. Leigh had a lot of questions to answer. And this time he wasn't going to be distracted by a pair of soft blue eyes.

ALEXIS MISJUDGED the depth of a pothole. She went down hard on the muddy driveway. Instantly she was on her feet and moving again, veering off the chewed-up tarmac onto the grass. She didn't look back to see if Jacob was chasing her. Her only goal was to put as much distance between them as she could manage.

She was pretty sure her kick to his kneecap had missed its intended mark, but she consoled herself with the thought that Jacob would be hurting all the same. He probably wouldn't shoot her. Not only hadn't he displayed a gun, but he wouldn't want her dead until she told him where she'd hidden the briefcase.

The grass wasn't proving to be a better alternative to the driveway. Not only was it wet and slippery, but the soggy ground sucked at her shoes, threatening to pull them from her feet with every step.

She heard a bark behind her. Lucky had come charging around the house and was giving chase. Obviously the dog thought this was some sort of new game for his entertainment. He romped up beside her as she neared the road. The light, playful contact of sixty-plus pounds of dog was enough to send her sprawling facedown in another puddle. Alexis scrambled to her feet, wiping futilely at her face. Sopping tendrils of hair clung to her skin. She brushed them aside—and Lucky, as well. The dog's tongue lolled happily to one side. She raced across the empty two-lane road with him at her side.

A stretch of open field, looking more like a marsh this morning, lay spread out to dry beneath the midday sun. She reasoned that Jacob would expect her to stay on the house side of the road where there were trees for shelter. The field was open and exposed, but there was a drainage ditch below the road, in front of the field. The ditch might offer her a better chance of going undetected—if she could keep Lucky from announcing her position.

Alexis had been listening hard for the sound of his car engine. She heard it as she began to slide down the embankment. Her feet landed in the drainage ditch and a good four inches of water. Her plan to lay flat and wait was useless, but there was no time to change her mind.

"Lucky! Here, boy. Good boy. Down! Down, Lucky!"

She had no idea whether he'd been trained to respond to the command, or if he plopped down beside her just so he could swipe his sandpaper tongue across her face. She didn't care either way. She wrapped her arms around him and held him there against the side of the embankment as the car backed out onto the street.

"Alexis!"

For a dizzying minute she thought he'd seen her. But from the sound of it, he was inching the car along the other side of the road, yelling into the trees.

"Stay, Lucky," she told the dog sternly when he started to wriggle. If he got up now, Jacob would spot them. The only reason he hadn't so far was that he wasn't looking in this direction.

"You've got it all wrong, Alexis! I came here to protect you!"

Did he think she was stupid?

"You have to trust me, Alexis!"

Not in a million years.

Lucky wriggled harder. He was tired of this game. Alexis was no match for the big dog. He raised his head alertly. But he was looking away from the direction Jacob had taken.

She heard it then. A car or truck or something was coming down the road. "Lucky, stay! Stay, boy!"

He whined, looking at her with quizzical chocolate-brown eyes. For a moment she was tempted to run up to the road to flag down the driver. The vehicle didn't sound as if it was moving all that fast, but the memory of Wyatt's shattered radio held her still.

"Stay!" she repeated more firmly to the dog, praying he wasn't the sort who liked to chase cars. To her great relief, Lucky stayed, though he whined in complaint.

"Good boy. Good boy!" She ruffled his fur. Jacob's car suddenly sped up. He must have seen the oncoming car. As the new vehicle came abreast of their position, Lucky pulled free and stood, shaking to clear his fur of lingering moisture.

Alexis didn't bother to wipe it away. She was wet clear through as it was. She waited until the other car was well past before she raised her head to look. Neither vehicle was in sight. Still, there was nothing to prevent Jacob from turning around and coming back.

She could climb the fence that separated her from the field, or cross the road and make her way back to the house. Maybe the telephone lines were working again. If she chose the field, Lucky wouldn't be able to go with her and he might get hurt trying. On the other hand, the house was essentially a trap. Jacob had already proven that much. Better to start walking and to flag down the next car she saw to ask for help.

"Come on, Lucky." She'd always preferred action to inaction. If Jacob did turn around to come back this way, he'd be more likely to see her this time. The trees offered some cover, and being on the opposite side of the road from his car might give her the head start she'd need to outrun him.

As she scrambled back up to the road, she snatched up a fist-size rock. It wasn't much, but if she hit Jacob in the right spot with it, the rock could do some damage and give her a fighting chance.

Last night's storm had swept away the extreme heat and humidity, but already she could feel it creeping back. The sun and the heat, at least, were welcome. Her sodden clothing made her feel chilled despite the temperature. Her sister's once-white pants were history. So were the tennis shoes. The mud and grass stains would never come out of either one. Looked as though she owed her sister a whole new outfit, and R.J. a new dress shirt.

Thinking about clothing was a whole lot better than thinking about what she might have to do when she heard Jacob's car again. But minutes passed as she trudged along the side of the road and the only thing she heard was Lucky crashing about in the brush beneath the trees. He seemed perfectly content to be going for a walk and investigating unseen quarry to his heart's content.

As she pushed at her dripping hair, it occurred to Alexis that Jacob might not be planning to turn around. The road

took a sharp bend up ahead. A smart man might park and
wait there out of sight for her to come walking right into
his trap. Simple, practical, effective. Except that he
couldn't know which direction she'd take, or even that
she might not have gone back to the house to wait for
help.

She slapped at a mosquito that landed on her bare,
muddy arm. She was hopeful that the area had been
sprayed for the West Nile virus. She'd hate to survive all
this only to succumb to a mosquito bite.

Alexis slowed as she approached the curve in the road,
debating her options. The sound of a car engine speeding
toward her from beyond the bend stopped her cold. The
vehicle came flying around the curve before she could
react. Lights flashing, the police car zipped past, only to
slam on its brakes and skid as it did a one-eighty and
headed straight for her.

"Wyatt! Thank God."

Lucky gave up his pursuit of a startled bird to investigate this new development. Wyatt pulled off onto the
shoulder and stepped out of the car, looking bigger and
safer and sexier than ever.

She started to run toward him, but stopped when she
saw his expression. Something was wrong. He was taking
in her bedraggled condition with cold, dark eyes that made
her stomach lurch. Anger sheeted from him in waves as
he strode around the car and opened the back door, calling
to Lucky.

She tried for a smile as the big dog leaped onto the
back seat of the car.

"What, we didn't rate a siren, too?" she asked with a
bravado she was far from feeling.

"I turned it off."

A muscle twitched in his cheek. His expression was
hard and controlled. She'd been right. Wyatt was coldly,
quietly furious.

Her heart sank right along with a barely acknowledged

hope that there might be a future for the two of them. She had waited too long to tell him the truth. Somehow he knew she'd lied to him.

"Get in the car."

The flinty command made her blink. Her muscles clenched.

"Gee, how could I refuse such a gracious invitation?"

His eyes narrowed.

"Are you planning to hit me with that rock?"

She looked down at the forgotten stone in her hand and let it drop. While her stomach did flips, she squared her shoulders and faced him.

"Tempting as the idea seems right at this moment, I'd planned to use it on someone else."

Once again he let his gaze travel over her, from top to bottom. She stood perfectly still and let him look while a childish taunt went through her mind. After all, he wasn't exactly looking like a poster boy himself. He still wore the same clothing he'd had on last night. What had he been doing all morning?

"Who were you planning to hit? R.J.?"

"Why would I want to hit *him?*"

His lips pursed and she knew he'd understood the emphasis.

"I planned to hit Jacob when he came back."

Chapter Eight

"Jacob Voxx?"

Wyatt stared at her bedraggled condition while he waged an internal battle against pulling her into his arms and demanding to know if she was all right. She was alive, and basically unharmed, but she was a real mess from her muddy wet hair to her filthy clothing and the scratch down her arm.

"You're saying Voxx was here?" He turned back to the car and reached inside for the microphone. "What was he driving?"

"Some sort of silver sports car."

He told the dispatcher to let the state police know Jacob's car had been spotted. He gave his location and that of the nearest Interstate exit.

She watched in regal silence with her arms crossed over her chest until he finished. "You just missed him, you know. I half expected him to be parked around that bend in the road waiting for me."

Wyatt hardened his heart and his tone. "Get in the car."

"You know, I don't think I will," she said, her eyes sparking in defiance. "I've decided it's a lovely day for a walk and I can use the exercise. I think I'll just walk back into town."

It was hard to hold on to his anger when she stood

there so bravely, spitting at him in defiance like some tiny, scraggly kitten facing down a Great Dane. Only the slight tremor in her hands belied her bold front.

"Town's that way," he said, gesturing behind him. "The way you're heading will take you to the Interstate or Heartskeep."

"I'll head there, then."

His humor evaporated. "To get the briefcase?"

She regarded him calmly. He glimpsed what could have been hurt, even regret, in those large blue eyes.

"You've really got a fixation with that briefcase, haven't you?"

He took an instinctive step toward her. She tensed warily and his stomach contracted.

"Are you afraid of me?"

"No. But if you try to grab me, I'm going to drop you the same way I did Jacob."

She'd had to defend herself physically? A hot wash of rage swept over him. "Did he hurt you?"

Amazingly her stance relaxed at his savage tone.

"He never got to lay a hand on me," she said, as if *she* were trying to reassure *him*.

Her expression lightened in one of those instant transformations that so fascinated him. She offered him an impish grin.

"But I'm guessing he'll probably limp for a few days."

Wyatt found it hard to hold on to the edge of his anger. "You should have hit him in the arm. That gunshot wound of his can't be fully healed yet. I'll deal with Jacob later. What happened to you?"

Her gaze searched his face. "A disagreement with a mud puddle. I lost. What about you? Did you run out of clean clothing this morning?"

"No, I ran into my uncle before I could get to the locker room to change. And now that we've traded gibes—"

"Uh, Wyatt, not to interrupt the angry questions I sense

coming, but I think maybe you'd better let Lucky back out of the car before he takes another bite out of your back seat.''

He whirled to look at Lucky, a strip of gray material dangling from his mouth. Wyatt swore softly. He knew he had only himself to blame. R.J. had warned him the big dog had a habit of chewing on the furniture when he was bored.

He opened the door and the dog jumped out with what he'd swear was a triumphant doggy smile. No wonder R.J. generally took the animal everywhere with him.

''Would you please get in the car?''

He hadn't meant to say please, but it proved effective. Some of the tension ebbed from her shoulders.

''I think it would be better if you yell at me out here while I finish drip-drying.''

Lucky gamboled off into the trees.

''Lucky, get back here!'' R.J. would kill him if the dog wandered away.

''He's all right. He just wants to terrorize a few squirrels. They know they aren't in real jeopardy from a goofball like him, so it's okay.''

Wyatt shook his head. ''What sort of game are you playing at, Leigh?''

She made no effort to conceal her surprise.

''Tony Raine tells me you and Gavin are engaged.''

Her eyes widened. He'd swear she looked shocked. She wiped at a strand of dripping hair.

''And you believe everything you're told?''

The curse was out of his mouth before he could think. ''I don't like games or the people who play them. Are you going to deny you and Gavin were in Saratoga Springs yesterday trying to claim Livia Walsh's body?''

''I'm not going to confirm or deny anything. Why should I?'' she demanded.

''There's a name for women who like to play men off each other.''

"And here I thought a person was innocent until proven guilty."

His radio squawked before he could retort. He listened and responded. "Get in the car, Leigh. There's a problem at Heartskeep. Lucky! Get over here!"

The dog emerged from the woods.

"Come on, Lucky," she called to him. "Let's go, boy."

The dog trotted obediently over to her. Wyatt wasn't sure why he was the one feeling defensive, but he didn't like it a bit. Tony had had no reason to lie to him, yet his instincts were telling him that Leigh wasn't lying, either. They couldn't both be telling the truth. He slid behind the wheel as she fastened her seat belt.

"What's wrong at Heartskeep now?" she asked.

"That's what we're going to find out. What did Voxx want?" he asked. He was determined to reestablish his professionalism despite his churning emotions.

"For me to go with him."

"Where?" He glanced over at her, but her gaze was fastened on the road in front of them.

"He didn't say. When I declined, he attempted to force the issue. You men need to learn the caveman approach went out with the dinosaurs. Women have learned how to hold clubs, too."

Wyatt ignored the barb. "You said you dropped him?" He was suddenly reminded of the lookout on Alexis Ryder.

"And kicked him," she added smugly.

"Where did you learn self-defense techniques?"

"In school," she replied promptly. "Every woman should know a few basics. You never know when they'll come in handy."

He ignored the barb to concentrate on what she'd said as well as what she hadn't said. "Why would Jacob want you?"

"Gee. I don't know. Maybe *he* likes my winning personality."

"Enough, Leigh," he told her sharply. "I'm not going to sit here and trade quips with you. This is a police investigation. I want to know exactly what he said to you."

For several seconds she didn't reply. "Am I under arrest?"

His fingers gripped the steering wheel more tightly in sheer frustration. Lucky stuck his head over the seat and whined. Leigh immediately began to stroke his head. It wasn't until Wyatt saw the tremor in her hand that he reassessed the situation. She wasn't as calm as she'd have him believe. She was deliberately provoking him in an effort to conceal something.

"What's going on, Leigh?" he asked quietly. "What are you trying to hide?"

Her hand stilled in Lucky's fur.

"What does Jacob want from you?"

"You'll have to ask him."

"I'm asking you." For a second he didn't think she was going to respond.

"He's looking for the money," she said softly.

"The blackmail money? Why would he come to you—" Wyatt broke off as they came upon the entrance to Heartskeep. Two police cars and several gravel trucks blocked the driveway and most of the street. R.J. was standing out front, arguing with one of the officers.

"Wait here," Wyatt told Leigh as he pulled up behind the scene.

"Wyatt!" R.J. called to him. "Would you explain to Officer Feilding that I am not trying to be difficult? He can have all the access he wants to the house, but these men have to finish laying the gravel this afternoon. Can't your units use the back entrance?"

As soon as Wyatt got out of the car, Alexis reached for the door handle. "Come on, Lucky."

The dog jumped over the seat and bounded free. Alexis

stepped behind the nearest truck, aware that the driver was eyeing her curiously. He didn't call out and neither did anyone else. She skirted around the congestion and started jogging toward the house. The wet clothing was starting to chafe and her feet squished with every step. How ironic that she hadn't wanted to put on damp underwear this morning. She'd have to remember to retrieve her sister's personal items from R.J. later.

Alexis noticed that Wyatt's car was gone and so was the tree that had been lying across the driveway. A pile of cut wood was all that remained. She wondered what had happened to her purse. Obviously, Wyatt hadn't yet found it or he'd know she wasn't Leigh.

She sighed as she thought about telling him the truth. Wyatt was already furious. The longer she put it off, the madder he was going to be. But she'd be darned if she'd tell him the truth looking like the loser in a mud-wrestling contest.

She half expected him to come chasing after her. She was pretty sure he'd seen her going up the driveway, but she'd made it all the way to the house without anyone stopping her. The front door stood open. She could hear the banging and pounding sounds coming from inside even over the blare of a country-western song. Even so, nothing could have prepared her for the transformation inside.

Jacob had been right. R.J. and his men had been tearing down walls. The balcony was no longer cut off from the second floor. Where once there had been dark corridors, now there was open space and an incredible profusion of light. It didn't even look like the same house.

Alexis hurried up the main staircase, awed by the difference. She smiled at a pair of workers who were dismantling the remains of what appeared to be a linen closet in the upstairs front hall. They stared at her curiously and she tossed them a wave as she hurried to the bedroom she'd used the night before.

The tree limb was gone, but leaves and bits of glass and other debris littered the room. Two men were replacing the glass window. They looked up as she entered the room.

"Hello. Don't let me interrupt."

The furniture had been shoved against a wall to give them more room to work. With a small wave, she cut through the bathroom to the room next door. She'd intended to take a quick shower, but not with men working right there.

Wyatt would be coming after her any minute now, so there wasn't time to be choosy. She went through the other closet quickly and selected a bright red-and-white sundress from a hanger. A pair of red sandals perched on the shoetree, and she grabbed some lacy underwear from a dresser drawer.

She might as well borrow from each sister. The sizes were the same so it didn't matter. She stepped back into the bathroom and paused to collect a few toiletries. The two workmen had moved to the doorway where they were talking with someone. Alexis turned around and exited through the other bedroom into the main hall.

A bedroom door stood open at the rear of the hallway. Alexis hoped it contained a bathroom. She really wanted a quick, warm shower before she faced Wyatt again.

White French Provincial furniture and pastel-flowered wallpaper dominated the room. Her mother's bedroom? Probably once, but Wyatt had mentioned Eden's bedroom last night. Alexis didn't care either way. There was nothing of a personal nature in the room or the closet and the bedroom had the only amenity that concerned her at the moment—a bathroom whose only exit was through the bedroom. She locked both doors and turned on the shower.

If Wyatt planned to arrest her, she would do her best to look presentable for her mug shot.

WYATT SPOTTED LEIGH as she hurried up the driveway. He swallowed his anger, knowing she was heading for the house and a change of clothing. It wasn't as though there was anywhere else for her to go.

"Wy, you told me our crews could start back to work today," R.J. was saying. "It never occurred to me you'd need those walls because of what happened last night. We already pulled them down."

That got his full attention. Luke Fielding groaned.

"We can probably find the one that the slug went through," R.J. was saying, "but we dumped everything in the bin. I even have the glaziers here. They've already replaced the window over the back door."

Wyatt closed his eyes. His uncle was going to go through the roof.

"What do you want us to do, Wyatt?" Luke asked.

He looked at the men his uncle had sent over to retrieve possible ballistics evidence.

"Let me call in. In the meantime, let R.J.'s crews get back to work on the driveway. We'll use the back road if the chief wants us to dig through the garbage, but there isn't much point to dust for clues now."

"It's your noose."

"Tell me about it. I don't suppose your men found any shell casings?" Wyatt asked R.J.

"I don't know. We can ask."

"Did Beamer tow my car yet?"

R.J. nodded.

"I don't suppose you thought to get my cell phone?"

"Sorry. I wasn't even here when he came, but he'll hang on to the stuff inside your car for you."

"I know. May I borrow your cell phone?"

His uncle ranted loud enough to be heard without the cell phone. Wyatt knew he deserved the dressing-down and more. In the end, he sent the other officers back to town and drove around to the back entrance to the estate. The glaziers were getting in their truck, preparing to leave.

They exchanged nods as Wyatt set off through the woods to the front of the house.

R.J. had moved his crew outside to help spread the gravel being dumped over the driveway. Wyatt left them to it and entered the house. Even though he'd expected it to look different, the change inside was astounding. With the dark walls that had surrounded the balconies gone, the house was immeasurably brighter and far more open than he would have imagined. An agoraphobic's worst nightmare, he decided. He wondered what Leigh thought of the transformation. Then he wondered where she was.

WHILE IT FELT GOOD to be clean and dry again, Alexis adjusted the spaghetti straps of the sundress and wished she'd made a different choice. The dress was something she might have worn when she was younger. The snug bodice emphasized her breasts and left entirely too much of her shoulders and upper chest bare. She felt self-conscious and wondered if she could find a short jacket or something to put on over the dress.

Running a comb through her wet hair, she realized she'd neglected to look for a blow-dryer. The men should be finished putting the glass in the window by now. With luck she'd have time to grab another outfit and change before Wyatt came stalking her.

She gathered up her dirty clothing and the wet towels and unlocked the bathroom door. She stepped into the bedroom and stopped. Something wasn't right. Was it her imagination, or did she smell the faint but distinct odor of spearmint chewing gum?

Her heart stopped.

She wasn't imagining the bedroom door. She'd locked that door. She knew she had. But it wasn't locked now. Someone had been in here.

Alexis opened the door. The back hall was empty in both directions.

"Leigh?" she heard Wyatt call.

Alexis hurried around the corner and a saw him standing outside her sister's bedroom door. She ran to him in relief.

Wyatt had guessed right about the clothes and the shower, but he hardened his heart when he saw the sexy outfit she'd chosen. He didn't care how beautiful she was. Leigh wouldn't play any more games at his expense. If she and Gavin had had a fight, that was their problem.

Then he raised his eyes and saw her expression.

"There's someone in the house again!" she gasped.

"Where?"

"I don't know. I was taking a shower in the corner bedroom."

Eden's room.

"I locked the doors because there were men up here fixing the window and tearing down the walls, but when I came out of the bathroom I could smell chewing gum. The bedroom door was unlocked. Someone had been in there."

Wyatt frowned. "Maybe one of the workmen opened the door, realized you were in the bathroom and left." Except all the workmen were out front with R.J.

"How did they get the door unlocked?" she demanded.

"Let me have a look."

The corner room didn't have a second exit. There was only the one way in and out. The lock was a small bolt, no defense against someone who wanted in, but neither the door nor the lock showed any signs of being forced.

"Someone must have used a key," Leigh said.

Wyatt couldn't argue. "You're sure the door was locked?"

"Positive."

"Could someone have been hiding in the bedroom when you locked the door?"

"I checked the room," she insisted stubbornly. "It felt empty. The closet only opens into the bathroom. Even if there was a hidden door in there, I would have seen anyone going from the closet to the bedroom. The shower stall is clear glass.''

''Then the obvious answer is someone opened the door with a passkey.''

''Who?''

''You tell me. This is your home. Who has passkeys?''

She looked at him helplessly. ''I don't know.''

She probably didn't. She and Hayley hadn't lived here for the past seven years. Anyone could have keys.

''All right. There's nothing we can do about it now. I have to get back to town. I'm supposed to be working right now and I'd like to at least change out of yesterday's clothing and get into my uniform.''

''So go already.''

She was annoyed. Well so was he, but he tried to keep it from showing. ''I'd like you to show me the contents of that briefcase.''

Leigh stilled. ''Why?''

''You tell me. What's inside?''

She faced him mutely. The Thomas twins had a reputation for being stubborn. He had no legal grounds to push the issue, just a gut feeling that the briefcase was important.

Wyatt held her gaze. ''If you tell me there's nothing in that briefcase that relates in any way to my investigation, I won't ask about it again.''

Her eyes slid away from his face.

''One way or another, everything has meaning, doesn't it?'' she said. ''I put it in the closet in the first bedroom.''

''Show me?'' he asked in relief.

They didn't speak as they walked down the hall. Wyatt wondered at the decided slump to those creamy shoulders. What was in the case that made her feel defeated? Had she worn that sexy dress in an effort to distract him again? If so, it was working more than he'd like. The dress emphasized her slender waist and full curves. Even worse, the bright, strappy sandals called a man's eye to the delicate grace of those long, sleek legs. The skirt swirled around her calves in a flirty way that was far too appealing.

She entered the room and stopped. Dropping her laundry on the bed, she gestured toward the closed closet door.

"Behind the blankets," she said dejectedly. "You'll need the chair. The shelf's pretty tall."

He managed to keep his hands off her shoulders as he faced her. "Leigh, I promise, your family's secrets will stay secret unless they pertain to the investigation."

She didn't respond. He strode over to the closet. The shelf was high, but he stretched up and pulled down the blankets and the pillows that were bunched there. There was no briefcase.

His temper rose. "Is this another game?"

"I'm not playing games! The briefcase was right there. I swear it was."

There was a flash of fear in her eyes, but was she telling him the truth, or stalling again?

"I didn't think anyone would look for it there. I was wrong and you were right last night. He was looking for the briefcase, after all."

He crossed to where she stood and grabbed her forearms. She raised her face defiantly. He studied her expression and he believed her. If she was lying, she'd missed her calling as an actress.

He let her go when he realized he was starting to notice the subtle, feminine scent of her shampoo and how soft her skin felt under the pads of his fingers.

"Let's go."

"Where?" she demanded.

She rubbed at her arms where he'd grabbed her. His gut twisted in consternation. "Did I hurt you?"

"No."

He was unprepared for a physical rush of awareness as their eyes met and held. His body seemed finely tuned to hers, taking in the sudden dilation of her pupils, the abrupt hitch in her breathing, the way the pulse in her neck suddenly began to throb. His body responded, stirring with unwanted desire.

Leigh reached toward his cheek. With a whisper-soft touch, she ran the tips of her fingers lightly down the side of his jaw. They brushed over a small patch of missed stubble from his quick, early morning shave with R.J.'s borrowed razor.

The touch stirred his loins, demanding a response. Her eyes held him captive, crystal pools of blue. Their sparkling depths were a lure that held him fascinated by the way the color changed and deepened in passion.

He needed to kiss her as much as he needed his next breath. As he lowered his head, her fingers pressed lightly against his lips, stopping him.

"You need to know," she said quietly. "I'm not engaged to Gavin."

Gavin. The name was a slap of reality that lifted his head. "The two of you—"

"Are not a couple," she said decisively.

He wanted to believe that. His body was hard with a desire to believe that.

"We have never been a couple, no matter what you've been told. I'm not a tease, Wyatt. I don't play men against one another."

The intensity of her stare demanded that he believe.

He didn't remember taking hold of her arms again, but the satin of her skin under the roughness of his hands tore his gaze from her face to travel over the appealing curve of her chin, down the gentle arch of her neck to the expanse of creamy bare skin.

The tiny, bright red spaghetti straps were beacons of enticement. He slid his finger beneath one of them, pushing it lightly aside so he could trace its path down over the fragile curve of her collarbone to the starting swell of her breast where it disappeared behind the bit of red cotton.

Her chest rose and fell rapidly as her breathing quickened, turning shallow with desire. Wyatt slipped one finger beneath the naughty tease of red-and-white material and followed the top of that rounded curve until he reached the natural valley her breasts created.

He felt her quiver pass straight through to him. He backed her against the wall, sliding his leg between hers. A small gasp parted her lips, soft and moist. Exquisitely inviting.

She gazed up at him without trepidation, her cheeks flushed a beguiling bright pink. Her fingers clung to his upper arms, making no effort to push him away. They slid up over his neck, urging his face down toward hers.

"No ties?" he whispered, moving his leg against her and watching her startled reaction closely at the intimate contact. The thin material of her skirt offered little protection from the hardness of his muscled thigh.

To his surprise, she smiled and traced one hand along the side of his face, rubbing his jaw with the pad of her thumb.

"No ties."

She raised her face and shocked him into immobility by nipping demandingly at his jaw.

"And no commitments."

Her tongue licked the tiny bite scattering tiny shocks of current clear through him. His control ebbed with frightening ease. He cupped her face with both hands and took possession of her mouth. She arched against him with a tiny mew of pleasure and he was lost.

His hand delved inside the top of her dress, finding the firm round globe of her breast. He pulled it free and took the nipple into his mouth, sucking strongly. She cried out and the restless hand that had been running across his back, stilled.

Quickly he muffled her cry with his lips. A sane portion of his brain reminded him that there were people all over outside—people who could be coming back inside any-time now. The bedroom door was wide open next to them.

He pulled free and went to close it. Turning the lock, he gazed at her in sharp hunger. Her eyes were half closed in passion, her lips swollen from his kiss. With her dress in disarray, one strap hanging off her shoulder, the ex-posed breast damp from his mouth, Wyatt knew he'd never seen anything sexier in all his life.

"C'mere."

She came to him shyly, though excitement shimmered in her expression. He touched the nipple and she trembled.

"Take it off. I want to see you."

Shock gave way to a tremulous smile. "I will, if you will."

The outrageous dare set him on fire. From outside they heard Lucky's deep woof of happiness.

"Get away from there, you silly dog," R.J. yelled. Other voices chimed in. There was the sound of a truck bed rising, of rocks falling.

Wyatt stilled. He sensed the sudden hesitation in her.

"What were we thinking?"

She covered her breast and tugged at the dress to adjust it once more. "We weren't. At least, I wasn't."

"Me, neither. I'm..."

"Don't you dare say you're sorry," she warned.

He found a smile. "Only that I had such rotten timing. It's just as well. I don't have any protection with me."

Her lips parted in consternation.

"I gather you aren't on the pill?"

"I've never had a reason to be."

That pleased him until a sudden, scary thought reared its head. "What do you mean, never?"

Her cheeks suffused with color. She looked away.

"You aren't going to tell me you're a virgin."

That snapped her head up. Her eyes glittered in warning.

"I'm not going to tell you anything at all."

He took the step that closed the distance between them. "Are you?" he demanded.

"Is there an anti-virgin law or something?"

He swore softly.

"I thought that was what we were trying to do," she said on a shaky breath.

He ran a hand through his hair. "I don't seduce virgins."

"Then we have a problem, don't we?"

Chapter Nine

Her body still quaked with the aftershocks caused by his mouth and his hands. Her nipples were painfully aroused, her blood still pounding with latent desire.

"There's no problem," Wyatt said fiercely.

"That would be why your hair is in danger of being ripped out by the roots."

He dropped his hand to his side. "What is wrong with you?"

"Do you want a list?"

He shook his head. "I've never met anyone like you."

"At last, something in common. I've never met anyone like you, either."

"This is crazy. We're crazy. It's the middle of the morning."

"Actually, I'm betting it's close to noon right now, but you're right. This is crazy. Why don't you run along and get back to work, or whatever you were doing, and we'll pretend this never happened."

His expression softened to one of regret. "You're upset."

"Upset? Why would I be upset? Because you get me all hot and bothered and then pull away and tell me it was a mistake. I'm not upset. I'm angry. And the more I think about it, the angrier I'm getting. Please leave."

"Leigh..."

"I mean it, Wyatt. I don't want to stand here and hold a postmortem, all right? Just go."

He started to protest. She summoned every ounce of anger she could manage and glared at him.

"If you dare say you're sorry I'm going to scream so loud every one of those men will come running in here to find out why. Get out!"

Without a word, he turned and opened the door, closing it gently behind him.

Alexis sat on the edge of the bed. Her emotions were so confused, she didn't know whether to laugh or to cry, but she was shaking all over in reaction to his lovemaking.

The door suddenly slammed back open. Wyatt filled the doorway, looking impossibly large and devastatingly masculine.

"Go ahead and scream," he told her. "I'm not going to leave here feeling like I've kicked a kitten."

She came up off the bed in outrage. "A kitten? You think I'm some weak little kitten?"

His intensity faded. "Maybe that was a poor choice of words."

"No maybe about it. I may be smaller than you, but I am nobody's kitten."

His lips twitched.

"I stand corrected."

"Darn right you do. And don't you dare laugh at me."

He smiled with his eyes and the twitch lifted the corners of his mouth.

"Wouldn't think of it."

He reached out a hand toward her. She was so infuriated by his aura of masculine superiority she didn't stop to think until he was sprawled on the carpet on his back, blinking up at her with a stunned expression.

Instantly contrite, she bent over him. "I'm sorry. I didn't mean to do that. Are you all right?"

"I'm not sure. I'll let you know when I try to move."

"Oh, come on, I didn't drop you that hard. And you'll have to admit, not many kittens can do that."

She extended her hand to help him up. He grasped it and pulled her down on top of him. Before she could do more than squeal in protest, he rolled them over, pinning her to the carpet with his weight.

"No," he admitted, "they can't. But then, I never had any desire to do this to a kitten."

He claimed her mouth before she could think to turn her face away. The kiss was hot and searing and scattered coherent thought to the wind. She kissed him back, feeling him stir against her. When he lifted his mouth, they were both breathless.

"Why did you do that?" she whispered.

"I don't know. I think you've cast a spell on me."

"First a kitten, now a witch?"

He shook his head. "A sorceress. A very powerful, very beautiful sorceress."

Someone rapped sharply on the wall outside the door. The person cleared his throat loudly.

Wyatt rolled away and came to his feet in the blink of her eye. He strode to the door.

"Sorry," a voice said, "but the chief sent me out here with a message. You're to get your sorry, uh, *person,* back to town or, uh, see if Connecticut wants you back."

"Understood," he said grimly. "I'm sorry you had to drive all the way out here, Jim."

"No problem. I didn't mean to, uh, interrupt."

"That's okay."

In voice almost too low to hear, she heard the man called Jim add, "Is there something wrong with the bed?"

"Yes," Alexis said boldly, sidling past Wyatt to face a red-faced police officer in full uniform. "The springs creak something awful."

Satisfied that she'd gotten the last word, she headed for the stairs. Wyatt grabbed her and spun her around before she could take the first step. "We aren't finished."

She glanced at his friend and then at him. "We certainly are. I don't give performances."

"Whoa. I think on that note, I'll be leaving now," the man called Jim said. "If you two will excuse me?"

"Certainly," she agreed.

Wyatt growled, but stepped aside so Jim could get by them.

"Someone should have spanked you as a child," he told her.

"Try it. I'll toss you over the railing."

Jim began whistling off-key as he hurried down the stairs.

"As much as I'd like to show you how wrong you can be, I need to get back to work before my uncle actually fires me."

"Go ahead, I'm certainly not going to stop you."

"Are you sure you aren't Hayley? I thought you were supposed to be the quiet twin."

"Shows what you know, doesn't it? I'm not a twin at all, I'm the evil triplet, the one they tossed out at birth."

"I'm beginning to believe that. Do you want a ride back into town?"

"Yes, please."

"Then let's go. My uncle isn't known for his patience and I'm already at the top of his list today. Of course, I could always take you with me. He might even forget about me after one of your tongue-lashings."

"Thank you, but I have better things to do than visit with your uncle."

Alexis hurried down the steps, totally aware of him at her back. Hadn't she told herself from the day they'd first met that going anywhere with this man was dangerous? Too bad she hadn't realized just how dangerous.

On the porch, she spotted the young officer talking with R.J. She knew her cheeks were flushed, so she gave the two of them a jaunty wave, glad when Lucky bounded over to her.

"Hey there, Lucky. Are you behaving yourself?"

The dog woofed acknowledgment and paused to sniff Wyatt's hand and to accept a pat before he trotted away, satisfied. Alexis was glad that Wyatt's annoyance was strong enough to send him striding ahead since she had no idea where the back driveway was located. And if he stayed angry, maybe he'd forget to ask about the contents of the briefcase again until she could decide how to tell him the truth.

She let him get several yards in front of her, following him through the trees until they came to a clearing near several old barns and an old forge. The clearing was being used for parking.

Wyatt paused and waited for her.

"Are you going to threaten me again if I try to apologize for embarrassing you?" he asked.

"Nope. I figure you got the worst of that scene. Your buddy Jim was out there giving R.J. an earful. I suspect you're going to get a lot of teasing about that."

"I can handle it. It's your reputation I'm worried about."

She started to tell him she didn't give a fig for her reputation and then she realized it wasn't *her* reputation that was going to suffer. Everyone thought she was Leigh.

"Wyatt, this has gone on long enough. You need to know—"

"Wait here!"

Startled, Alexis watched him run to the nearest barn. Her heart leaped to her throat when she saw a gun appear in his hand.

"Now what?" She was starting to hate Heartskeep.

Like some television drama, she watched Wyatt disappear into the barn. He'd told her to wait, but her brain clamored for her to run back to the house to get the other police officer. She hesitated, afraid to go, afraid not to go. Seconds turned into minutes. The minutes began to stretch. Alexis began to edge closer to the barn.

She could still scream if something happened. But would anyone hear her over the noise made by the dump trucks and the gravel?

Wyatt had been in there too long. He should have come out by now, or at least called out to her. The clearing was too quiet. There weren't even any birds chirping nearby.

Her unease turned into certainty. Something was wrong. "Wyatt?"

There was no answer. Every instinct told her to go for help. She turned around to do just that.

"Wyatt can't answer you right now."

Alexis gasped. Jacob stepped from the woods directly into her path. He brought up his hand and she saw the gun he pointed at her.

"Don't move. All I want is the money, Alexis. You're going to inherit more than you can possibly spend. You won't miss the money in that briefcase."

As he moved forward, she saw that he was favoring his left leg slightly. She began to back away. There was little left of his boyish charm at the moment. Jacob was still a good-looking man, but his features were hard, almost desperate.

"What did you do to Wyatt?"

"I didn't do anything. He had an accident."

Fear gripped her.

"What sort of accident?"

"He fell down the rabbit hole." Jacob came toward her with a sardonic smile. "Oh, don't worry. He's all right, but it should take him a while to climb out of there, so he won't be interrupting us right now. I need that money, Alexis."

"Why?" She changed direction and began backing toward the parked vehicles. If she could get close enough, she might be able to dodge between the cars and trucks and get away before he could shoot her. "Have you got a drug problem or something?"

"Something. It doesn't matter. What matters is that if

you want all this to stop, you need to give me the money.''

"I can't. Even if I wanted to, I can't. It's gone."

"Damn it, Alexis, don't lie to me! Give me the money!''

"I told you, I can't! You can shoot me if you want, but I can't give you what I don't have."

He stopped moving. So did she. She was only a few feet from the cars now. Worry lines marred his features. He was obviously upset.

"Who has it?"

"I don't know. Whoever was shooting at us last night, I guess."

"Someone shot at you?"

Fear underlay his concern. Enough to convince Alexis that he hadn't been the gunman, but she suspected he knew who had been.

"Talk to the person who broke in last night during the storm,'' she told him. "He's the only one who can tell you where the briefcase is now. When I went to give it to Wyatt, it was gone."

Jacob appeared shaken. "Alexis, if you're lying to me—''

"You know I'm not. I don't have the briefcase and I don't have any way of getting it back even if I wanted to give it to you."

"Drop the gun, Jacob."

Wyatt's voice came from the mouth of the barn. Relieved, Alexis looked at him. His clothing was soaked and appeared to be covered in thick, wet mud. Clumps of it dripped from his pants. That didn't lessen the menace of his appearance. If anything, he looked larger and more dangerous. He held his weapon in one grimy hand, fixed rigidly on Jacob.

Alexis caught the flash of fear in Jacob's eyes as his fingers tightened around the gun in his own hand. His voice, however, was steady as he moved slightly to one side so he could see both of them. He kept his weapon trained on her.

"That was fast. I thought it would take you a whole lot longer to climb out, Wyatt. That shaft looked pretty deep to me. Other than a lot of mud, you don't look any the worse for your clumsiness."

"I said, drop the weapon!"

"You know I'd like to, I really would, Wyatt, but I don't have time to go into town and answer a lot of questions right now."

Wyatt started forward. Jacob shook his head. "Move again and I'll have to shoot her. I don't want to, but I will, Wyatt."

Wyatt stopped. Jacob didn't. He motioned for Alexis to keep moving past the cars scattered in the clearing. She tried to stay calm, mentally reviewing all the moves she'd learned. Her muscles bunched, ready to take action the moment Jacob came close enough.

"Leigh, step behind the truck and run into the woods," Wyatt ordered. "Jacob isn't stupid. He won't shoot you."

"Don't do it, *Leigh*," Jacob warned her.

The fierceness of his words was offset by a glint of amusement at Wyatt's use of the wrong name. Jacob wanted her to know he wouldn't give her away.

Perplexed, Alexis didn't move. Instinct told her that Wyatt was right. Jacob had no intention of shooting her. The problem was she wasn't so sure he wouldn't fire at Wyatt if he felt trapped.

"Help me," Jacob mouthed inaudibly.

His eyes pleaded for her cooperation even as he raised his voice.

"I know you can take me, Wyatt, but not before I put a bullet in her chest. Can you live with that? Don't force me to do something we'll all regret."

Wyatt had edged a step closer. Now he stopped as if considering the seriousness of Jacob's threat.

"Don't do anything stupid, Jacob. Let's talk."

Jacob grinned, using every bit of his boyish charm. "Sorry. I don't have time for extended conversation. Leigh, here, is going to walk me to my car. Right, Leigh?"

He motioned her to start moving. Alexis glanced at Wyatt. Tension showed in every muscle of his body. He was all cop right now, dangerous and focused. He would shoot Jacob to protect her. She wasn't sure exactly what was happening here, but she didn't want anyone getting hurt.

"It's all right, Wyatt. I'll walk Jacob to his car." Alexis began to move in the direction Jacob had indicated.

"No! Leigh, stay where you are!"

Jacob's lips nearly disappeared in a tight line of determination. His desperation was almost tangible.

"It's all right, Wyatt," she said as she continued moving past the nearest car. "Let him go."

"Stop, Leigh! I can't do that."

Alexis glimpsed the gratitude in Jacob's eyes as she assessed her odds of bringing the situation to a safe close. But Jacob had learned his lesson. Obviously he had no intention of getting close enough to let her take him down again.

As Alexis came abreast of R.J.'s truck, she cast a quick look around the clearing. She didn't see Jacob's silver sports car. What she did see was Lucky bounding down the trail from the house, coming straight toward them. Wyatt was unaware of the animal. He strode after them, his grim expression intent on Jacob and the gun in his hand.

Jacob, keeping one eye on Wyatt and one on her, didn't see the dog coming either, but he began to swear as he realized how quickly Wyatt was gaining on them.

"Stay back, Wyatt. I mean it!"

Without warning, Wyatt launched himself at Jacob. Alexis flattened herself against the truck as the two men came together with an audible thud. They hit the muddy ground hard.

"Lucky! No!" she screamed as the dog, barking happily, threw himself into the fray. He knocked against Wyatt, catching him unawares as Wyatt reached for Jacob's gun hand. The sheer weight of the animal sent him sprawling instead.

That was all the advantage Jacob needed. He scrambled to his feet and bolted around the front of the truck. Wyatt shoved his way free of the dog and leaped to his feet to give chase.

"Lucky!" Alexis yelled again at the large animal. Intent on this new game, the dog ignored her completely to chase after Wyatt. He ran up alongside Wyatt, bumping into him. Wyatt staggered to one side. Jacob disappeared into the woods.

Wyatt cursed the dog, pointing toward the trees. "Get Jacob, you fool dog. Get him, boy!"

Lucky barked in excitement and plunged into the woods, Wyatt at his heels. Alexis started to go after them, then saw R.J. and the cop called Jim pelting toward her.

She met them halfway. "Wyatt and Lucky are chasing Jacob. He has a gun."

"Where?" the officer demanded.

Alexis pointed.

"The two of you wait here," Jim instructed.

"We should go with him," she said anxiously.

They heard Jim calling to Wyatt.

"It's not safe to come up behind a cop when he has a gun in his hand," R.J. told her. "That's how fatal accidents happen. We need to do what he said."

"Then you should call Lucky. He thinks this is a game. He might get hurt."

R.J. hesitated before nodding. "Lucky! Here, boy! Lucky!"

They heard an answering woof from somewhere in the trees. R.J. continued calling the dog, and Alexis added her voice to his. Minutes later the animal burst from the trees several yards away. Tongue lolling, he gamboled up to them.

"That's it, Lucky. Come here. Good boy," R.J. crooned. He grabbed the dog's collar with both hands as soon as the animal was in reach.

"Good boy, Lucky," Alexis told him, stroking the top of his silky head.

"What's going on?" R.J. asked.

Alexis offered him an abbreviated version. She liked R.J., but she couldn't tell him what Jacob had said without telling him about the money. The only person she was willing to trust with that information at the moment was Wyatt.

Lucky began to struggle in an effort to break free of R.J.'s hold. He was more than ready to resume his interrupted play.

Alexis shared the animal's agitation. Her stomach knotted in concern. Someone was going to get hurt—or worse.

"Where are they?"

R.J. pointed down the rutted lane that served as a driveway. "There!"

He released his hold on Lucky and the dog loped down the path to greet the two returning men. There was no sign of Jacob. Alexis didn't know whether to be relieved or sorry that he'd gotten away. She didn't trust him—wasn't even sure she liked him—yet he hadn't given her away and he hadn't really hurt her.

She shook her head at her chaotic thoughts, knowing Wyatt was going to be plenty annoyed with her.

"What did you do, roll in the mud?" R.J. asked him.

"I fell into an abandoned shaft out behind the barn."

"You're kidding."

Wyatt offered R.J. a glare as Lucky pranced up to him, looking hopeful. "Forget it, dog. If I didn't know better, I'd figure Jacob bribed you to help him get away."

"Lucky tripped him," Jim explained.

"He tripped Jacob?" R.J. asked.

"Wyatt," Jim said succinctly.

R.J. winced. "Oh."

"Yeah, oh," Wyatt snarled.

"Don't snap at R.J.," Alexis protested. "It wasn't his fault."

"No," Wyatt said with quiet intimidation. "It wasn't *his* fault."

"It wasn't Lucky's fault, either," she defended. "He's just a dog. He was trying to play."

"I know exactly whose fault it was," Wyatt told her. He strode up to her. Despite the leaves and other debris clinging to the mud that stained his hair and clothing, Wyatt managed to look quite dangerous.

"It wasn't my fault, either," she objected.

"Why didn't you do as I told you?"

"Because Jacob felt trapped. I was afraid he might shoot you."

"The gun was aimed at you, not me."

"Okay, but you said yourself that he wasn't really going to shoot me. I wasn't so sure what he'd do about you. He likes me better than you."

The officer called Jim choked back a chuckle, reminding her that the two of them were not alone. Wyatt spared the man a dark glare.

"Would someone mind telling me what the heck is going on?" R.J. asked. "What was Jacob doing with a gun?"

Wyatt drew in a breath, though he continued to scowl at Alexis. "That's a real good question. R.J. I spotted someone moving in the barn, and when I went to check it out, Jacob Voxx took off running. I never saw the blasted shaft until it was too late. The sides were covered in so much ooze I kept slipping when I tried to climb out. I finally realized there were ladder rungs under the mud at my back, but when I did get out, I found Voxx holding a gun on Leigh. If she'd done what I told her, I'd have taken him down."

"No, you wouldn't," she argued. "He would have felt forced to shoot you. I was going to walk him to his car so no one would get hurt."

"And what would you have done if he insisted you get in the car with him?"

"I would have refused."

"And you think he would have stood there meekly and said okay?"

Alexis lifted her chin. "Why not? I took him down once. He knew I could do it again."

"For crying out loud, Leigh. The man was holding a gun on you this time!"

"I told you he wasn't going to use it!"

"At least we got a broadcast out on him," Jim temporized, gesturing toward the radio on his shoulder. "Someone will pick him up. He can't get far, even in that fancy car of his. In the meantime, you should go up to the house and clean up."

"I've got to get back into town," Wyatt said tersely.

"Like that?" Alexis asked skeptically. "It'll take you a week to clean all the mud out of your car."

"I'm going to have to clean the mess you made anyhow."

"I wasn't half that dirty."

"I've got a change of clothes in the truck," R.J. offered. "Cutoffs and a T-shirt. They might be a little big, but they'll be better than what you're wearing now."

Wyatt tried wiping at some mud on his face and only succeeded in making it worse. With a sigh, he agreed.

"Go on up to the house and I'll get them," R.J. told him.

"All right, but do me a favor and reconnect the phone line, will you? I need to call the chief."

"Sure thing."

INSIDE HEARTSKEEP, Alexis discovered there were two bedrooms and another full bath on the first floor behind the office. She couldn't get over how immense the house was.

Wyatt's friend Jim got a call and had to leave, but R.J. agreed he'd be more than happy to have her make him some lunch while Wyatt took a shower. Alexis raided the enormous walk-in pantry and found more than enough ingredients to make a tasty pasta and vegetable dish. She popped some biscuits into the oven to go with the casserole. By dividing a large can of pears into three small bowls, she was able to chill them quickly by setting the bowls in the freezer while the pasta cooked.

Lucky waited hopefully near the door, watching her work. She figured he deserved a reward, so she put a small portion of the casserole in a dish for him, as well. Wyatt came out holding his soiled clothing while she was setting things on the large kitchen table.

"Much better," she told him approvingly. Actually he looked terrific in R.J.'s cutoffs, loose T-shirt and a pair of open-toed sandals. Between the two of them, they looked ready for a day at the beach.

"Dump your dirty clothes in the laundry tub and I'll soak them after we eat. Did you make your call?"

"I made it," he said grimly as R.J. came out to the kitchen and washed his hands at the kitchen sink. "The chief is not happy."

"It wasn't your fault Jacob got away," she said, then realized she was repeating their earlier argument.

Wyatt dumped his clothes as instructed. "In his place, I'd be hopping mad, too. I took the rest of the day off."

"Good thinking," R.J. said, pulling out a chair. "What smells so good?"

"Just a casserole."

"And biscuits? Do I smell biscuits?"

"Biscuits," she agreed. "I'm not sure how good the butter is. Most of the stuff in that refrigerator is going bad, but I did find a jar of honey in the pantry."

"You know something, Leigh? All this wealth is

wasted on you. A person who can cook like this should be a working man's wife. How would you like to chuck this overgrown mansion and come and live with Lucky and me in a ramshackle old farmhouse?''

Alexis laughed at his teasing, but Wyatt scowled at his friend. "Shut up and eat your lunch."

"Hey, until someone puts a ring on her finger, I figure she's fair game," R.J. told him. "Besides, I don't want to marry Leigh for her money, I want to marry her for her culinary abilities."

"You're all talk, R.J.," Alexis told him.

"Not *all* talk. I can eat, too. Quit hogging the biscuits, Wy. Some of us have been working hard all morning."

"No one was talking about your crew," Wyatt gibed.

"Oh. I didn't think about them," Alexis said, feeling embarrassed. "I could make some more."

"That's okay, Leigh. They all piled into one of the trucks a little while ago and drove out to the highway. One of the guys found a sub shop they like. They were supposed to bring me back something. I'll take it home and have it for dinner unless I can convince you to elope with me."

"You know, R.J., that's a very tempting offer."

Wyatt turned his scowl on her.

"But I'll have to decline." She picked up her fork. "I'm hoping for a different offer."

R.J. raised his eyebrows, shot Wyatt a quick glance and plunged his fork into the casserole on his plate. "Too bad. Lucky was counting on you."

The dog had polished off his portion in seconds and sat between Alexis and Wyatt watching them eat. She avoided looking at Wyatt and smiled at the dog instead.

"Maybe I should reconsider. I always did want a dog."

"Yeah," Wyatt growled. "Especially one as *helpful* as Lucky."

Lucky wagged his tail.

R.J. reached for another biscuit, looking from one of them

to the other. "I'd still like to know what Jacob was doing out there with a gun," he said.

Leigh shifted uncomfortably. She finished swallowing and set her fork down on her plate. Time was up.

"He wants the briefcase."

Chapter Ten

Wyatt set down his half-eaten biscuit. "Why?"

"What briefcase?" R.J. asked. "That heavy thing you had with you the other day? Looked more like a suitcase than a briefcase."

The telephone rang on the wall behind Wyatt, making them all jump. Wyatt didn't take his eyes off her.

"Aren't you going to answer that?" she asked.

"No. What's in the briefcase, Leigh?"

His stomach clenched at her guilty expression.

"It's a long story."

The phone stopped ringing.

"I've got the entire day."

Leigh nodded sadly. R.J. said nothing at all. Wyatt debated asking him to leave, but decided the younger man had earned the right to stay. They owed him, and R.J. knew how to keep a secret.

The phone began to ring again.

"Money."

R.J. sucked in a breath. Wyatt felt his muscles contract. "How much money?"

The phone stopped ringing.

"I don't know," Leigh said. "I didn't count it."

The phone began to ring again.

"You want me to get that?" R.J. asked.

Wyatt stood and looked at the Caller ID. He recognized

Jim's cell phone number and swore. Jim wouldn't be calling him repeatedly unless it was urgent.

"I need to take this," he told them.

"Big briefcase," R.J. said mildly.

Leigh nodded sadly. "There was a lot of money."

Wyatt scowled and answered.

"Wyatt? It's Jim. I'm on my way back to the house. Meet me out front right away."

There was an edge of carefully controlled excitement in the younger man's voice.

"What's wrong?"

"Meet me. I'm turning in the driveway right now."

"All right." He clicked off. "I have to meet Jim out front. How much money, Leigh?"

"As I said, I didn't count it, but the briefcase was full."

"Where did you get it?" Wyatt demanded.

Leigh pushed back her chair and stood to face him.

"That's where the long part of the story comes in. It can wait. I'm not going anywhere. Go meet your friend."

Mentally he cursed Jim and his lousy timing. "Stay with her, R.J. Don't leave her alone for a second."

"I told you I wouldn't go anywhere."

"Jacob may still be lurking nearby. I'll be right back."

He strode down the hall to the front door. Jim's cruiser was coming up the drive, trailing a plume of dust from the newly laid gravel. There was someone in the back seat of the car.

Jim pulled to a stop, got out and came around to meet him, waving a sheet of paper in his hand. Wyatt crossed the porch and started down the steps. As the dust began to settle, he recognized Hayley.

"What's going on, Jim? Why is Hayley in the back of your car?"

"Before I try to answer that, have a look at this."

Wyatt took the paper. "Is this a joke?"

Jim shook his head. "N.Y.P.D. put this out."

He stared at the picture of a woman who looked just like Leigh and Hayley.

"You know that call I had to take when I left here? It was Miller. He gave me the picture because he knew you and I were the ones who found the Ryder woman's car. He made a traffic stop about a mile from here and didn't know what to think when he saw the driver. He went to school with the Thomas twins, but N.Y.P.D. says this is a picture of Alexis Ryder."

"So who's in your car?"

"I don't know. She *claims* she's Hayley Thomas, but she doesn't have any identification. Miller stopped her for speeding. She was driving a rental car with New York City plates. She didn't have the rental contract in the car, either."

"What's her explanation?"

"She says she must have left everything in Bram's truck."

Wyatt rubbed at his jaw, suddenly more tired than he'd felt in a long time. "She knows about Bram?"

"Uh-huh."

"But you don't believe her."

Jim shrugged. "You're the former big-city detective, pal. Given what's been happening here, I figured you could decide who she is—and what this picture means."

All sorts of thoughts were running through his mind. None of them good. Wyatt walked over to the patrol car and opened the door.

"It's about time! Wyatt, will you kindly tell this…this *officer,* who I am?"

Wyatt looked at Jim. He raised his eyebrows and shrugged.

"You sound like Hayley," he said mildly.

"I *am* Hayley, you morons! That…*cop*…won't even tell me what's going on."

"Wy," Jim said at his back. "The stain on that jacket tested positive for blood."

Wyatt nodded in acknowledgment, but he didn't take his eyes from the woman who looked exactly like Leigh.

"What jacket? What blood?" the woman demanded. "What's going on?"

"Where's Bram?" Wyatt asked her.

She took a deep breath as if to steady her temper.

"He's on his way to Murrett Township to see his father. We stayed overnight in New York last night. I rented that stupid car because we were using his truck and Bram decided to go back to check on his dad again. I wanted to give him a chance to visit with his family alone so I was going to drive to Boston to check on our apartment and pick up the mail." Her shoulders rose and fell. "I changed my mind and decided to come straight back here. I had no idea leaving my purse in Bram's truck could get me arrested. Now what's going on? Is Leigh okay?"

The question and her worried expression convinced Wyatt of her identity as nothing else could have.

"Leigh's fine. Why don't we go inside and you can see for yourself." To Jim, he added, "She's Hayley. Leigh can verify her identity. She'll know her own sister when she sees her."

"Leigh's here?" Hayley asked in surprise. "What's she doing here? I thought she and Gavin were…oh, never mind. May I get out of the car now?"

"Sure." He stepped back.

"What about that?" Jim asked, nodding to the paper in Wyatt's hand.

"What is that?" Hayley demanded.

Wyatt held it out so she could see for herself. "You and Leigh don't happen to have another sister, do you?"

Hayley paled. "Oh, my God."

Wyatt felt his stomach contract.

"You can see the problem, Hayley," Jim was saying. "This picture looks exactly like you. Even your hair is styled the same way."

Hayley stared at them with wide, shocked eyes. Eyes that were identical to Leigh's.

"This has to be a mistake. They think she murdered someone?" Hayley asked in a hushed tone.

"Her father," Wyatt confirmed.

"Oh, my God," she breathed.

Wyatt tensed. Her shock was genuine, but something felt off.

"You said Leigh's inside?" she asked, pulling herself together with obvious effort.

"Yes, she's in there with R.J."

"Gavin isn't with her?"

His stomach twisted. "No."

She shook her head with something close to panic in her eyes.

"I need to see Leigh," she told him.

His jaw clenched. He had a foreboding sense of impending disaster. "I think we'd both better go see Leigh."

"You want me to wait?" Jim asked.

"I can handle it. But Jim? Ask Miller to keep this quiet right now."

"I already did. He figured as much."

"I owe you both one."

"Two," Jim told him. "You owe me two."

Wyatt nodded but didn't return his smile. One of the work trucks was bumping its way up the drive. R.J.'s men were back from their lunch break.

"Who's Alexis Ryder, Hayley?" Wyatt asked as they headed up the steps.

"Oh, God, it's a mess. Gavin told us we were taking a chance. I think he'd prefer we explain everything when he gets here."

"Gavin," Wyatt said tersely, "has his own explaining to do." He held open the door for her.

"Don't be mad at him, Wyatt. He wanted to tell you. We pleaded with him to wait. We wanted to find her first."

He stopped when she would have stepped inside, yanking her to a stop, as well. "Are you saying Alexis Ryder *is* your sister?"

She trembled slightly. "Yes. At least, we think she is. It's complicated, Wyatt."

"Well you'd better uncomplicate it real fast." His emotions settled on anger and it churned inside him, burning like acid. Leigh had lied to him—by omission if nothing else.

"What does the briefcase have to do with Alexis Ryder?" he demanded.

"What briefcase?"

Her expression was baffled.

"Get inside."

She didn't move. Her features tightened. "You know something? I'm not real fond of orders, nor of the people who give them."

"I'm not fond of people who withhold information during a police investigation, so I guess that makes us even."

With a mutinous glare, she stepped inside and came to a complete stop.

"Oh!"

She moved into the living room with an expression of total shock. She stared up at the open ceiling as if she couldn't take it in.

"Wow! I mean, *wow!* Look at this! It's fantastic! I had no idea the rooms would look like this."

She crossed into the dining room and R.J. came around the corner from the kitchen with a wide grin.

"I thought I heard voices. Hi, Hayley. Looks a little different, huh?"

"Different? R.J., it's incredible! This doesn't even look like the same house. It makes everything so much bigger and brighter. I can't get over it."

"I know. Even I was impressed. You never did say what you thought of the change, Leigh."

Wyatt stiffened as she came around the corner and

stepped forward hesitantly. Her eyes went first to her sister, then to him. Comprehension hit him in a rush that robbed his lungs of air.

Hayley turned around. Her lips parted in shock.

"Oh, my God. You aren't Leigh!"

Her gaze remained riveted on him. "No. I'm not."

Wyatt struggled to marshal the incredible mix of emotions threatening to rip him to shreds. He barely heard R.J.'s startled exclamation. Hayley looked at them uncertainly. The woman who wasn't Leigh never took her eyes from his—as if she was afraid to look at the woman who was her exact replica.

Wyatt didn't move. "Why didn't you tell me?"

ALEXIS COULDN'T THINK. She'd known her sisters were identical to her, but the reality of her first glimpse of Hayley had left her shaken, so she'd centered her focus on Wyatt. Now, panic squeezed the air from her lungs. Numb, she could only stare at him. The hurt in his eyes was tearing her apart.

"I tried to tell you," she forced past stiff lips.

"When? When did you try? A few minutes ago? What was wrong with when we met? Or yesterday afternoon? Or last night? Or this morning when I nearly made love to you?"

His words flayed her soul. He would never forgive her. She couldn't blame him. She should have told him. Nothing she could say now would make it right.

Helplessly, she spread her hands. "I didn't know you when we met. You were just a good-looking stranger who thought I was someone else."

"And you didn't want to give me your name because you knew you were wanted by the police," he snapped furiously.

"No! I didn't know I was wanted, and I didn't know you were a cop until R.J. told me! When you first walked up to me, I'd just found out the lawyer was dead. I didn't know what to do, where to go.''

''What lawyer? Rosencroft? What does he have to do with anything?''

''I don't know. He was dead, so I couldn't ask him. My father's note warned me not to trust anyone except him and someone named Kathy.''

''Wait a minute,'' Hayley interrupted.

Alexis had been trying not to stare at the other woman. It was horribly disorienting to look into a living mirror.

Her face, but not her face.

''Are you saying you've been here at Heartskeep all this time pretending to be Leigh?'' Hayley demanded.

''That's exactly what she's saying,'' Wyatt said. ''What's this note you're talking about?''

Alexis pulled her gaze from Hayley's with effort. Wyatt's hard, tight features left no room for compromise. With a stab of remorse, she realized that whatever he might have felt for her before was gone without a trace. There was only anger and the residue of hurt in his expression.

''I told you it was complicated.''

He strode up to her then. She pulled back her shoulders, raised her face, and waited for the lash of his words. But the front door opened suddenly. R.J.'s crew stepped into the main hall. They were noisy, joking and laughing together until someone spotted the tableau in the dining room.

''Why don't you guys go to the kitchen?'' R.J. said. ''I need to get the men started upstairs.''

Wyatt gave him a terse nod. ''After you,'' he told her.

Her heart thudded painfully as Hayley followed them into the kitchen. A tumult of emotions threatened to overwhelm her.

Alexis saw Lucky out back chasing a passing butterfly. She wished R.J. hadn't let him out. She would have given a lot for a nonjudgmental friend about now.

"Have a seat," Wyatt ordered.

"I'd rather stand," she told him. She was far too stressed to sit.

"Tough. Sit down."

From somewhere a spark of defiance urged her to stop castigating herself. He was going to be angry no matter what she said or did, so it didn't matter.

"Does the bad cop image generally get results? Personally, I find it annoying."

The vein in his neck began to throb. "Why'd you shoot your father?"

Alexis blinked. She shook her head as if it would clear the words from the air and make her hear an entirely different question.

"I didn't shoot my father."

"That's not what the New York City police think."

Her mouth went totally dry. "They think *I* killed him?" Her head continued moving in denial.

Hayley didn't offer up a sound. Alexis could only imagine what she must be thinking as she stood there, watching them.

"You were there," Wyatt said relentlessly. "There was blood on your jacket."

"Of course I was there!" she blurted. She remembered the horror as vividly as if it were happening all over again. "I came home and found him there. I watched him die!"

Her eyes filled with tears, but she blinked them back fiercely. She would not let him see her cry. The tears for her father were private. She might have shared them with Wyatt, but not this cop. *He* was stranger.

"You watched him die. You didn't call for help. Then you walked out the door and drove away."

"Wyatt, cut it out," Hayley said abruptly, to Alexis's surprise. She moved to stand between them. "You can see she's upset."

"Sit down and be quiet, Hayley."

Alexis shot her sister a look of gratitude. "It's all right,

Hayley. He's right. I watched my father die. I didn't call for help. I did walk out and drive away.'' She lifted her chin and looked him in the eyes. ''You left out the briefcase full of money. I brought that with me. It still had his blood on it.''

Though she trembled from head to toe, she refused to bow to the pain. For a long moment there was only silence.

''No more lies. No more games. Tell me what happened,'' he commanded savagely.

''Why bother? You've already decided what happened. Arrest me.''

''I don't know a damn thing. Who is Alexis Ryder?''

Alexis swallowed hard. For a minute she wasn't sure she could answer him. Hayley's presence made it all the more difficult to come up with an answer.

''I don't know. I used to know.'' She shook her head helplessly. ''Everything's changed now. Alexis was just a girl who grew up in New Jersey with a mother and a father and an unremarkable life like everyone else she knew. The only tragedy she ever faced was the death of her mother when she was seventeen.''

Hayley made a startled sound. Alexis sent a quick glance her way.

''Ironic, huh? I guess in some ways our lives weren't so different, after all. Except my mother wasn't murdered. She died in a simple car crash on a slippery road. Her death left my dad so devastated, he climbed in a bottle and refused to come out.''

She shrugged off the acrid memory. ''Alexis Ryder went to college, got a degree, got a job and moved into an apartment in New York City with her college roommate. The biggest problem in her life was a date with her roommate's cousin. She was searching for a way to tell him she wasn't interested in more than friendship.''

Her laugh sounded brittle even to her.

''Funny. That date was all I could think about all week.

Seth's a nice guy. I didn't want to hurt his feelings, but when he came to pick me up, I didn't even open the door. My father was dead, and I didn't even open the door.''

Pain creased her face.

"You were in shock," Wyatt said. He controlled the impulse to comfort her. He couldn't do that. He had a job to do—even if she hated him for doing it.

"Why didn't you call the police?"

"Dad told me to run. He said they'd be coming for me next. He was right."

"Who came?" he demanded.

"I don't know. I hid in the closet. I've gotten pretty good at hiding lately. Closets, beds, hidden rooms—heck even my identity."

His gut tightened. He worked at keeping his voice even. "Tell me what happened."

"Why not? I expect I'll have to tell it a number of times now. Do you want to see the note? My father wrote me a note to tell me he wasn't my father." Her eyes closed in pain.

"Where is the note?" Wyatt asked.

She opened her eyes. "Upstairs. I took it out of the briefcase. I'm not sure why, but I put it inside the pillow-case in the room where I fell asleep. If no one found it and it didn't get ruined when the branch blew through the window, it should still be there."

"A branch blew through a window?" Hayley asked.

"A big one," Alexis told her with a remembered shudder. "You actually grew up in this house?" She tried to imagine that and failed. The house was so large. So creepy. "Maybe I was lucky, after all. Come on, I'll show you the letter," she told Wyatt.

"Is the letter the reason you came here?" Wyatt asked as she headed for the back staircase.

"Yes. It rambles a bit, but the gist of it was I should come here and see a lawyer named Rosencroft. I wasn't to trust anyone else except Kathy."

"Kathy? You mean, Kathy Walsh?" Hayley asked.

She and Wyatt exchanged surprised looks. Alexis shrugged.

"Dad wasn't good with names, but that's who Jacob thought he meant."

Wyatt stopped her when she would have started up the steps. "How does Jacob know about this note?"

"I don't think he does, but when he showed up at R.J.'s house he said he wanted the briefcase Kathy had given my…Brian Ryder."

She faltered over the name. Wyatt could empathize. She'd grown up thinking of Ryder as her father. It was hard to make a sudden adjustment. He was having the same problem with her name.

"How did Jacob know about the money?" Hayley asked.

"You'll have to ask him. He's the one who told me my father had been shot. I didn't even know what had happened to him. There was a lot of blood." She shuddered, then went on. "Jacob seems to know a lot more than I do about everything. He isn't the easygoing innocent you seem to think he is, Hayley. You and your sister need to look a little deeper. You might not feel the same way about him if you saw him pointing a gun at you."

"Jacob pointed a gun at you? Are you sure it was Jacob? Jacob Voxx?"

Alexis shrugged. "That's what he said. It's a little hard to tell all the players around here without a cast list and pictures."

"Pictures don't help much, either," Wyatt told her wryly. To his surprise, she almost smiled, glancing at Hayley.

"No, I guess they don't. Shall I get the letter?"

Wyatt nodded. They reached the landing and Alexis started across on a diagonal. Hayley faltered. Wyatt turned to look at her.

"Sorry. I just can't seem to take this in. The house looks so different."

"To me, too," Alexis admitted, "and I've only been here a couple of days."

"Stare later," Wyatt prodded.

"There's no hurry," Alexis chided. "Either the letter is still there or it isn't. A few minutes either way isn't going to matter, is it?"

"I guess not," he admitted reluctantly.

"That's okay," Hayley told him. "I want to see this letter, too. We've been trying to find you, you know, Alexis. We wanted to be the ones to tell you the truth."

"Jacob said you were looking for me."

"How could Jacob possibly know that?" Hayley demanded. "We just found my grandfather's files three days ago. We didn't even know you existed until then."

"He did."

Hayley's eyes widened. Wyatt filed the information away for later. "Where did you find these files, Hayley? In the hidden room across the way?"

"You *know* about that?"

Alexis nodded. "We hid there last night."

Wyatt frowned. R.J. and his crew were across the way, working in what had been her grandfather's suite. "Let's save this conversation for a more private location."

"There's no such thing in this house," Alexis told him.

She was right. He followed her into Leigh's bedroom. She went straight to the bed and pulled a large manila envelope from inside the pillowcase.

"It doesn't prove I didn't kill my—Brian Ryder, but maybe it will show you I was telling the truth about some of what happened anyhow."

He looked her straight in the eye. "You didn't kill anyone."

There was a flicker of relief, but she shook her head with that familiar stubborn expression on her face. "You don't know that."

"I know."

"How?"

"You teach self-defense classes to battered women. You counsel runaways and pregnant teens. You get too involved in your work and you cross the line at times. You worry about hurting a date's feelings and there's pain in your voice every time you mention Brian Ryder."

She blinked in surprise. "Thanks, I'll have them call you as a character reference at my trial."

"You aren't going to trial."

"I'd like that in writing please."

Wyatt took the slightly soggy envelope from her hand and smiled. "At least you didn't ask for it in blood."

"Only your signature," she responded.

Hayley watched the exchange with intense curiosity. "*How* long have you two known each other?"

Two bright spots of color appeared on Alexis's cheeks. Wyatt turned his attention to the envelope self-consciously.

"So if this is Leigh's room, yours is the one next door?" Alexis asked instead of answering her question.

"Yes. And you know something? I have an old dress exactly like that one."

"I know. I borrowed it. I hope you don't mind, but I didn't have any extra clothing with me when I arrived. To tell you the truth, I was hoping to change it for something else. I grabbed it in a hurry this morning and didn't realize it was quite so—"

"I know what you mean. I only wore it once myself for the same reason. I'm afraid most of the stuff we left here at the house is pretty dated. We haven't really lived here since we graduated from high school."

"I suspected as much."

"If you want to change into something else, I've got a pink peasant blouse and print skirt I was meaning to take back to Boston with me. I think I know exactly where it is."

"Not to interrupt such a serious fashion discussion," Wyatt said, "but Alexis looks fine, and we have a few things left to discuss."

He handed her back the letter. With an almost imperceptible nod of thanks, she handed it to her sister. Hayley took it, but didn't start reading it immediately.

"Cops in general don't rate high with me," she told Alexis. "A few rate only marginally higher than an amoeba, but Bram and Gavin trust Wyatt. They could be right."

"I'm flattered."

"Who's Bram?"

"My fiancé. You'll like him. He designed and built the gates out front. I didn't think he'd ever get past the whole money issue, but he proposed to me in front of his entire family the other day," Hayley told her proudly. "His father was lying in a hospital bed, hooked up to all these monitors, looking two steps from death's door. His three brothers were standing around the room looking bleak and, out of nowhere, Bram looks at me and asks me to marry him."

"Romantic," Wyatt said wryly.

Hayley grinned, unconcerned. "It certainly broke the ice."

Wyatt nearly smiled back. "Do you have some way of reaching Gavin, since he isn't returning my phone calls?"

"It isn't personal. The battery on his cell phone went dead and his recharger was in the apartment when it blew up."

"He could have bought a new one."

"True, but then he would have had to take your calls and he'd promised us three days to try to find Alexis before we came and told you about the files we found."

"Exactly what did you find?" he asked.

Hayley's expression turned grim. "Alexis. My grandfather hired a private investigator more than seven years ago. We aren't sure why, but Bram said maybe someone told him about a teenager who looked identical to us. Anyhow, the investigator found her and told Grandpa. Gavin's going to see about having his body exhumed. Leigh and I don't think his heart gave out the way everyone believed at the time.''

''You think it had chemical help?'' Wyatt asked.

''Marcus killed my grandfather,'' she said flatly. ''Then he killed my mother so no one would know he'd sold his own child.''

Chapter Eleven

Wyatt finally got them settled downstairs in the library. Hayley called her sister, who was with Gavin, and then called Bram. All of them were now on their way back to Heartskeep.

Haltingly at first, Alexis told Wyatt and Hayley what had happened. As much as it still bothered Wyatt that she hadn't trusted him with the truth, part of him understood. Her father's letter had told her not to trust anyone, but in trying to protect her, his instructions had left Alexis with too little information and no one to ask for help.

Hayley took her sister's hand when she finished. "I hope you'll believe me, Alexis. Leigh and I don't care about the money. We're thrilled to have another sister. And, to tell you the truth, neither one of us wanted to be responsible for Heartskeep."

"I can see why," Alexis said, glancing around.

"Yes. It wasn't like this when we were growing up. I wish you could have lived here then. You would have loved Mom and Grandpa." She released her hand and smiled sadly. "On the other hand, you got the best of the deal when it came to fathers. I can't think of any word vile enough to describe Marcus."

"I don't understand why he…" She couldn't bring herself to say he'd sold her to strangers, but that was what he'd done. As if she was an unwanted puppy or something.

"Don't bother trying to understand. No one understood Marcus. I know it doesn't help to say it could have been any of us he gave away. I can't imagine how I'd feel if it had been me, but he totally lacked empathy, Alexis."

"He was a doctor! It doesn't make sense. He must have had something," Alexis protested. "After all, your mother married him."

"Eden married him, too," Wyatt put in.

"She's easier to understand," Hayley told him. "The one thing Eden and Marcus had in common was a love of money and the things it could buy. Greed kept them together—greed and guilty secrets as it's turning out. And Marcus could fake emotions. I've seen him do it with patients. He just never bothered with the rest of us."

Alexis shook her head. "Maybe I was lucky then. Both of my parents loved me." She shared a sad smile with her sister.

"Well, at least now you won't have to worry about someone coming after you anymore."

"How do you figure that, Hayley?" Wyatt asked.

"Eden has the money, right? It's too late for her to try to conceal the truth now. We already know what she and Marcus did, and we can prove it. There's no point in killing Alexis anymore."

"We don't know who has the money," he corrected.

"It was a man who shot at us," Alexis added. "And I don't think it was Jacob. He seemed really upset to learn someone had the briefcase."

Hayley pursed her lips. "Look, as hard as it is for me to believe Jacob even had a gun in the first place, maybe it *was* him who shot at you. What if Jacob was acting alone last night and didn't know his mother was in the house, too? She could have found the money after Wyatt chased Jacob away."

"Or someone else took the money," Wyatt pointed out.

"We simply don't know enough, Hayley. I'd like to know where this money came from in the first place."

"It has to be the blackmail money," Hayley said.

"The briefcase is big, but I don't think it could have held six hundred thousand dollars," Wyatt argued. "I can't envision that much money in cash."

"Me, neither."

Alexis frowned thoughtfully. "There was a lot of money in there, but I didn't want to touch it, let alone count it. I did take out two one-hundred-dollar bills," she admitted. "I didn't have much cash on me and I don't have an ATM card. I intended to replace the money."

"Don't apologize," Hayley said. "It was our money anyhow."

"Maybe," Wyatt argued. "But, maybe not. We won't know until we can find Kathy Walsh. I'd like to know how she figures into this. If she was blackmailing Marcus, why give the money to Brian Ryder? Unless they were working together."

Alexis tensed but remained silent. He realized that was one of the reasons she hadn't told him the truth. She wasn't entirely convinced her father was innocent.

"We still have a lot of unresolved questions. Right now, my biggest concern is you, Alexis."

"Gee, there's a surprise," Hayley murmured.

Wyatt ignored her. "As a cop, it's my job to turn you over to the New York City police department."

"You can't!" Hayley objected instantly.

Alexis remained silent on the couch beside her sister.

"They'll arrest her for her father's murder!"

"That isn't how it will work, Hayley. They're investigating right now. Alexis is their only lead." He held up his hand to forestall her interruption. "They need to talk to her, but they won't arrest her without evidence."

"By her own admission, she was there!"

"When he died," Wyatt said evenly. "But was he shot there?"

He watched Alexis's eyes widen in comprehension.

"I don't think so," Alexis told him. "I saw the blood almost as soon as I opened the door."

"Was there blood in the hall? On the elevator? On the stairs? How did he get to your place? Was there blood in his car, in the cab he used?"

"I don't know."

"Of course not, but these are things the investigators are looking at. You left work and took your usual bus home, right?"

"Yes."

"That can be verified. They can pretty well figure what time you arrived at your apartment. Depending on the wound, a gunshot victim can live quite a while after being shot. I'm sorry," he added as her features twisted in pain. "But these are facts. You need to know how this is being investigated."

"It's okay, Wyatt," she said softly. "You're right. I do need to know."

"They'll be looking at the evidence inside your apartment. They'll be going door to door asking if anyone heard a shot. They'll be waiting for the autopsy report to pin down the time of death."

"The police were at his house when we drove up," Hayley said, biting on her lip guiltily. "We had an old address from the private investigator's file. The phone book confirmed Brian Ryder still lived there, but he didn't answer when we called, so Bram and I drove out there. When we saw all the police activity, we went past without stopping and called Gavin. He said we should come straight back here because something must have happened and we were out of it. He insisted we had to talk to you."

"Glad to hear he still had a grain of common sense left."

Hayley groaned. "Okay. We should have told you what we found from the start."

"It certainly would have simplified things all around," he agreed mildly.

Alexis interrupted. "What do you want me to do?"

Wyatt knew what police procedure demanded, but he'd already broken so many rules, a few more weren't going to matter.

"We'll wait and talk to Gavin. This is a dicey situation for a number of reasons. There's a jurisdiction issue among other things. Now that this picture of you has been released, someone will make the link to Heartskeep and Hayley and Leigh."

He mulled over that thought for a minute and rose to his feet. "I need to make a phone call."

Alexis stood, as well. "I don't want you getting into trouble, Wyatt."

"Let me worry about that."

Her hand went to his arm. "Your uncle is already mad at you."

"He'll get over it." He glanced down at her hand. She left it there.

"He's your boss."

"He's an idiot," Hayley muttered.

Wyatt turned to her. "Not really, but he is opinionated and stubborn, and he likes things simple and tidy. Everyone believed your mother disappeared in New York City. While I'm not trying to defend him, Hayley, from his point of view you and Leigh were making waves without a shred of evidence to substantiate your allegations."

She glared at him. "If he'd bothered to look, all the evidence he needed was right there, buried in the maze."

"I know. And I'm more sorry than I can say about that. He should have done more and he knows it. For what it's worth, your mother's death is going to eat at him for the rest of his life. He took this job in Stony Ridge because he wanted a nice quiet town, where big crime was considered an occasional drunken squabble or a traffic violation."

"Someone should have warned him about the Hart family before he took the job," Hayley said bitterly.

"Why?" Alexis asked. "Do you have a reputation for trouble?"

"Grandpa implied our family has a lively history."

Wyatt cut in. "While you two discuss Hart family history, I'm going to use the phone in the office next door."

Her hair swayed against her cheek as Alexis squeezed his arm lightly. "Don't do anything foolish to risk your job, Wyatt."

"I'm just going to make a telephone call, Alexis."

But he appreciated her concern. Though aware of Hayley watching them curiously, he was unable to resist touching Alexis. He covered her hand, rubbing the back of it lightly with his thumb.

"It'll be okay."

His uncle could be as angry as he wanted. The Crossley men owed this family. Wyatt was going to do his best to pay back some of that debt by protecting Alexis.

"Okay," he heard Hayley say as he stepped into the office. "What's going on between you and Wyatt?"

And though he paused to hear her answer, Alexis spoke too softly to make out the words. Maybe that was just as well. The pull of attraction she exuded was almost impossible to ignore. He still wanted her and he wasn't sure he had enough willpower to resist her a second time.

He sank down on the leather chair behind the desk and glared at the telephone. Maybe it was petty, but it still bothered him that Alexis would have trusted him enough to make him her first lover, yet hadn't trusted him enough to tell him who she really was.

Except that she had told him, he realized. In the bedroom when he'd accused her upstairs of being more like Hayley than Leigh, she'd told him she wasn't either one. She'd said she was their evil sister, or words to that effect. He hadn't paid any attention, thinking she was just trying to goad him.

Aggravated, he lifted the receiver and began to punch in his uncle's phone number. He was going to have to start listening more closely to what Alexis said. That would require putting a more professional distance between them so he could stop thinking about how exciting it would be to be her first lover.

Maybe Alexis really was a sorceress. He was certainly feeling bewitched. Just thinking about her was enough to stir all sorts of crazy thoughts he shouldn't be having.

The phone began ringing on his uncle's desk. He could lose his job over this request, but if his uncle insisted on playing by the rules, Alexis could lose her life.

One way or another, Wyatt wasn't about to let that happen.

HAVING TWO SISTERS who looked exactly like her was strange in ways Alexis couldn't begin to define. Stranger still was how comfortable she was with them now that the initial impact was starting to fade.

Meeting Leigh hadn't been quite as startling as her first view of Hayley. By the time Leigh arrived, Alexis had had a little time to get used to seeing someone who looked just like her. Yet seeing two of herself had been disorienting all over again.

For her part, Leigh had welcomed Alexis warmly. In some ways it was as if the three of them had always known each other. They shared many of the same personality traits and they liked many of the same things. They even thought a lot alike. And when it came to the male of the species, the three of them definitely gravitated toward a similar type.

Alexis liked Bram and Gavin right away. Like Wyatt, they were quiet, confident men, comfortable in their skin.

Bram reminded her of a large, gentle giant with a core of inner strength. His muscles weren't simply for show, however. He would protect what was his, and that definitely included Hayley. Alexis saw him watching her sister once or twice as if she were some exotic creature that he couldn't believe was really his.

Gavin was a big man, as well, though not nearly as tall or broad as Bram. Yet he carried himself in a way that commanded respect. He moved with an imperious, catlike grace. His watchful eyes had a way of looking directly at a person that was slightly disconcerting—as if he could see below the surface to what they were thinking. Alexis decided he would make a formidable trial lawyer until he looked at Leigh. Then his eyes seemed to soften and warm with an inner contentment that spoke volumes about what he felt for her.

Alexis envied them. Both couples maintained physical contact with each other in small ways they probably weren't even aware of. Her parents had been like that. Those little touches and intimate looks could block out the rest of the world. No fortune on earth could buy that sort of bond.

Too bad she'd never share that sort of relationship with Wyatt. The impossibly sexy, aggravating man wasn't likely to forgive her deception anytime soon. Oh, he'd risk his neck and his job to help her, and the chemistry between them was stronger than anything she'd ever imagined, but he considered her virginity on par with some sort of disease.

Leave it to her to finally meet a man who could produce the sort of fireworks she'd always wanted to experience, and he turns out to be the one man she can't have. Why couldn't she have found this spark with someone like her roommate's cousin Seth? Or someone as genuinely nice as R.J.? Nope, not her. Alexis had to be drawn to an impossible cop with standards.

What was wrong with being a virgin, anyhow? Weren't men supposed to respect chastity in a woman?

Alexis reigned in her thoughts as she realized R.J. was getting ready to leave again. He'd been halfway out the door earlier when Gavin and Leigh had arrived bearing an armload of pizza boxes. He'd refused to stay and have dinner with them, but he'd hung around long enough to listen to their accolades over the changes to the house.

"By the way, I called the security company," he told Gavin. "They'll be out tomorrow to activate the alarm system. And, Leigh, I need to know what you want done with your grandfather's former suite and the front parlor and ballroom."

"Don't look at me," she told him, leaning smugly against Gavin. "You'll have to talk to Alexis. Heartskeep belongs to her now."

Startled to find herself the sudden focus of six pairs of eyes, she immediately looked to Wyatt.

"What am I supposed to do with a place this big?"

"Whatever you want to do," he said gently.

"It's always reminded me of a hotel," Gavin offered. "You could turn it into a bed-and-breakfast."

Leigh rolled her eyes. "You've got a fixation with turning this house into a hotel."

"How can I not? It's got eleven bedrooms!"

"You could rent it to some Hollywood studio," Bram suggested. "I always thought it was the perfect setting for a horror movie."

Hayley nudged him in the side.

"Ow! You need to file those sharp elbows."

She smiled up at him unrepentantly. "Sorry. Next time I'll stomp on your foot."

"You don't have to decide tonight," R.J. told Alexis, grinning at the byplay. "Sleep on it and we'll go over the rooms tomorrow and discuss possibilities."

"Are you sure you don't want to stay for pizza, R.J.?" Leigh asked. "We bought plenty."

"Thanks, anyhow, but I've got a ham-and-cheese sub and the rest of that casserole Alexis made us for lunch. Lucky's getting the sub."

"Where is he?" Leigh asked.

"Out front. He was busy chasing a squirrel across the

lawn the last time I saw him. Oh, and before I forget, power's back on all over the house and the phones were reactivated. Answer at your own risk. The media still wants an interview with you. I'll see everyone tomorrow.''

'''Bye, R.J. Come on, guys, I'm hungry,'' Hayley said. ''I missed lunch again. I'll warm up the pizzas while Alexis brings the rest of you up to date.''

''And the four of you can fill me in on all the little details you've been withholding,'' Wyatt told them with a pointed gaze at Gavin.

They trouped out to the kitchen where Alexis gave them a condensed version of events while Hayley and Leigh got drinks and set out plates and napkins. All three pizzas had meat, so Alexis chose the pepperoni and tried to be subtle about picking the meat off and sliding it into the napkin in her lap. If R.J. had stayed for dinner with Lucky, she would have slipped the meat to him. As it was, Gavin's sharp eyes caught her in the act when she took a second slice.

''Would you rather try this one?'' Gavin asked. ''It has sausage, but no pepperoni.''

''No. Thanks. This is fine.''

Wyatt twisted to study her. She knew the moment he made the connection to the two meals she'd prepared for him. ''You couldn't even bring yourself to tell me you're a vegetarian?''

Her cheeks warmed, but Alexis lifted her chin. ''No. I couldn't take the chance that you might have known if Leigh wasn't.''

''Oh. I would never have thought of that,'' Hayley said.

''It must have been incredibly difficult pretending to be someone you knew nothing about,'' Leigh added.

''Alexis is a gifted actress,'' Wyatt told her.

Alexis narrowed her eyes at the taunt. ''Thank you, but it didn't require all that much talent. It's quite easy to fool some people.''

"Ouch," Gavin said sotto voce.

Wyatt's jaw set in reaction. "Maybe I should have let you talk to the city police after all."

"Maybe you should have," she agreed, her anger goaded by his. She set the napkin full of pepperoni on the table and stood.

"I'm not going to apologize for doing what I had to do. You're the one who mistook me for one of my sisters. I tried to walk away, if you'll recall, so get over it, Wyatt. Excuse me," she said to the others. "I'm not very hungry tonight."

Wyatt pushed back his chair and stood before she could move. He seemed to tower above her, a large dark force to be reckoned with. But even as she faced him, she watched his expression gentle with regret.

"Sit down," he said quietly. "You're right. I was out of line. I apologize."

That wasn't what he'd intended to say at all, but the hurt in her eyes canceled his annoyance and left Wyatt feeling small and petty.

"Apology accepted," she told him after a moment. "But I'm really not hungry anymore."

"Leigh—I mean, Alexis. Please sit down. We need to discuss what we're going to do tomorrow."

He hated the vulnerability he glimpsed before she lowered those thick dark lashes to hide her expression.

"All right. I'll be back in a minute. I need to use the bathroom."

She started around the table toward the main hall.

"There's one right over there," he pointed out.

Alexis paused and held his gaze. He didn't know what she was thinking, but her expression scattered the rest of his anger.

"I'd rather use the one near the office. Excuse me," she said to the table at large.

Wyatt stood there, feeling the weight of the undigested

pizza in his stomach as he watched her disappear around the corner.

"You know, I'm usually considered the mild twin," Leigh said. "But I'm not feeling real mild right now."

Gavin covered her hand as if in warning, but she ignored him.

Hayley nodded. "Neither am I. Alexis has enough on her plate without a moody lover."

"We aren't lovers," Wyatt told her.

Leigh scowled at him. "Maybe that's the problem."

"We just met!"

Hayley shook her head. "So what? I knew the first time I laid eyes on Bram that he was special."

Bram leaned back with a wry expression. "I never had a chance," he admitted.

"Darn right you didn't."

"You'd better go talk to her," Gavin told him. "We don't need sideline emotions while we're plotting our strategy for tomorrow."

"She went to the bathroom!"

"No, she didn't," Leigh corrected. "She went down the hall to cry in private."

"Men can be so obtuse," Hayley complained.

"It's genetic," Bram told her. "We aren't responsible."

"What are you waiting for?" Leigh demanded. "Go after her."

Wyatt left. Alexis wasn't in sight. He walked down the hall to the bathroom door and knocked. There was silence on the other side. He realized there was no light showing under the door so he twisted the handle. Leigh had been right. Alexis hadn't gone to the bathroom.

Wyatt looked toward the living room, in the office, then the library. Alexis wasn't in any of those rooms. The knife edge of fear nicked him.

"Alexis?"

He looked toward the front door. The dead bolt was in

place. She hadn't gone out that way. He took the front stairs by twos.

"Alexis?"

The nick became an artery of fear, pumping panic along his veins.

"Alexis!"

Chapter Twelve

Alexis started down the hall, but as she came abreast of the first bedroom on her left, a movement caught her attention. A woman stood inside the room, motioning to her urgently.

"Alexis!"

The whisper was so faint she barely heard it, but Alexis stepped toward the door. There was nothing frightening about the slender woman. She was dressed in a pair of light blue pants and a matching T-shirt. Her short brown hair showed flecks of silver, but it was the bruises on her face that took Alexis into the room without a qualm.

She recognized the signs immediately. The battered women she taught self-defense classes to often had similar marks on their faces and arms.

"Quickly," the woman said.

She hurried to an opening in the wall between the bathroom and what Alexis guessed was the closet. Alexis hesitated.

"Please," she whispered urgently. "I need to talk with you in private. My name's Kathy Walsh. You are Alexis, aren't you?"

"You're Kathy? I wasn't sure you existed."

"Will you come with me?"

"Just let me tell Wyatt—"

"No! Please. Just you."

Pain clouded her eyes. Pain mingled with fear. Reluctantly, Alexis followed her inside the opening.

Like the hidden room off the closet upstairs, Alexis found herself in a space where the walls were bare studs and exposed nail tips. Only this wasn't a room, more like a passageway. A set of steep stairs led both up and down, while a short corridor ended in what appeared to be a dead end.

Kathy did something Alexis couldn't see. The panel closed.

"Thank you for trusting me," the woman said.

"No offense, but I'm not real sure that I do trust you. What is this place?"

The woman tried to smile, but her healing split lip and the fading bruises on her face made the expression look more like a grimace.

"I'm sorry about the steps," she said, "but we should talk upstairs."

"Why can't we talk right here?"

The woman began to climb slowly. It was obvious that each step was painful.

"I left the briefcase upstairs."

Alexis couldn't prevent a soft gasp. "*You* have the briefcase?"

Kathy continued to mount the steps stiffly, pressing a hand against her chest under her breasts.

A broken rib, Alexis decided. Maybe more than one. She gentled her voice. "Are you all right?"

"I will be."

Alexis bit her lip. It was obviously taking a great deal of energy for the woman to climb the stairs. Questions could wait. But there were more stairs when they reached a landing on what must have been the second floor. The area replicated the space below.

"Where are we going?" Alexis asked.

"The attic. We'll be safe there."

She wanted to ask safe from whom, but Kathy's

breathing had become labored. Alexis didn't like the sound.

At the top of the stairs Kathy opened another panel to reveal a long, narrow room under the eaves.

Someone had furnished the area sparsely with discarded furniture. A mattress neatly made with a sheet and blanket and pillow sat on the floor. A damaged end table sat between two battered wing-backed chairs with faded upholstery. There were two bottles of water on the table. The remaining furniture consisted of a scarred, drop-leaf table and two dilapidated folding chairs leaning against a stud. Alexis spotted a backpack on the floor between the wall and the mattress. The briefcase sat in the farthest, darkest corner of the room under the eaves.

Alexis looked away from it as Kathy sank into the nearest chair and closed her eyes.

"How long have you been living up here?"

"Not long."

Alexis crouched beside her chair. "Have you seen a doctor?"

Kathy's tired eyes opened and she tried to smile again. "I'll be all right. I think I have a couple of fractured ribs. They take time to heal. There isn't much a doctor can do for them."

"You need an X ray, Kathy. A broken rib can be dangerous. It could puncture a lung. Or you could have other internal damage."

"It isn't that bad. It's just those stairs are so steep."

"Was it your husband or your boyfriend who hit you?" Alexis asked gently.

She gave a tired shake of her head. "I never married the bastard, thank God. My mother was so right about him. I was a fool, but he could be so charming. So much fun."

"They usually are at first."

She smiled crookedly. "I forgot you were a social

worker. Alexis Mary Ryder Hart.'' Her voice softened.
''You look just like your sisters.''

''So I've discovered. You and your mother used to
work for my grandfather.''

''Yes. Please sit down. I really am okay.''

She didn't sound okay. Her breathing was too shallow
and sounded too raspy.

''I'm afraid all I have to offer you is some chewing
gum or bottled water.'' She hunted in her pocket and
pulled out a package of spearmint gum. ''The water's
probably warm by now.''

''That's all right, I'm not thirsty.'' And she shook her
head at the gum. She stood and crossed to the other chair.
It rocked a bit as she sat.

''Careful, that back leg isn't real stable,'' Kathy said.
''It'll hold as long as you don't move around too much.
I'm sorry, Alexis. I tried to approach you sooner to tell
you I'd moved the money, but you were in the shower. I
didn't think you'd appreciate the interruption.''

''Actually, I'm relieved to learn that was you, even if
you did scare me to death,'' Alexis admitted. ''I smelled
your chewing gum when I opened the bathroom door. I
must have just missed you.''

''I'm so sorry. I didn't think you'd even know I'd been
there. I heard someone coming, so I left.''

''Why hide? Are you afraid your boyfriend will find
you?''

''That, too, but the police have been all over the
house.''

''You're afraid of the police? They were here because
they found a body out back.''

''Yes, I know. I'm so sorry. I know you never had a
chance to meet Amy, but she was your real mother.''

''So I've learned.''

Kathy sighed. ''Everything's so awful. I don't know
what to do anymore. When I heard voices in the kitchen
tonight I thought the police were back.''

''No,'' Alexis told her gently. ''Well, just Wyatt. Hayley and Leigh and their fiancés were having pizza with us.''

''The twins are engaged? How wonderful! They're such sweet girls. Just like their mother. But I guess I can't call them the twins anymore, can I?''

''Kathy, what's going on? Why are you afraid of the police?''

''How much has Brian told you?''

''Almost nothing before he died.''

''He's dead?'' Kathy's face bleached of color. ''How? When? It's because of the money, isn't it? Oh, God, I knew this was a mistake. I told her we should have given the money to Mr. Rosencroft. My mother put us all in grave danger. She meant well, Alexis. You have to believe that!''

Her mother?

Kathy began to cough and the sound was even more distressed than her breathing. She pulled a wadded handkerchief from her pocket and pressed it to her mouth until the spell stopped. Truly worried, Alexis reached for one of the bottles of water and handed it to her.

Kathy gave her a grateful look and took a couple of sips, stuffing the handkerchief back into her pocket. She handed the bottle back with a shaky hand, then pressed her arms against her midriff and rocked back and forth, looking ready to cry.

''We worked for the Hart family ever since I can remember. My father used to tend the grounds here when I was little. You have to understand, my mother was devoted to the Harts. We both were. It nearly broke her heart when Dennison died.''

Kathy suddenly leaned forward, her expression intent.

''I went to visit my mother several weeks ago. I'd decided to admit she was right and to ask if I could move in with her until I could find a job. But she was terribly agitated. She claimed Amy Hart had given birth to triplets.

I didn't know what to think until she showed me the file she'd found. There were pictures of you."

Questions filled her, but when Kathy paused to drag in a ragged breath, Alexis shunted them aside. "Kathy, let me get Wyatt."

"No! I can't go to the police! Don't you understand? She was blackmailing him! My own mother! I couldn't believe it. Even when she showed me the money, I couldn't take it in."

"Who was your mother blackmailing?"

"I know this makes her sound like an awful person, but she didn't want the money for herself. She wanted him to pay."

"Marcus?"

"Marcus." Kathy agreed. She spat the name as if saying it out loud left an evil taste in her mouth.

"All these years she's been taking his money and hiding it away. You see, Dennison took care of us after my father died. He paid for my college education, saw to our health needs, gave us a place to live…he made us feel like Heartskeep was our home, too. My mother would have done anything for him. And then he died."

She closed her eyes for a second in remembered pain.

"Mom was convinced Marcus caused his fatal heart attack somehow. She knew Dennison had a bad heart, but—" she shrugged, then winced in pain "—it doesn't matter anymore. What matters is that she decided to make Marcus pay. Amy and Marcus argued all the time after Dennison died and Mom was convinced Marcus was trying to steal from the estate. That's when she decided to type up a vague threat and leave it for him to find."

"Did she know what really happened to Amy?"

"Oh, no! She suspected, of course, especially when he paid the blackmail. The twins were so adamant, it was hard not to think they might be right. But the police insisted Amy vanished in New York. She was seen early that morning and then never again. Mom and I had gone to Stony Ridge that day. We met some friends for lunch and went shopping afterward. We didn't get home until late, but everything seemed normal. It wasn't until the next evening that anyone knew something was wrong.''

She sighed sadly. ''I wish I'd known. Mom left the blackmail note for Marcus to find that very morning. And he paid.''

''I'm confused, Kathy. When did your mother leave Marcus the blackmail note?''

''The morning after we went to Stony Ridge. The very day they learned Amy hadn't gone back to the hotel the night before. Don't you see? My mother left the note for him before the alarm was even raised. Mom was sure he murdered Dennison. Then, afterward, she wondered if the twins could be right. Except Marcus had an unshakeable alibi for the day Amy disappeared. There wasn't time for him to have driven to New York to kill her.''

''But Amy didn't die in New York. She died here,'' Alexis pointed out.

Kathy sagged more deeply into the chair. ''We didn't know that. No one even suggested the possibility except the twins. They got the police to dig up the fountain because of all the publicity they stirred up, but there was no body under there.''

''Why didn't your mother tell someone?''

''She was afraid,'' Kathy said sadly. ''She knew she could go to jail for leaving that note. She actually blackmailed someone! And she really didn't *know* anything.''

''Except that only a guilty person would have paid her.''

''And he kept paying her,'' Kathy said morosely. ''Right up until the last time, right before he was killed.''

Alexis wanted to ask how Marcus had been killed, but the question would have to wait. She really didn't like Kathy's color at all.

''Let me get Wyatt. You need to tell him all this.''

''No!'' She jerked up and winced. ''I only wanted you

to have the money back before Eden found it. I hid the jewelry in the room where we keep the silver. I was sure she didn't know about that room, but she must have found it. Your grandfather's box and the jewelry are gone,'' she said sadly.

Alexis shook her head. "What jewelry? Amy's jewelry?"

"No. Mom hid that up here in the attic right after the girls left for Boston. Marcus moved Eden in right away and Mom knew not to trust her. Two of a kind, they were. All they cared about was money. That's why Mom wanted to take him for every cent she could. It was the only way to hurt him back.''

"And you think Eden knows about the briefcase?"

"She knows. Eden followed my mother into the maze the last time Mom tried to collect money from Marcus. Marcus was already crazy by then and he started shouting he wouldn't pay anymore. Mom got scared and went back to the house. She hid here for several days. Hayley had come home, you see, and she was worried about her safety. She kept trying to find a way to talk to Hayley in private, but Hayley kept falling asleep and Mom couldn't wake her.''

Alexis struggled to take it all in. It was hard to contain her questions, but Kathy kept talking and she didn't want to interrupt.

"Then Mom discovered Marcus had installed a fake wall in his office. Once she found the way inside, she discovered the box the jeweler had mailed to Amy after Dennison died. She also found a copy of the investigator's report. She hid it and the box in the room under the back stairs. She was sickened by what Marcus had done and she was more convinced than ever that Marcus murdered your grandfather.''

Alexis was pretty sickened herself. She'd been blithely living her life, never imaging such intrigue could be happening because of her existence.

"If the fire hadn't destroyed everything, who knows what other secrets might have been revealed?"

Alexis shook her head. "How many hidden rooms are there in this house?"

"Quite a few. They aren't all rooms, of course. When your great-great-great-grandfather rebuilt this house back in the early nineteen hundreds, he had a passion for strange architecture and secret passageways. I'm not sure even Dennison found them all."

Alexis was out of her depths.

"Kathy, you have to talk to Wyatt."

"No!"

She became so agitated she began to cough again. This time she couldn't seem to stop. Alarmed, Alexis went to her, but there was nothing she could do until the spasm finally subsided. The woman needed immediate medical attention.

"Kathy, what do you want me to do? How can I help you?"

"I'll be all right. I only wanted to give you back the money and explain. But now that you've told me she killed Brian, too—"

"Are you saying Eden killed my father?"

"She must have. I'm pretty sure Eden saw him that day at Marcus's funeral."

The nurse who brought you to us was there at the cemetery that day. That was what his note had meant.

"He needed to go to know I wasn't lying. Brian thought I was trying to blackmail *him* the first time I called."

"Why would he think that?"

"Your adoption wasn't legal. I'm not sure what sort of trouble he would have been in, but he knew it would be bad. He refused to believe me when I told you were a triplet, so I told him to go to the funeral and see for himself. I know he came because I saw him running through the cemetery. Your sisters were there, of course, so Brian had no choice but to believe me. He agreed to meet me after that.''

"Why didn't he tell me?"

"I don't know. I wanted to meet you, to give you the money myself, but he refused. He said he wanted to tell you himself. I believed him. I couldn't risk holding on to the money because my boyfriend, Bernie, was desperate for money and might have found it. I gave Brian the briefcase, but I warned him about Eden. I told him not to trust anyone. Eden must have killed your father to get the money. No one else knew about it.''

"Jacob did."

Kathy paled even further. She looked as though she wanted to cry.

"So Eden corrupted him, after all." She closed her eyes and leaned her head back wearily. "I'm sorry, Alexis. I should never have contacted your father."

She sighed and began to cough again. This time when she pulled out the soiled handkerchief Alexis saw a trace of blood on the white linen.

"Kathy, I'm sorry, but you need medical attention."

"I'm just tired," she gasped.

"You're dying," Alexis told her bluntly.

There was no other way. The woman would sit there until she bled to death internally. Alexis couldn't let that happen. She crouched in front of her.

"Listen to me, Kathy. I'm going to get Wyatt and get you to the hospital."

"But the police—"

"No one will arrest you or harass you. I won't let that happen. I promise you!"

"But my mother—"

Oh, God, she didn't know that her mother was dead. Alexis couldn't tell her now.

"Kathy, your mother doesn't have to worry, either. I give you my solemn word of honor. The police will not prosecute her. You asked me to trust you and I did. Now

I'm asking the same of you. Trust me. I don't want you to die. You're too important to Hayley and Leigh—and to me. You're family.''

Kathy stared at her through pain-filled eyes, but there was relief in her expression, as well. Alexis rose to her feet.

''Family takes care of family, Kathy. Hayley and Leigh and I will take care of you now, all right?''

Kathy nodded. Alexis didn't wait for her to change her mind. She was halfway down the first flight of stairs when she realized she had no idea how to open the hidden door. She prayed it worked the same way as the one in the hidden room.

Thinking to save time, she stopped on the second floor instead of going all the way down. But she couldn't find an exit at either end. She forced down an instant of pure panic. If she couldn't find the way out, all she had to do was go back up and ask Kathy.

Then she heard the muffled sound of Wyatt calling her name.

''Wyatt! I'm in here!''

She ran to the wall across from the stairs.

''Wyatt!''

''Alexis! Where are you?''

''I'm in here. In the wall. I'm not sure how to get out.''

''Keep talking.''

''I found Kathy. Well, she found me. She's hurt, Wyatt. Someone beat her. I think she's bleeding internally.''

''Gavin! Bram! Leigh's room!''

Though he was shouting, she could barely hear him and she couldn't hear anyone else.

''Alexis! Move to your left. The opening must be in the closet.''

Alexis did as he told her.

''Talk to me! The opening has to be in here somewhere! Knock on the wall, Alexis, as loud as you can.''

As she did, she spotted the opening. Unlike the main

floor, the opening on this level was on the side of the wall, not at the far end.

"Wyatt, I see the mechanism! Let me see if I can—"

She jumped back as the panel began to move. Wyatt didn't even wait for it to open all the way. He moved inside, gathering her into his arms in a quick, hard embrace that took her breath away.

"Are you all right?" he demanded roughly.

"I'm fine, but Kathy's in bad shape."

"Where?"

She pointed toward the steps. One by one, Gavin, then Hayley and Bram stepped inside the narrow space.

"Up there," she told them without preamble. Leigh came through last as the others were disappearing up the stairs.

"Wyatt told me to call for an ambulance. It's on its way, but it's going to take at least twenty minutes. It's on another call."

"I'm not sure we should wait," Alexis told her. "Kathy's coughing up blood."

"Oh, no."

As Leigh hurried upstairs after the others, Alexis recognized Leigh's walk-in closet stretched in front of her. The hidden entrance was concealed behind the closet door each time the closet was opened. Even if they'd been looking for an opening in here, she doubted they would have found this one.

Alexis started up the stairs after the others, but Bram was already on his way down with a terrifyingly still Kathy in his arms. Wyatt followed on his heels with Hayley then Gavin then Leigh behind him.

"We'll take my cruiser," Wyatt was saying. "It will be faster than waiting for the ambulance. I can radio ahead and let them know we're coming."

Alexis stepped back to let them pass. Kathy's eyes were closed. The fading yellow-green bruises stood out starkly against her pale skin. Wyatt continued issuing orders as they hurried down the hall.

"Alexis, you'll have to stay here. We don't want to have to explain why there are suddenly three of you to anyone tonight."

"I can stay with her," Gavin said.

"I'll stay, too," Leigh offered as they plunged down the staircase.

Wyatt held open the front door to allow Bram and Hayley to hurry onto the front porch. Wyatt turned to Alexis instead of following them immediately.

"You're sure you're okay?"

"Yes."

"Stay with Gavin and Leigh. And I mean," he added forcefully, "stay right with them. If you have to go to the bathroom, you take Leigh with you. Give me your word."

She held his gaze. "You'd trust it?"

"Yes."

Alexis felt as if a band around her chest had suddenly loosened. "Then you have my word," she promised.

"We'll go to the Walkens'," Gavin told him.

"Even better. They have an alarm system, right?"

"Yes."

"Put it on as soon as you get inside."

"We'll keep her safe," Gavin promised.

"You need to keep them both safe," he told Gavin. "I'll call you as soon as we get to the hospital."

"All right."

To her stunned surprise, Wyatt grabbed her by the shoulders. The kiss was so hard and fast she had no time to react at all.

"We're going to talk as soon as I get back."

Her heart raced like crazy as Wyatt followed the others.

"Grab your purse," Gavin told Leigh. "We're out of here right now."

"We have to clean the kitchen first," Leigh protested.

"Now!"

Alexis suddenly remembered the briefcase. "No. Wait! Gavin, we need to close the door in the closet."

"Leave it!"

"We can't." She lowered her voice to a bare whisper of sound. "Kathy hid the money up there."

Gavin swore. "Wait here with Leigh."

"We have to go to the kitchen to get my purse," Leigh told him.

"All right, but hurry."

As he plunged up the stairs, Alexis followed Leigh to the kitchen.

"Wyatt's crazy about you, you know," Leigh said as they rushed to gather the remains of the meal from the table. They worked in unison as if they'd done it all their lives.

"I didn't think he'd ever forgive me for deceiving him."

"There's nothing like a spot of danger to rearrange a man's priorities. Trust me, I know."

Alexis looked up from the dishes she was putting in the dishwasher.

"Why are we in such a hurry? We aren't in any immediate danger. Kathy was injured days ago. The bruises are healing."

"I don't know." Leigh handed her the last glass. "You disappeared and Wyatt went nuts." She snatched up her purse. "And don't be so sure about the danger part. If Kathy could be hiding in this house, so could others."

Leigh was right. They were on their way back down the hall when they heard Gavin calling them.

"On our way," Leigh yelled back.

He stood in the opening to the living room so he could watch them coming. In his hand was the briefcase.

"Let's go."

The sun hadn't even finished setting yet. Somehow it felt to Alexis as if more time should have passed. She twisted around in her seat for another look at the house as Gavin drove down the rock-filled driveway. She would have sworn the somber house was watching them leave.

"What am I going to do with a place that big?"

"Sell it, donate it to charity, turn it into an animal shelter, tear it down if you want," Leigh said.

"But you grew up there," Alexis protested.

"Yes, and we have some wonderful memories of Heartskeep. My mother—*our* mother—loved that old house. So did our grandfather. It's been in the Hart family for generations. But I don't care anymore. The Hart name died with Grandpa and I think the soul of Heartskeep died with him."

Alexis barely suppressed a shiver. "I think you might be right."

Leigh twisted around to look at her. "Maybe you could turn it into something useful. An artists' retreat or something. It's just a big, ugly tax drain now."

"Not an artist's retreat," Alexis said, "But maybe a retreat for battered women."

Gavin made a sound that could have been a snort. "Don't you think being battered is enough punishment? Heartskeep isn't exactly a warm and cozy haven."

"No," she said, warming to the idea, "but it could be made a lot more welcoming. Look how much better it is with those ugly, dark walls gone."

"You're right," Leigh agreed. "The rooms are big. There's plenty of privacy."

"Hidden rooms aside?" Gavin asked.

"No, really. I think she could have something there," Leigh said enthusiastically. "When the mazes are trimmed and you plant a few flowers back there—but not roses. Promise me you'll never plant roses."

Alexis met Gavin's eyes in the rearview mirror. Amy's body had been found in Marcus's rose garden, Jacob had told her.

"No roses," she agreed.

"Good. Mom had beautiful gardens full of all sorts of

flowers. The mazes can be beautiful again, even soothing. There's a nice breeze that comes in off the river in the evenings. You could even fix up the stables, maybe get some riding horses."

"Leigh, before you get carried away here, something like you're talking requires a business plan," Gavin told her.

"So? I think we can handle that. You're a lawyer, after all," Leigh reminded him. "Hayley has an MBA, I've got computer skills, and Alexis is a social worker. If that's what she wants to do with the place, we can help."

"Let's not put the cart in front of the horse," Gavin told her. "Not to dim your enthusiasm, but our first step needs to be addressing a few more pressing problems at the moment."

"Like keeping me out of jail?" Alexis asked.

Chapter Thirteen

"Don't look now, but your uncle just walked in the door," Hayley said to Wyatt.

The emergency room was busy, but the chief of police was hard to miss. "Good. I'll be right back," Wyatt told them.

"Good?" he heard Hayley say to Bram. "How can that possibly be good?"

Maybe it was the bright lights, but Wyatt thought he'd never seen his Uncle Nestor look older or more haggard than he did right now. As Wyatt approached, he straightened his shoulders and plastered a sour scowl across his face.

"Is that her?" his uncle demanded, nodding at the couple.

"No, that's Hayley."

"Do you know what you're doing, Wyatt?"

"Trying to solve our case."

For a moment his uncle said nothing. "I got the information you asked for. Brian Ryder was shot inside his New Jersey home, not the woman's apartment. There were signs of a struggle and the place had been burglarized. The current theory is he escaped and went to his daughter's place while his killer was searching the upstairs."

His uncle looked over to where Hayley sat talking with Bram.

"Her time's been accounted for. They know she's out of it, but they also know she came home at some point and found him. They want to know she's okay, and why she ran."

Wyatt nodded. "Did Lois Ryder die the same day as Amy Thomas?"

With a deep sigh, he nodded. "Your theory holds, but I'm not sure we'll be able to prove it."

"We don't have to prove it. We simply have to give them closure. Amy Thomas drove to the city to see for herself that a third daughter existed. She waited for Alexis to leave for school and then went to the house to talk to the mother. After that, she drove back to Heartskeep to confront her husband."

The older man nodded. "It would explain why Lois Ryder, normally a careful driver, was speeding on rain-slicked streets when she lost control of her car. And before you ask, she was two blocks from her husband's office."

"We need to find Eden Thomas," Wyatt told him. Quickly he related what Kathy Walsh knew and had told them in the car on the way to the hospital.

"I already made finding the Thomas woman and her son first priority," his uncle said testily. "What more can I do?"

"Buy me a little more time with Alexis. I think this whole thing is about to come to apart."

"You don't ask for much, do you?"

"Someone wants that money badly enough to kill for it. Alexis is not going to be the next victim."

His uncle dropped his hand to his side and narrowed his eyes. "Sounds to me like you have a personal interest."

"I do," Wyatt told him honestly.

Instead of the explosion he expected, his uncle shut his eyes wearily for a moment.

"I'm a small-town cop, Wyatt. It's all I ever wanted to be. I had my gut full of big-city crime when I was young like you. I came here because I thought it would be a nice quiet place. Someone should have warned me about the Hart family."

"That's exactly what Hayley said earlier today."

They both looked toward the couple sitting across the room watching them.

"Seven years ago, Amy Thomas's disappearance looked open-and-shut to me. I didn't want to probe any deeper. I believed Marcus Thomas was a respected member of the community with two mouthy young daughters. I was wrong. I owe those girls and their mother. Do what you can to repay that debt. I'll buy you as much time as I'm able."

He sighed heavily and looked at Hayley. "I may as well start with an apology."

"You don't have to do that," Wyatt told him.

"Yes," he said carefully. "I do."

"She won't thank you for it."

"No, I don't imagine she will."

Wyatt found new respect for his uncle. He turned and called to the couple, "Bram! See you a minute?"

Bram stood and ambled over to him. His uncle inclined his head in acknowledgment as they passed.

"What's up?" Bram asked, but his attention was on Hayley.

"My uncle wanted to talk to her for a minute."

"Is that wise?"

"No, but I couldn't talk him out of it. Don't worry, Hayley can handle herself."

"She wasn't the one I was worried about," Bram said dryly.

The conversation didn't last five minutes. His uncle met Wyatt's eyes as he headed for the door. Wyatt would swear he looked relieved.

"Everything all right?" Bram asked as they joined Hayley.

"Don't look now," Hayley replied, sounding shocked, "but I think hell just froze over. Chief Crossley came over to apologize for not doing more seven years ago. Can you believe it?"

Bram slid an arm around her waist. Hayley looked at Wyatt. "He said he knew it didn't change anything, but he wanted me to know he was sorry anyhow." She leaned her head against Bram's side and he rested his chin on her head in wordless support.

Wyatt turned away. He wondered if the couple knew how lucky they were to have a bond like that. He couldn't help thinking he'd only met one woman in his life who had ever made him feel anything remotely similar, and he barely knew her. But he wanted to.

THE WALKEN HOUSE looked almost as big as Heartskeep from the outside. Though no one should have been home, there were welcoming lights on inside.

"Did George and Emily come back?" Leigh asked Gavin.

"I don't know. They were supposed to stay with their friends until tomorrow. Maybe Nan came back early."

"Who's Nan?" Alexis asked.

"Technically, the cook and housekeeper," Gavin answered. "In reality, she runs the house and everyone in it."

Leigh reached for the door handle.

"Wait!" Gavin ordered sharply.

Alexis stared anxiously into the darkness, looking for something out of place.

"I don't see any cars," he said softly.

"Wouldn't they have parked around back or in the garage?" Leigh asked.

Gavin didn't answer. The easygoing lawyer had turned into someone very different. There was a tense watchfulness about him. Alexis could tell Leigh was spooked, as well.

"It doesn't feel right," he said.

"Who'd look for us here?" she asked nervously.

"Anyone who knows you. Call the house. Let's see who answers."

Leigh opened her purse and pulled out a cell phone. After a minute, she shook her head. "No one's answering." Her voice was hushed.

Gavin started the engine. "We're out of here."

"Couldn't the lights be on timers?" Alexis asked.

Gavin paused, considering that.

"See if you can raise Wyatt."

After a minute of tense silence, Leigh shook her head and began speaking. "Wyatt, this is Leigh. Would you call us back as soon as you get this message?"

As she recited her cell phone number, they heard the sound of a shot. Gavin put the car in gear and sped down the driveway.

"Did someone just shoot at us?" Alexis asked, shaken.

"I think it came from behind the house. Call the police, Leigh. Report the gunshot and suggest they investigate, but don't give your name."

"George or Emily might be hurt!"

Gavin looked grim. "I know."

His job was to keep them safe, Alexis realized. No matter how much he wanted to check on the couple, keeping them safe was what he intended to do.

Leigh reported the sound of the shot and hung up quickly. "Where are we going?"

"R.J.'s?" Alexis suggested when Gavin didn't say anything right away.

He glanced at her in the rearview mirror. "Do you know how to get there?"

"I think so."

"His place is in the woods, isn't it?"

She nodded.

Wyatt gave a negative shake of his head. "Too isolated. We'll be safer at The Inn. I want people around."

"I'm sorry I brought all this trouble here," Alexis said.

"You didn't bring it," Leigh protested. "It was already here."

Leigh told her how they'd discovered her existence and gone looking for her.

"We were sidetracked when we learned about Mrs. Walsh. She and Kathy were so much a part of our lives growing up. We were hoping she'd come out of her coma and be able to help us, but she never did," Leigh said sadly.

"Kathy doesn't know about her mother," Alexis told them.

"Hayley will tell her," Gavin said. "Kathy's tough. She'll handle it. Her boyfriend was a gambler who latched on to her for her money. He ran through most of it, so he needed a new source."

"Is he the one looking for the briefcase?" Alexis asked.

"I don't think so," Leigh said. "Kathy wouldn't have told him about the money. She told a neighbor she was fed up and planned to leave him."

"But he beat her up," Alexis reminded them. "She was hiding from him."

Leigh shook her head. "If she'd told him about the money, she would have warned you."

Alexis wasn't so sure, but she didn't argue. "Kathy did mention some missing jewelry she'd hidden."

"Kathy hid the emeralds?" Leigh asked in surprise.

"I don't know if they were emeralds, but..." Alexis repeated what Kathy had told her.

"It's okay. We found them in the hidden room behind the pantry," Leigh explained.

Alexis groaned. "Another hidden room?"

"Afraid so," Gavin told her. "Leigh and I went to see the jeweler who made the pieces for your grandfather. The timing fits. We think Amy first learned you existed when the package arrived shortly after Dennison died. Your grandfather told him to mark the boxes with your names.''

"Mom would have gone looking for an explanation when she saw your name. That's probably how she found the investigator's file. We spent most of yesterday trying to track him down, and guess what? He was killed during a burglary of his office right after Grandpa died.''

Alexis stared at her sister. "You think Marcus killed him, too?''

"Don't you?'' she asked.

Alexis had to admit, it seemed a likely assumption. But one they probably wouldn't be able to prove now.

"Bram and Hayley went to find out if the address for Brian Ryder was still valid while we started going through telephone books trying to find a listing in your name.''

"The phone and the lease are in my roommate's name,'' Alexis said.

"That explains why we couldn't find you.''

Gavin turned the car into a large parking lot. The Inn was a sprawling, rustic place tucked in among the trees. The lot was filled with cars.

"Maybe this wasn't such a good idea, after all,'' Gavin said as they waited for a car to pull out so they could park.

"Someone must be having a birthday party or something. But having people around us is a good thing, isn't it?'' Leigh asked.

Gavin frowned. "That depends. Alexis, you did such a great job pretending to be Leigh, do you think you can be Hayley for a couple of hours?''

"I'm wearing her dress so I guess that's a start.''

"I'll try to clue you in with names if anyone comes over to us,'' Leigh promised.

"Let's see if we can get a room,'' Gavin said, getting out of the car. He carried himself alertly, sweeping the area with his gaze as they crossed the parking lot toward the building.

"That should boost your reputation around town," Leigh told him.

"What do you mean?"

"One room, two women, and no luggage. Gee, I can't imagine what people will think," she teased.

"I don't care what anyone thinks as long as I can keep the two of you safe."

Leigh linked her arm with his. "From bad boy of the county to hero. You have come a long way, haven't you?"

Gavin muttered something under his breath. Leigh grinned up at him. Watching them, Alexis tried to ignore a stab of envy. They were so easy with one another. So right together.

They made her think of Wyatt. He was angry with her, but that kiss he'd given her right before he'd left gave her hope. Anger was something they could deal with—if time gave them the chance.

As it turned out, Gavin didn't have to worry about what people would think, after all. There were no rooms available. A local couple was celebrating their fiftieth wedding anniversary and had booked most of the rooms for their out-of-town guests. Added to that, the restaurant was coping with three separate birthday parties as well as the normal local trade.

Gavin thanked the harried desk clerk and told him they'd be in the bar for a while in case someone canceled a room at the last minute. The man agreed to let them know but doubted he'd be able to help.

As they started for the bar, Leigh tugged on his shoulder. "Gavin, I just remembered the briefcase. Should we leave it sitting in the car?"

Gavin swore. The bar was packed with people waiting to be seated in the restaurant. The music wasn't loud, but the room was hot and noisy.

"I'll see if I can get a table, then I'll go out and get the briefcase."

"You have to be joking," Leigh said, looking around. "We'll never get a table in this crush."

"We will if I have enough cash. I'll be right back."

"He's going to pay someone for a table?" Alexis asked as he disappeared into the crowd

"Apparently."

He returned before they had time to become overly nervous. Two college-age males relinquished their chairs as soon as the three of them approached their table near the back wall of the room.

"Heck, we'd have given the chairs to ladies as pretty as these," one of them said with an appreciative grin.

Alexis fixed him with a smile. "You can always give him the money back."

The youth laughed, wiggled his bottle of beer at her, and followed his friend into the crowd.

"Let me have the phone, Leigh. I'm going to try Wyatt again."

"You'll never be able to hear in here, even if you get through," she warned.

"I'll take it with me on the way to the car. Order me a soda if the waitress ever shows up."

Several minutes passed before one did make it over to them. Leigh ordered three soft drinks and some pretzels to munch on, handing the waitress several bills.

"Sorry I can't offer to pay," Alexis apologized. "My purse is probably still in Wyatt's car, wherever that is."

"Don't worry. From what you told us, Beamer towed the car. He's a good guy. He'll hold your purse for you."

Alexis noticed a young male eyeing her and quickly looked away. "I really wish I'd chosen a different dress from your sister's closet."

Leigh smiled in sympathy. "It's definitely drawing more than one eye tonight."

"Thanks a lot. That makes me feel so much better."

The drinks arrived, but Gavin didn't. The crowd showed no signs of thinning out. If anything, it was growing larger as several boisterous college friends arrived to join the others already standing around.

Leigh drummed her fingers restlessly against the table-top. "Gavin should have been back by now."

"Maybe he got us a room," Alexis suggested. But the weight of apprehension was sitting heavy in her mind, as well. As the minutes continued to stretch, so did their nerves.

"Something's wrong."

Privately, Alexis agreed. "If we move, he'll never find us."

"I know, but I can't sit here anymore. You stay and watch the table—"

Alexis shook her head. "We stay together."

After a second Leigh nodded. "You're right. Let's go."

Their table was immediately claimed by an older couple waiting nearby. Alexis followed her sister as she squeezed her way through the mob.

Small clusters of people stood outside talking or moving about the parking lot, but there was no sign of Gavin.

"We should have waited," Alexis said.

Leigh suddenly tensed. "I don't think so. See that cream-colored car over there? I think that's Eden's car."

Alexis felt a twist of fear. "She's here?"

"Let's have a look."

"This is not a good idea," Alexis objected even as they hurried across the lot.

"There's no one in the car," Leigh pointed out. "I just want a quick look inside. Maybe there will be something sitting out to tell us where she's staying."

The front seats were empty. The back wasn't. At first Alexis thought it was a pile of clothing. Then she realized the clothing was attached to a body, and the body wasn't moving.

Leigh gave a slight gasp and stepped back quickly. They shared a frightened look.

"Is she dead?" Alexis whispered.

"I don't know."

Tentatively, Alexis reached for the door handle. Leigh shook her head violently. "We need to find Gavin."

Leigh was right. They didn't want to wake Eden if she was only sleeping, and if she was hurt—or worse—she needed more help than they could offer.

Together, they ran back to the building.

Almost no one stood outside now, but a glance inside the bar showed why. It had been crowded before. Now it was jammed. Alexis tried to follow as Leigh pushed her way through, but an older couple stepped between them, forcing Alexis to wait.

She lost sight of Leigh for less than a minute, but it was long enough for Leigh to be intercepted by a tall blond man.

Jacob!

He'd taken Leigh by the arm and was leading her toward an emergency exit near the spot where their table had been.

"Leigh!"

Her sister didn't hear her over the din. She appeared to be moving with him almost eagerly. Alexis struggled to catch up with them.

"Leigh! No! Wait!"

"Gavin's been hurt!" Leigh tossed back over her shoulder as she reached the exit.

"It's a trick! Let her go, Jacob!"

He turned with a scowl. "It's no trick, Hayley!" he called to her. "I came in here to get some help."

Leigh stepped outside with Jacob on her heels. Alexis had no choice but to follow them into the hot, muggy night.

A single lightbulb above the door threw a small circle

of yellow over the ground. The rest of the area was in darkness.

Ahead stretched a shadow line of trees, to the right, one edge of the parking lot. Alexis wasn't surprised when Jacob turned left. Three large Dumpster containers blocked the view to form a black, evil wall of metal.

Her sister trusted Jacob, despite what Alexis had told her.

And why not? Leigh had known Jacob all her life. She'd only known her sister for a few short hours.

Alexis raked the ground with her eyes. A skinny length of dark metal drew her attention. She had no idea what the slender rod of broken pipe had been used for, but when she picked it up she found it was heavy. That was what counted. She'd probably only get one chance to use it.

Alexis chased after them around the Dumpster wall. On the other side, a figure lay crumpled in the dirt. The figure stirred as Leigh flew to his side with a terrified cry.

"Gavin!"

"I saw him heading around the building when I pulled into the parking lot," Jacob was saying. "I knew something was wrong. That's why I followed him back here."

Alexis hung back. She stopped several feet away and gripped the pipe more firmly, concealing it against her skirt.

"Gavin, it's Leigh. Don't try to move. We're going to get you some help."

Leigh reached for something in the pile of debris next to the Dumpster. She rose with a flimsy strip of wood in her hand that looked as if it had come from a broken fence.

"What did you hit him with, Jacob?"

At her cold, hard words, Jacob took a step back in surprise. Alexis was surprised, as well. She'd underestimated her sister.

Gavin attempted to sit up. Alexis tore her eyes from

him and closed in on Jacob from behind as her sister strode toward him.

"Hey! What is this?" Jacob demanded, twisting to look at Alexis.

"Where's your gun?" Alexis demanded.

"What gun?"

"The gun you pulled on Alexis," Leigh told him.

His hand started toward his pocket. "You mean this?"

Leigh swung the board at his arm before he could pull his hand free. There was a loud crack. The wood snapped in two and bounced off his arm. Jacob yelped in surprise.

"What are you doing? Are you crazy?"

Alexis swung the pipe as hard as she could toward his upper arm. Wyatt had mentioned a prior injury, but he hadn't said which arm. Jacob cried out in pain and grabbed his arm below the shoulder.

"It's a toy!" he yelled at them. "It isn't a real gun!"

The kitchen door opened behind Leigh.

"Call the police! Get an ambulance!" Leigh hollered without turning around.

"Touch that pocket again and I'll go for your head," Alexis warned the stunned man. "What did you do to Gavin?"

"I didn't do anything! I found him like this! What's the matter with you two?"

"Police! Drop your weapon!"

Alexis didn't turn to look at the voice coming out of the dark to one side of her. "He's got a gun in his pocket," she called without moving.

"Drop your weapon! Do it now!" the voice commanded.

Alexis released the length of pipe.

"You two, down on the ground. Keep your hands spread above your head where I can see them! Move!"

Alexis started to obey, but the man ran up to her.

"Not you! You stand right where you are!"

He grabbed her forearm in a crushing grip, yanking her

against a body that smelled of stale sweat. She knew a moment of sheer panic as she saw his gun hand come around to aim at Leigh. A cop would never do it this way. He wasn't a cop!

"Don't move! Any of you!"

Gavin was still trying to rise. The fake cop moved his hand in that direction. Alexis didn't stop to think. She came down on his instep as hard as she could, bringing her free arm up and against his outstretched gun arm.

The weapon discharged with a sound that left her ears ringing, but Alexis was already following through. Twisting, she brought her knee up, aimed at his groin.

He blocked the blow and she struck his thigh instead. The mistake cost her. He grabbed a fistful of her hair and shoved the hot muzzle of the gun under her chin.

"Move again, you bitch, and I'll kill you where you stand."

The fetid stench of his body odor nearly made her gag as he brought his arm across her chest to pin her against him.

"Back down on the ground or I'll kill her! Do it!"

There was a countermove she could have made to his hold, but she didn't. This was the man who had stalked her through the house—the man who'd shot at Wyatt. He was pumped and ready to pull that trigger right now. She could feel the adrenaline rushing through him. She couldn't risk what he might do to the others.

He tugged her toward the parking lot. She went with him, waiting for an opening.

"Excuse me, would you be Officer Crossley?"

Wyatt looked up at the young woman approaching his chair.

"I am," he acknowledged.

"There's a telephone call at the desk for you, sir."

"I'll be right back," he told Hayley and Bram.

His uncle's voice filled his ear without preamble as soon as he picked up the phone and identified himself.

"Someone called in a report of shots fired out at the Walken estate. Isn't that where you said Jarret was taking the other two women?"

Alexis!

"I'm on my way," Wyatt told him. He ran back to Hayley and Bram. "I have to go. I'll be back for you as soon as I can."

"What's wrong?" Bram asked.

"Is it Leigh?" Hayley demanded.

"I don't know. Let me borrow your cell phone?" Hayley pulled it from her purse and handed it to him.

"Leigh's number is in the directory," she told him. "So is Bram's."

Wyatt nodded. "Thanks."

He sprinted for his cruiser.

He should never have left Alexis. Starting the car, he hit the lights and siren and punched the accelerator. If anything happened to her, he'd never forgive himself.

He took the twisty two-lane roads at speeds that scared even him, but he was making good time when the police radio crackled to life. Dispatch requested he switch frequencies to talk to his uncle. An officer had already responded to the Walken home. The house had been breached and searched. There was no one inside, but there was blood on the back porch. Indications were that a car had been parked behind the house. His uncle Nestor was sending a car to Heartskeep for a quick look around. Wyatt promised to meet him there.

No sooner did he switch back to the main frequency than dispatch reported a disturbance at The Inn. Wyatt would be coming up on that cross street in just a few seconds. A dishwasher reported two women and a man involved in an altercation behind the restaurant.

Instincts screaming, Wyatt responded that he'd take the call, but requested backup. He hoped he wasn't wasting valuable time, but he had a strong hunch he couldn't ignore.

Wyatt careened into the parking lot a minute later, nearly sideswiping an exiting car. A man in a white bus-boy uniform hurried over to meet him.

"Out back by the kitchens!" the excited youth sputtered. "There's two women beating up—"

The sound of a single gunshot nearly stopped his heart. Wyatt got out of the car, handing the startled youth his microphone.

"Press the button. Tell them an officer needs help. Shots fired."

He sprinted across the parking lot, yanking out his gun as he ran. The Inn was the most popular restaurant around for miles. Tonight it was busier than usual. The parking lot was full of cars and people.

"Police officer," he shouted as he ran past. "Clear the area!"

As he neared the corner of the building closest to the bar, two figures emerged. He recognized Alexis at once. The man holding her was of average height, lean and blond. He had the muzzle of a gun pressed against her throat.

Chapter Fourteen

"Police!" he yelled. "Drop—"

The man brought the weapon around. It spat a streamer of flame at him. He heard the bullet slam into the car parked beside him even as he dove for cover.

Alexis suddenly twisted in the man's grasp. Wyatt wasn't exactly sure what she did, but the man suddenly bellowed. Instead of running, she turned into him, smashed her forehead against his face and punched him in the breastbone with surprising force. The man's weapon discharged into the air.

"Alexis get down!"

She twisted away and plunged between two parked cars. Blood streamed from the man's nose. He aimed the weapon at her, giving Wyatt a clear shot. Wyatt squeezed off a round and the man staggered. Someone else burst out of the darkness from behind the building. Wyatt fired at the new threat and missed.

The second figure kept coming. He tackled the gunman, sending them both crashing to the ground. The gun spun away as they disappeared behind a parked car. Wyatt rushed forward.

"Jacob! He's going for the gun!" Alexis yelled.

She darted back toward the struggling men, yelling, "No you don't!"

Alexis kicked the weapon away from the gunman's outstretched fingers and stomped on his hand. He screamed in rage and pain bucking Jacob off his back as he grabbed for her ankle. Jacob reached into his pants pocket and pulled out a gun. At the same time Alexis kicked the gunman in the face and went after his weapon.

Jacob jammed his gun against the back of the man's neck. "Don't move!" he yelled.

Wyatt sensed more movement near the corner of the building. He spun, pointing his weapon as two more figures appeared. Only instinct kept him from firing at them as Leigh, supporting Gavin, stepped into view.

"Who else is back there?" he demanded.

"No one we know about," Alexis replied, running over to him.

"State police!" a voice called from behind Wyatt. "Drop your weapons."

Wyatt glanced back and saw a man in a suit and tie, holding a drawn gun. Thankful to have backup, he signaled the man that he was a cop and turned back to Jacob who was straddling the original gunman.

"Jacob! Toss the weapon to your left and stand up slowly."

"No problem. It was just a toy gun anyhow."

"I need a pair of handcuffs over here," Wyatt called to the other officer.

"Only one?" the man asked, eyeing the situation as he ran up to them. "I don't have mine on me. Farnsworth," he told Wyatt. "The wife and I were having dinner inside when I heard the first shot."

"Glad you could join us," Wyatt told him. "You want to cover me while I pat him down?"

"Go. My wife called for backup."

"It should be on the way already," he told the man. "Jacob, stay where you are and keep your hands in plain sight until I get this sorted out."

"Hey, no problem. I'm a statue."

Alexis hurried over to Leigh and Gavin. "Gavin needs an ambulance," she called out.

Gavin mumbled something that could have been, "I'm fine."

"You're seeing double," he heard Leigh argue.

"You're twins. I'm supposed to see double."

Relieved that he sounded rational, Wyatt kept his attention on the man on the ground who'd begun to stir again.

"Hold still!"

The man ignored the order and started to rise. Wyatt placed his knee in the small of the man's back. The man went berserk. He struggled to reach inside his pants' pocket. Farnsworth and Jacob immediately dove in to lend a hand. The crazed man thrashed blindly. It took all three of them to subdue him. His nose was spurting blood and his chest was bleeding, but it didn't slow him down any.

A uniformed officer ran up, a pair of cuffs in hand. Wyatt looked up, surprised to see his uncle. It took another brief struggle before they got the cuffs on the man so that Wyatt could pat him down. He found a snub-nose revolver in his pocket and a knife strapped to his leg.

Wyatt rolled him faceup.

"Mario Silva."

"Well, fancy that," Farnsworth said.

Jacob took a step forward. "Where's my mother, you bastard?"

"Stay where you are, Jacob," Wyatt warned him.

"He did something to my mother."

Wyatt shook his head. "I'm not going to tell you again," he said in his most authoritative voice. "Stay where you are!"

Wyatt was relieved when he obeyed. Alexis watched anxiously. He could see that she wanted to say something to him, but he warned her off with a shake of his head. The situation was still too explosive for conversation.

Not until another unit arrived did he step back. The

fight suddenly went out of Silva, who began to groan in pain.

"Ambulance is on the way," his uncle said. "I heard the call and figured I was closer than anyone else."

"Thanks for responding." He was relieved to be able to turn the scene over to someone else. "I'm still trying to sort out what happened."

"Wyatt," Alexis said urgently, "Eden's in the back seat of her car on the other side of the parking lot. I don't know if she's asleep or dead or unconscious."

"Go!" his uncle told him. "We'll cover this."

Sirens screamed in the distance.

"Show me!" Wyatt ordered. He ran with Alexis past the gathering crowd, but stopped to flag down the cop who rolled into the lot. "Get crowd control started. Nobody in or out. Where?" he demanded of Alexis.

She pointed to the car.

"Wait here!"

He ran to the vehicle and found the doors locked. The woman on the back seat wasn't moving. Wyatt ran to his cruiser and grabbed a tool to force open the door. A state police car pulled up.

"We're going to need another ambulance," Wyatt called to the officer, who waved in acknowledgment.

Wyatt ran back to Eden's car and popped the door lock. The minute he was inside he smelled the copper scent of blood. Eden was facedown. She didn't stir when he reached for her neck, searching for a pulse.

"I need an EMT now!" he called out.

"She's alive?" Alexis asked anxiously at his shoulder.

"For the moment."

He pulled Alexis aside for the EMTs who'd arrived. "We've got another gunshot victim on the other side of the building," he told the pair.

Having done what he could, he turned to Alexis. "Are you all right?"

"I am now."

He tilted her face up and brushed the hair back from her forehead. "You're starting to bruise."

"Since I broke his nose and some bones in his hand, I figure we're even," she replied with a shaky smile.

He started to pull her into his arms when she held up a gun by the barrel.

"Would you mind taking this? Guns make me nervous."

He stared at the weapon in shock. He'd forgotten that she'd picked up Silva's weapon after kicking it away from him.

"Are you sure you're a social worker and not a cop?" he asked as he took it from her.

"Uh-huh. We don't take a lot of crap from creeps, but we usually don't have to shoot them, either. Thanks for coming."

"I wouldn't have missed it," he told her, and opened his arms.

Shaking all over, Alexis stepped into them and buried her face against his chest.

IT WAS A SUBDUED GROUP that gathered in the library of Heartskeep two weeks later. Amy Hart Thomas had finally been laid to rest in the family plot overlooking the Hudson River. Only a select group of invited guests had been in attendance for the double funeral that afternoon. The services had been delayed until Kathy was out of the hospital and able to attend as they laid Livia Walsh to rest, as well.

The past two weeks had been rough on all of them. Wyatt was grateful for the support George and Emily Walken had given the women. They had even traveled to New Jersey with them to be with Alexis when she buried Brian Ryder next to his beloved Lois.

The older couple had opened their home and their hearts to Alexis from the moment they'd met her. Wyatt hadn't been surprised. The couple hadn't just been neighbors and family friends, they'd acted as surrogate parents to Hayley and Leigh for years. Alexis had accepted their warmth and friendship shyly at first, but the couple was so open and giving that her hesitation hadn't lasted long.

Wyatt studied the group, reluctant to tell them what he had to say, knowing everyone was tired of death and funerals. But Hayley gave him the perfect opening.

"Why didn't Jacob come back to the house?" she asked the room in general. "I saw him standing off to one side talking to R.J. Doesn't he know we don't blame him for anything that happened?"

Wyatt cleared his throat, attracting every eye. "Jacob had to get back to the hospital. Eden slipped into a coma this morning. The doctors don't expect her to make it through the day."

"But she was on the mend," Leigh protested.

"So the doctors hoped, even though they knew she wasn't entirely out of danger. They said sometimes it happens like this."

Alexis held his gaze as the others chimed in. "You talked to her, didn't you?"

Her quiet question created a sudden well of silence.

"Yesterday," he confirmed. Wyatt expected a volley of questions, but no one said a word. Bram rubbed Hayley's upper arm lightly. Leigh reached for Gavin's hand. Emily and George Walken shared a worried look, while Kathy Walsh twisted the ring on her hand. Alexis sat still beside Leigh and waited.

"Eden gave us a statement. As you know, Mario Silva shot her when she tried to get away from him at the Walken estate. He'd dragged her there, looking for the money. He kept insisting she was holding out on him. He didn't believe Marcus could have died broke."

"I have to say, we found it hard to believe, as well," Gavin said. Leigh nodded.

"Marcus was involved in all sorts of illegal activities," George Walken agreed. "If most of the blackmail money came from the estate, what happened to the money he must have raked in over the years?''

Wyatt leaned against the door frame and crossed his legs at the ankles. ''Good question. It's going to take time to untangle all this, but we expect to recover a lot of the answers from the computer we took from his office. We're betting Marcus stashed a lot of his money in a Swiss bank account or in one of those offshore banks.''

''There's only one question I want answered,'' Hayley told the room at large. ''Did Marcus kill our mother?''

Wyatt frowned. ''According to Eden, her death was an accident.''

''Her skull was crushed! How is that an accident?'' Hayley demanded.

''Eden claims Amy had a car accident on the way home from the city—similar to the one that killed Lois Ryder.''

''Hayley, let the man talk,'' Bram said when she began to protest.

Wyatt waited for the outbursts to die down before he continued. ''According to Eden, Amy said she wasn't wearing her seat belt and hit her head on the window when she slid off the road. Since there was no one around and the car was driveable, she drove home. Eden saw Amy pull up out front, saw the damaged fender and went outside to see what had happened. She claims Amy verbally attacked her.''

''She probably did,'' Leigh said.

Wyatt nodded. ''Eden says they argued and Amy tried to hit her.''

''No way,'' Hayley said immediately.

''Eden claims she went to push her away and Amy fell. Her injured head struck the side mirror on the car. When Amy didn't get up, Eden discovered she was dead.''

''What do you think?'' George asked quietly.

''The autopsy doesn't rule it out,'' Wyatt said with care. ''It could have happened that way.''

''I sense a 'but' in there,'' Bram said.

"A big one!" Hayley agreed. "She lied."

Wyatt rubbed his jaw. "You may be right. She and Marcus went to great lengths to bury your mother's body and get rid of the only evidence that could have substantiated Eden's claim."

"What *did* they do with her car?" Emily Walken asked.

"According to Eden, they hid it in one of the barns until late that night after everyone had gone to bed. Eden followed Marcus to New York City. They drove to a rough part of town and parked it there, leaving the keys in the ignition. As an added inducement, they set Amy's purse on the front seat in plain sight."

"It's actually a pretty ingenious way of getting rid of the evidence," Gavin said. "An expensive car like that would have been worth something to a chop shop, damaged or not. If her driver's license or any part of the car turned up, it would be there in the city and would point to her having been killed there."

Wyatt nodded. "That's why I question her version of the story, but I'm afraid we'll never know what really happened."

"Did they murder Dennison and his private investigator, too?" Bram asked.

"Eden claims she didn't know anything about a private investigator—and that could be true. As you know, Dennison did have a bad heart. We could have him exhumed, as you'd planned. An autopsy might show something, but even if it did, it wouldn't prove who committed the crime. My feeling is we should let it go, but that's up to Hayley and Leigh."

"There isn't much point," Hayley said bitterly. "There isn't anyone left to punish."

"Except Mario Silva," Wyatt corrected. "Ballistics matched the bullets they took out of Brian Ryder and Eden to the gun Mario stole after his prison break. We also found a matching shell casing by the Dumpster at Heartskeep.''

''I hate to sound stupid, but I'm confused. You're saying it was Mario Silva who killed Brian Ryder?'' Emily asked.

Wyatt nodded.

''Then how did Brian Ryder get to Alexis's apartment?''

''We surmise from the evidence that Brian Ryder played dead after he was shot. Silva went upstairs looking for the money. While he was tearing the house apart, Brian staggered out to his car and drove to the city to warn Alexis.''

''He should have driven to the hospital instead,'' Alexis murmured.

Wyatt wished he could take the shadows from her eyes. ''It wouldn't have mattered,'' he told her gently. ''I think he knew he was dying. He must have had the briefcase in his car. He wanted to get it to you and warn you before Silva found your address and came after you next.''

''If you found a shell casing here at Heartskeep, that means Silva was also the one who shot at you and Alexis, right?'' Gavin asked.

''Yes,'' Wyatt agreed.

''But—how did he know to come here?'' Bram questioned.

''Eden,'' Wyatt said succinctly. ''She was afraid of Mario. When she learned of his prison escape, she knew he'd show up sooner or later.''

''Why?'' Hayley asked.

''Because Mario was Marcus's half brother.''

''What!'' several voices chorused.

''They shared the same mother, but different fathers. Marcus's father died and left him money in some sort of trust, but only if he used it to become a physician,''

''Good heavens,'' Emily whispered.

''Mario's father didn't leave him anything at all.''

"And Marcus felt responsible for him?" Leigh asked in surprise.

"Not exactly. I think Marcus was intimidated by his older brother. Mario met Eden through Marcus when they were working at the same hospital. They married, but divorced before Jacob was born. Eden claims Marcus got her involved in some unspecified illegal activities." Wyatt grimaced. "To be honest, I suspect it was the other way around, but it doesn't matter. They became partners in crime. They never got caught, so Mario felt free to come around in times of need—which were generally any time he wasn't in prison."

"Did Jacob know?" Leigh asked quietly.

"He says not, and I don't think he's lying," Wyatt told her.

"Eden wasn't much of a person," Hayley said, nodding in agreement, "but Jacob always said she was a good mother."

"I still don't understand how this Mario person knew about the briefcase," Emily said.

Wyatt rubbed his jaw absently. "Eden told him she didn't have any money, but she knew where he might be able to get some. She'd known for some time that Marcus was being blackmailed. She'd always suspected Kathy. Ironically, Marcus believed it was Jacob, despite Eden's assurances to the contrary."

"Marcus never did like Jacob," Hayley agreed. "But then, he never liked anyone."

"To answer your question, Emily," Wyatt continued, "Eden followed Livia Walsh into the maze one morning and heard Marcus refusing to pay her. Eden found out where Livia was living and arranged to run into her in town."

"Why would she tell Eden about the briefcase?" Brian asked.

Kathy sat forward and spoke for the first time, drawing all eyes in her direction. "My mother disliked Eden almost as much as Marcus. I can see her thinking the money was out of Eden's reach and taunting Eden with the knowledge that she'd given it to the child they'd stolen from Amy. She thought it was poetic justice and probably said as much to Eden. Mom was getting older. She wasn't as careful as she should have been.''

"So Eden sent Mario after Brian Ryder?" Leigh asked.

"That's how it looks," Wyatt said. "Silva isn't talking."

George spoke up again. "Who were the people Alexis heard outside her apartment? Did Silva follow Brian there?"

"No. Alexis heard Jacob and Eden." Wyatt staved off a barrage of questions and focused on Alexis. "Jacob discovered what Eden had done. He claims he went to New Jersey to warn Brian, but got there too late. He saw your dad stagger from the house to his car. Silva came charging out a few minutes later holding a gun. By then, Brian's car had turned the corner. Silva was parked at the other end of the street, facing the opposite direction. As soon as Silva left, Jacob went to the house. He says Silva left the front door standing open, so he went inside to see if he could find an address for Alexis."

"Yeah, right." Bram snorted in disbelief. "Obviously he had no interest in finding the briefcase."

Wyatt smiled at the sarcasm. "That's his story and he's sticking to it. As soon as he found Alexis's address, he called Eden to tell her he was going there."

"I feel sorry for Jacob," Leigh said.

This time it was Gavin who made a rude sound.

"No, really, Leigh's right," Hayley put in. "In his way, he was trying to protect all of us."

"Hayley, the man threatened Alexis," Bram reminded her.

"With a toy gun," Alexis reminded them.

Wyatt didn't want to argue over Jacob's possible motives. The man *had* helped to rescue Alexis, so he figured he owed him for that.

"Jacob says he believed if he could get the money and give it to his mother, Eden would take it and disappear, then Silva would go away, and everything would be all right. He claims he was sickened by what Eden and Marcus had done, but he didn't want her to go to prison. He didn't expect Eden to show up at your apartment. He was terrified they'd be seen there, but he knew he had to find you and get the money."

"So everyone headed for Heartskeep, figuring Alexis would show up there sooner or later," George said.

"Everyone except us," Hayley said. "We were out chasing shadows while Alexis was being stalked and shot at."

"Silva wasn't looking for the money or Alexis at Heartskeep," Wyatt corrected. "He was looking for Eden. He thought she'd gone back there to hide. What was it you called this earlier, Alexis? A farce without humor?"

She nodded.

"I just wish someone could explain to me why Mom married that miserable bastard in the first place," Hayley muttered.

Wyatt caught the troubled look George gave his wife. Emily Walken laid a hand on his arm and gave him a slight, encouraging nod.

"Or why she didn't divorce him," Leigh agreed.

"Because of me," George said. "Marcus wasn't your biological father. I am."

Alexis was stunned. She saw the expressions of hurt and betrayal on the faces of her sisters and understood exactly how they felt.

"Oh, my God," Leigh whispered.

"You can't be," Hayley said. "You just can't be."

Alexis stared at the face of the man who'd so recently befriended her and tried to absorb this new shock. She didn't know George or Emily very well, and while she genuinely liked the couple, George's words staggered her. It was like learning Brian Ryder wasn't really her father all over again.

"That's impossible," Hayley whispered.

"Twenty-five years ago, I found out I couldn't have children," Emily said, "and I fell apart. George and I went through a bleak time. Eventually I walked out, telling him I was going to file for a divorce."

"You had an affair with our mother?" Hayley was trembling.

George shook his head, looking miserable. "It wasn't like that. Amy was my best friend's daughter. She'd always had a bit of a crush on me. While it was flattering, I felt avuncular where she was concerned. One evening Amy stopped by with a book I'd asked to borrow from Dennison. I'd been drowning my sorrows all afternoon. She'd come home for the weekend because she'd had a fight with this doctor she'd been dating."

"Marcus?" Leigh asked.

"Yes. We got to talking and I invited her in to have a drink."

"I don't want to hear this," Hayley said hoarsely. "You had a one-night stand with our mother. She got pregnant and married Marcus. That's why he didn't care about giving away one of her babies. We weren't even his children."

"Why didn't you tell us?" Leigh demanded.

"I didn't know. I suspected it, but when I asked Amy if you were my daughters, she denied it."

"I didn't see it, either," Emily told them. "You look so much like your mother, I never looked for anyone else. It wasn't until you and I talked about taking down those walls at Heartskeep, Hayley. I was going through some old photo albums when I came across some pictures of you as babies. There was something in the way you looked then. I compared the pictures to George's old baby photos and the resemblance was impossible to miss."

She took her husband's hand and squeezed it lightly. "I knew something happened after I left, but when we reconciled, I decided it was my fault, so we never talked about it. But you can see I had to know." Emily apologized. "You were staying at the house so I found a lab to run the DNA test and sent them hairs from your brushes. The results came back while you were searching for Alexis. If you want, I can show you the report."

"I don't want," Hayley exclaimed.

Emily was practically in tears. "I know this is a shock to you. It's a shock to all of us. George didn't want to tell you, but I felt you should know. Your mother stayed with Marcus to protect all of us."

"So she ruined her life instead? That's just stupid," Hayley proclaimed. "We grew up thinking that abomination was our father!"

Leigh looked every bit as upset. Alexis wasn't sure exactly what she felt. She stood and crossed to Wyatt. The action brought conversation to a halt. Tossing back her hair, she faced the room.

"In the past week, I learned my entire life was a lie. I've been an inadvertent participant in this family drama. I never met Marcus, but I hated him for selling me like an unwanted commodity. And I hated Brian Ryder for buying me for his wife. He loved me. I know that. But there was always something missing in our relationship, and now I understand why. I understand a lot of things."

Alexis took in a deep breath. Wyatt twined his fingers with hers. She didn't look at him, but she squeezed his fingers to let him know how much she appreciated his support.

"I understand your hurt and bitterness," she told her sisters, "but all I feel right now is relief. Marcus wasn't our biological father. What he did to me—to all of us—it wasn't personal. He didn't sell his firstborn child. He didn't ignore his twin daughters. We weren't any part of him."

She regarded each of them in turn.

"What good are recriminations? If we don't accept what we can't change, we can't move forward. I didn't know Amy. I didn't have to make her choices, so I can't put myself in her place. And I don't want to. This happened twenty-five years ago. I'm not about to stand in judgment."

"Amy was like a sister to me," Kathy said. "She's the only one who lost anything by her decision, but I can tell you this, she would have suffered a lot more if she had ripped these two families apart by telling the truth. Think about that. She did what she thought was best. And you should also consider that an hour ago, you only had each other. Now you've got a father and stepmother who've always been there for you, even when they didn't know the truth."

The large room suddenly felt too small as everyone began to talk at once. Alexis tugged on Wyatt's hand. He followed her into the hall. Mrs. Norwhich was moving around the kitchen. The woman had been hired by Eden to cook for Heartskeep after Eden had fired Livia and Kathy, and Hayley and Leigh had kept her on retainer while the house was being restored after the fire. Alexis liked the dour-faced woman when they'd met a few days ago. She was especially pleased to see that Mrs. Norwhich and Kathy seemed to get along so well. Alexis had plans for Heartskeep, and if they worked out, she was hoping both women would stay and work together. But she didn't want to talk to the woman right now. She led Wyatt out the front door and down the steps to the path that ran around the side of the house.

"Are we going somewhere in particular?" Wyatt asked.

"The maze."

The landscaping firm Leigh had hired had done an incredible job of making the maze marginally presentable in time for the service today. There was still a tremendous amount of work to be done, but as with the house, Alexis could see the potential. It was nice to have something positive to focus on in the midst of all the grief surrounding them.

Wyatt continued to hold her hand as she bypassed the first entrance into the maze in favor of the one behind the kitchen that led to the fountain.

"Not to sound nervous or anything, but you do know where you're going, right?" Wyatt asked. "I'd rather not wander around in there for hour or so trying to find our way out again, if you don't mind."

She smiled up at him. "I'm only going to the fountain. We can even see the house from there, now that they've pruned back some of these hedges."

"Just checking."

They reached the gurgling fountain and Wyatt released her hand. Alexis sat on the bench that encircled it so she could trail her fingers in the cool water. The humidity was lower today, the temperatures not quite so hot for a change. And there wasn't a rain cloud in sight.

Wyatt took off his dark suit coat and laid it across the bench. Then he worked loose his somber tie and laid that on top. As he loosened the top button on his white shirt, he saw her watching him with a smile.

"What?"

"Nothing. Just enjoying the show."

Color reddened his neck. He sank down next to her.

"Don't stop now."

"Behave."

"I thought I was. Wasn't I showing admirable restraint?"

Alexis glimpsed a hungry spark of answering desire in his gaze before it was quickly banked and his professional persona was back in place. They'd been together almost constantly for the past two weeks. She wouldn't have gotten through her father's funeral without Wyatt at her side. Yet there had always been someone around and Wyatt had maintained an emotional distance that was driving her crazy.

"Are you okay?" he asked.

"Don't I look okay?"

"You look…fine."

But his eyes reassured her with a different message altogether. She'd bought the simple navy shirtwaist because of the bright, bold jacket and belt that went with it. She'd left the jacket off for the funerals, but she'd seen him eyeing her legs more than once.

"I'm glad the services are over," she told him. "But then, I guess they aren't, are they? We'll need to be there for Jacob, as well."

"You're pretty loyal to someone you don't even know."

"I sort of warmed up to Jacob after I bashed him in the arm with that iron pipe."

His lips quirked. "I gathered as much when you refused to press charges against him."

Lightly she touched his face with her dry hand, rewarded when his eyes darkened. "It's going to be okay, you know. They will forgive George and their mother."

"I think so, too, but what about you?"

She dropped her hand to her lap. "I'm not sure what I feel right now. I think my brain is on overload or something. I like George and Emily. How could anyone not like them? They are two of the kindest, most loving people I've ever met." She gave a light shrug. "I think, when it comes right down to it, no matter who my biological father really is, Brian Ryder will always be my dad."

Wyatt held her gaze with a tenderness that warmed her heart. "I think that's the way it should be, Alexis. I doubt George would want it any other way. The transition is going to be a little more difficult for your sisters."

"Yes, but they've always loved George and Emily. They'll work it out. We all will. It's just going to take a little time."

Alexis turned around abruptly, scooting back so she could lean against his chest. Wyatt had little choice but to support her weight. She liked the way his warm hands felt against her skin. She didn't want to think about the others right now. She had other things on her mind and she was through playing fair.

"It's nice," she told him.

"What is?"

"Sitting here like this."

She thought he kissed the top of her hair, and decided they were making progress.

"Yes, it is."

For several minutes they listened to the spill of the water, birds calling to one another, and an occasional plane overhead.

She toyed with the emerald necklace her sisters had given her from the grandfather she'd never met. They had worn the jewelry today for the first time and it had felt right—just as sitting here with Wyatt felt right. The two of them had had so little time to be alone together. She knew at least some of that had been by his design. The danger was over and he was pulling back, masking the desire she only glimpsed occasionally now.

"By the way," he said, "Kathy doesn't have to worry about Bernie Duquette anymore. The New Hampshire State Police found his decomposed body on the side of the road last week."

Alexis sat up and turned so she could look at him.

"He was beaten to death. A sheet of paper with IOU was taped to his chest. Paid In Full had been stamped across it."

"Have you told Kathy?"

Wyatt nodded. "She seemed relieved."

"I can imagine. I've decided to turn Heartskeep into a woman's shelter. I've already asked Kathy if she'd be willing to move in and run the day-to-day operation of the house. If Mrs. Norwhich works out, and I think she will, I'll ask her to stay on and continue to run the kitchen.''

''Sounds like you've given this some thought.''

''Oh, I've been doing a lot of thinking. Primarily about you and me.''

His whole body reacted to that, going tense and still. ''Alexis. You've been through a lot—''

''Hold it right there. You're talking to a social worker, Wyatt. I'll bet I've had more psych courses than you have. I did not fall in love with you because you came to my rescue. While you did a terrific job in that department, if you'll recall, I wasn't doing so badly myself. I don't need a hero. I need a partner.''

His gaze never left her face.

''Hayley told me I was going to have to take the initiative with you over this whole virgin issue. I gather taking the initiative is a Hart family trait.''

''You've discussed that with Hayley?''

''And Leigh,'' she admitted. ''I didn't have much choice.'' Her mouth was unaccountably dry. ''Hayley said you'd keep dragging your feet if I didn't do something. Of course, they thought it was because of the inheritance, so I had to tell them it was the virginity issue causing me problems.''

Wyatt closed his eyes. ''You're making this up.'' He opened his eyes. ''You are teasing, aren't you?''

She struggled not to grin. ''They suggested we have the wedding night before the wedding and get it out of the way.''

''I ought to turn you over my knee.''

It was so hard to keep a straight face. ''Sounds a little awkward for the first time, but if that's what you like…''

The answering gleam in his eyes kicked her desire into overdrive. She reached for the button on his shirt. He stayed her hand, his expression serious. She could see him picking his words with care.

"Being a virgin makes you special, Alexis. That's quite a gift to offer the man you marry."

"Then I guess you're going to have to marry me, huh?"

He took her by the shoulders. With a toss of her head, she swept the hair back from her face and regarded him calmly while her heart palpitated madly.

"Alexis, we've only known each other—"

She pressed her finger against his lips. "It's okay. I won't rush you into anything."

He lowered her hand. "You won't rush me?"

"No. I've given it a lot of thought. I don't mind waiting until you're ready. You can have all the time you need."

She smiled, but couldn't bring herself to look into his eyes. She was afraid of what she might see. Or worse, what she might not see.

"This is a perfect setting, don't you think?" she said, rushing on.

"I'm not even going to ask for what. I'm pretty sure my brain stopped working several seconds ago. About the time you proposed to me. You did just propose to me, didn't you?"

"Of course not! That's your job. I simply meant this was a good spot for a seduction. Maybe not right this minute with all those people in the house, but we could come back later, maybe bring a bottle of wine or something."

He tilted her chin up, forcing her to meet his eyes. Her heart soared. It was going to be all right. The laugh lines around the corners of his eyes deepened with gentle humor. With aching tenderness, he ran his thumb across her bottom lip.

"Do I get any say in all this?"

"Of course. 'I do' would be nice."

"I DO," Bram said.

"I do," Gavin said.

"I do," Wyatt told her, hoping Alexis could see all the love he felt for her as the six of them stood before the minister in front of the sparkling fountain and exchanged their vows.

"...you may kiss your brides," the minister intoned.

Wyatt felt himself growing hard as their lips met and clung.

"At last," she whispered against his mouth.

"I love you," he told her.

"I know."

Happiness radiated from her as they turned to face their friends and family—and Heartskeep. George beamed at them from the front row of chairs where he'd taken his place as the proud father of the brides. Beside him, Emily dabbed at her eyes as she smiled her pleasure.

The house stretched above them almost tranquil in the late May morning sun, as if it, too, watched the scene in silent approval. From somewhere in the maze, a single white dove took wing and soared above the wedding party.

"Lucky! Get back here!"

Guests scattered as the large dog gave a gleeful woof and set off in chase. Wyatt chuckled and lowered his head for another taste of those luscious lips.

"Nice," Alexis breathed against his mouth when he released her.

He cocked his head, framing her delicate face in his hands, everyone else forgotten. "I plan to do a whole lot better than nice," he promised softly.

The desire, never far from the surface between them, flared to life in her eyes even as a mischievous smile curved her lips. "I certainly hope so. We've waited a long time for this day."

He knew it all too well. His body urged him to pull her deeper into the maze, away from the crowd, and show her exactly how much better than nice their wedding night would be.

Lucky streaked past them, barking merrily.

"I don't suppose you'd settle for a cat, would you?" he asked as George came forward to embrace his daughters and welcome their husbands into the family.

Alexis's laughter filled the air.

HARLEQUIN®
INTRIGUE®

has a new lineup of books to keep you on
the edge of your seat throughout the winter.
So be on the alert for...

BACHELORS AT LARGE

Bold and brash—these men have sworn to serve
and protect as officers of the law...and only the
most special women can "catch" these good guys!

UNDER HIS PROTECTION
BY AMY J. FETZER
(October 2003)

UNMARKED MAN
BY DARLENE SCALERA
(November 2003)

BOYS IN BLUE
A special 3-in-1 volume with
REBECCA YORK (Ruth Glick writing as Rebecca York),
ANN VOSS PETERSON AND PATRICIA ROSEMOOR
(December 2003)

CONCEALED WEAPON
BY SUSAN PETERSON
(January 2004)

GUARDIAN OF HER HEART
BY LINDA O. JOHNSTON
(February 2004)

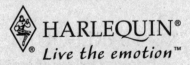

HARLEQUIN®
® *Live the emotion*™

**Visit us at www.eHarlequin.com
and www.tryintrigue.com**

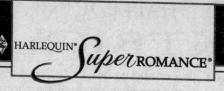

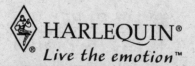

HARLEQUIN®
INTRIGUE®

Our unique brand of high-caliber romantic suspense just cannot be contained. And to meet our readers' demands, Harlequin Intrigue is expanding its publishing lineup to include **SIX** breathtaking titles every month!

Here's what we have in store for you:

❏ A trilogy of **Heartskeep** stories by Dani Sinclair

❏ More great **Bachelors at Large** books featuring sexy, single cops

❏ Plus outstanding contributions from your favorite Harlequin Intrigue authors, such as Amanda Stevens, B.J. Daniels and Gayle Wilson

MORE variety.
MORE pulse-pounding excitement.
MORE of your favorite authors and series.
Every month.

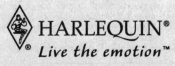

HARLEQUIN®
Live the emotion™

Visit us at www.tryIntrigue.com   HI4T06B

If you enjoyed what you just read,
then we've got an offer you can't resist!

Take 2 bestselling love stories FREE!

Plus get a FREE surprise gift!

Clip this page and mail it to Harlequin Reader Service

IN U.S.A.	**IN CANADA**
3010 Walden Ave.	P.O. Box 609
P.O. Box 1867	Fort Erie, Ontario
Buffalo, N.Y. 14240-1867	L2A 5X3

YES! Please send me 2 free Harlequin Intrigue® novels and my free surprise gift. After receiving them, if I don't wish to receive anymore, I can return the shipping statement marked cancel. If I don't cancel, I will receive 6 brand-new novels each month, before they're available in stores! In the U.S.A., bill me at the bargain price of $3.99 plus 25¢ shipping and handling per book and applicable sales tax, if any*. In Canada, bill me at the bargain price of $4.74 plus 25¢ shipping and handling per book and applicable taxes**. That's the complete price and a savings of at least 10% off the cover prices—what a great deal! I understand that accepting the 2 free books and gift places me under no obligation ever to buy any books. I can always return a shipment and cancel at any time. Even if I never buy another book from Harlequin, the 2 free books and gift are mine to keep forever.

182 HDN DU9K
382 HDN DU9L

Name	(PLEASE PRINT)	
Address	Apt.#	
City	State/Prov.	Zip/Postal Code

* Terms and prices subject to change without notice. Sales tax applicable in N.Y.
** Canadian residents will be charged applicable provincial taxes and GST.
   All orders subject to approval. Offer limited to one per household and not valid to
   current Harlequin Intrigue® subscribers.
   ® are registered trademarks of Harlequin Enterprises Limited.

INT03

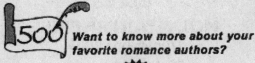

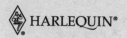

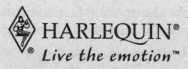